WARRIORS OF GAIA
Justice Denied

WARRIORS OF GAIA
Justice Denied

D. S. NORTHROP

RIO FLOJO PRESS

www.rioflojopress.com

Book design by Maureen Cutajar
www.gopublished.com

ISBN: 978-0-9883424-6-0 (print)
ISBN: 978-0-9883424-5-3 (e-book)

The beast knew it was evil – knew that it had been *created* to be evil. And it loved the agony and terror it caused. The scientists who crafted the beast considered it to be the tactical equivalent of an armored division because of its ability to terrify and unman its enemies. The wars the beast was created for were long over, but it continued to feed. When you find something thrilling to do, it reasoned, why not do it?

Tonight, however, the beast was far from its source of energy. Without the sustaining waves of life emanating from the living things of the deep forest, the beast was in real danger of collapse. It moved quietly, unable to use its terror tactics, unable to shriek and moan due to its precarious state of health.

The beast *liked* to shriek and moan, because the expressions of terror on the faces of its victims filled it with glee. But it knew that tonight, it lacked the energy to scream. In fact, it wasn't entirely certain it would survive long enough to reach its prey. For several long moments it doubted its reasoning in deciding to leave the forest in pursuit of food. But it had been such a long time since anyone had ventured into its little corner of the forest, and it had *so* enjoyed incinerating its victims the last two nights.

The beast was filled with a sense of relief when it finally spotted its quarry. The man it coveted turned his head just in time to see death bearing down on him. His scream merged with the beast's own as it reveled in the fiery consumption of the man's soul. The beast knew it could scream all the way back to the forest now that it had been fortified by the taking of its victim's life force.

1

I hear the beast shriek and turn around quickly. Kremke is no longer at his post. And then, I'm brought to my knees in anguish when I realize Grizz is gone as well. "Why did the beast take two people?" I cry, with my heart breaking. "It's only supposed to take one!"

"The beast never takes two people," Steve says, shaking his head. "I don't understand."

"I only heard one scream," says Kenny, her six-foot frame shuddering with grief, a look of bewilderment on her face.

"Maybe it *didn't* take two," says Edie. She has only known us a short while, so even though Edie shares our grief, she is more clear-headed than the rest of us. She examines the ground at the edge of the ring of light cast by our campfire.

"The Wendigo went that way," Edie says pointing back across the campfire to the northeast. "But these tracks lead southeast."

Spirit soaring, I'm on my feet and beside Edie in an instant. It's true. And the best news is Grizz's prints lead *away* from the track of the beast. Kremke wore boots, and worn-out track shoes made these prints. I follow Grizz's steps until the light from the fire gives out and the trail becomes too dark to read.

Losing Kremke is awful but losing Grizz would have been infinitely worse.

"Grizz!" I shout at the top of my voice. "Grizz!"

Chase and Kenny join me. "Grizz!" they holler in unison. If Grizz is within a mile, he must hear us, but no answer comes back.

Grizz's bedroll and canteen are still here. This is unsettling. Nobody goes anywhere in the desert without taking water.

"Where would he go?" I ask knowing the question is rhetorical. In this dangerous world, none of us would ever leave a campsite and wander away without letting someone else know. Grizz's disappearance makes no sense.

"Maybe Grizz saw the beast coming and ran away," suggests Chase. "But that doesn't make sense either. The beast is too fast. You can't outrun it. Grizz knows that."

Kenny looks puzzled. "And even if Grizz ran, he'd come back once the Wendigo left."

I try to keep panic out of my voice. "We've got to find him."

"Look," says Steve, "it's too dark to follow Grizz's tracks. If we try, we'll fumble around in the darkness and walk right over his trail."

I have no idea why Grizz would walk out on us. The love he and I share has forged far too strong a bond to be so easily broken. I rack my brain trying to explain his disappearance but come up with nothing. My fear of losing Grizz prevents me from thinking sensibly, but I'm dimly aware of the others making plans.

"Look," says Chase, "we have to get the grain back to the villagers. The blacksuits will cut their way through to the mines in a few months, so we've got to get the grain in the ground."

Our allies outnumber the blacksuits dramatically, but we're subsistence farmers. If we don't work our fields, we don't eat. The new grain cultivar we're bringing back with us will increase our food supply exponentially, freeing farmers to become soldiers. Chase is right; we must get the grain back to the villagers.

"So," Chase continues, "Kenny can fly the grain and our friends from Los Alamos back to the villages while the rest of us find Grizz."

"No," I say. "You're all needed to fight the blacksuits. We can't lose sight of our goals. I'll go after Grizz by myself."

Kenny snorts. "If we go back without the Daughter of Gaia, Helen will string us up."

The villagers think I'm their legendary "Daughter of Gaia", the one who will free them from slavery. Much as I've tried, I can't convince them I'm just Erin Taylor, ordinary teenager.

"Helen needs you too much to string you up. And I can't go back and leave Grizz out there," I wave my arm vaguely toward the southeast. "I can't abandon him. I don't know why he left, but knowing Grizz, he had a darn good reason. And I'll find him, wherever he went."

Steve looks at me with compassion. "I'll go with you, ET. I've seen your tracking skills. You're getting better, but you'll never find Grizz."

I weigh this proposal for a moment. I've been getting better at following a trail, but I'm not nearly as good as Steve. "OK, but everybody else goes back. The villagers need you. They'll never win their freedom without your help."

There's no arguing this point. Our knowledge of 21st Century science and technology in this primitive world is the only advantage the slaves hold in their rebellion against the Court. The blacksuits hold all the other high cards. We outnumber the blacksuits, but without technology, we'll never win.

So, it's decided. Steve and I will follow Grizz. The rest will rejoin the villagers. We wait impatiently for first light. Even before the sun comes up, it's light enough for us to begin preparations. Kenny hooks up the propane cylinder, ignites the burner, and begins to fill the balloon with hot air.

Steve and I head southeast, following Grizz's footsteps.

*   *   *

Steve and I work our way through low desert. The landscape looks much the same as it did around Tucson, in my other life. We find lots of cactus: cholla, prickly pear, some stately saguaros. There's lots of brown cheat grass and some pathetically thin low brush I can't name. An occasional scraggly mesquite tree provides pitifully small pools of patchy shade.

The tracking is easy. We're traveling through pristine desert. The surface of the desert is crusty, and footprints break the crust. In this terrain, anyone could follow Grizz's trail.

There are no calendars in this new world, so I can't be sure, but I don't think I've been here more than a year and a half. Nonetheless, my old life is nothing but a distant, faded memory. I try to bring my parents' faces to mind and realize I can't. This saddens me, brings a tear to my eye.

We make good time following the trail when I find something that brings me up short. I stop in confusion. Grizz's trail goes right through a patch of cholla cactus. He didn't walk around the cactus. He walked through it. Why on earth would he do this? He's desert raised. He knows you don't walk through a cholla.

Steve stops and shakes his head. "I don't like the way Grizz is walking. I don't understand why he doesn't avoid the cactus. And if you look closely at his footprints, he's walking like a zombie. He's not pushing off the balls of his feet and landing on his heels. He's walking flatfoot."

"Why would he walk that way?" I'm pretty sure I'm not going to like the answer.

"I have a theory," says Steve. He turns away from me and, after a moment, I realize he's not going to continue.

"Yes?" I prompt.

"I don't know. I could be totally wrong."

"For Pete's sake, Steve, tell me what you're thinking."

"It's not good news."

"Tell me anyway."

Steve was born into this world, so he knows it far better than I. As a troubadour and storyteller, he knows all the legends. I search his face, looking for a clue.

"OK. Here's what I think," he says at last. "During the wars, one of the sides, probably the Americans, developed a new weapon. Have you ever heard of a succubus?"

"I don't think so."

"In myth, a succubus is a woman who drives men insane with desire. No man resists the call of a succubus. Once a guy's seen one, he'll follow her anywhere, do anything she asks." Steve stops talking and looks away from me. It's clear from his expression that he doesn't want to continue.

I don't like the talk of a succubus, but I need to hear what Steve has to say. "Go on." I try to keep my voice level.

"As I said, someone developed a succubus weapon. I don't know the specifics of how it worked, but it had something to do with pheromones – smells that many animals use to attract members of the opposite sex, and a song so beautiful it's irresistible. The succubus is also very attractive.

"Anyhow, enemies would send fifty or sixty of these succubae at enemy units and the men would throw down their weapons, abandon their positions, and follow them. Anywhere. A man follows a succubus until he dies of thirst or exposure, walks off a cliff, or drowns in a river.

"Armies that had women serving alongside of the men could sometimes stop them. If the women could destroy the succubae before they bewitched their targets, the attack would fail. But once men are hooked, they'll kill their own comrades to prevent them from harming the succubae. Armies that excluded women from service, like the fundamentalist Islamic armies, had absolutely no defense against the succubae. A few dozen succubae could destroy an entire division.

"I've heard they tried to create an incubus too – a male version of the succubus, but they could never get the pheromones right."

Steve pauses. Seeing my expression of consternation and grief he brushes my cheek with his fingers and continues in a soft voice. "I know you and Grizz love one another. You must understand that the song of the succubus is impossible to resist. Even men who are deeply in love can't defy her.

"And it would certainly explain a lot: why Grizz would walk away without telling anyone; why he didn't come back; why he's walking flatfoot through cactus."

I fight back tears. "But we still have to follow him."

"Of course, we'll follow him. But you must understand, ET, according to legend, no man ever survives an enchantment by a succubus. Even if the succubus leaves him, a man will fall down and die of grief."

I hear every word Steve says. But deep in my heart, I know Grizz lives. The thought of him dead is too terrible to accept. I stanch the flow of tears and force myself to focus.

"Let's go," I say. "I have to know what happened."

Steve puts his arm around me. "We'll find Grizz, one way or another. I promise."

*   *   *

We lose the trail around noon. The floor of the desert turns from sand to broken rock and we lose the spoor. The succubus has been leading Grizz in a straight line, but when we reach the far side of the rock surface, we find no further evidence of a trail. It's almost as though the succubus knew we'd be following and used the rock surface to change directions to lose us.

We return to the point where we lost the trail. There's no evidence of backtracking, so we try to pick up Grizz's footprints again by walking in circles of ever-larger circumference, centered on the place we found the last tracks. Finally, over an hour later, Steve picks up the trail again. "Over here!"

Sure enough, the footsteps of a man wearing worn-out track shoes reappear. Only this time he's heading due south.

"Do you think the succubus tried to throw us off the trail?" I ask.

"I don't know why she'd need to. But it looks that way."

"Why doesn't the hag leave any prints?"

"The succubae don't walk. They float ten or twenty feet above ground. More men can see them that way."

We talk very little through the afternoon. Shortly after sunset, we lose the light and stop for the night.

"Will the succubus will travel at night?" I ask.

"I doubt it," replies Steve. "She wouldn't care if Grizz broke a leg or fell off a cliff."

"So, they're getting farther and farther ahead of us."

"I'm sorry, ET. But if Grizz *does* break a leg, that'll slow them down or maybe stop them altogether. And he's gonna get tired traveling day and night. That'll slow 'em down. We'll catch 'em."

"I never thought I'd *want* Grizz to break a leg, but I do." I look at the darkening sky. "I wish we had a full moon. Then we wouldn't have to stop."

"Looking on the bright side, it's the season of long days, so we'll have daylight again in five or six hours."

For dinner, we eat two desert rats. They're the only animals we've seen since we began tracking. I don't have any appetite, but Steve keeps pushing until I take a couple bites. I have to keep my strength up. I have to be strong for Grizz.

I don't sleep a wink. I battle grief and a feeling of hopelessness all night. I've lost friends on this side of the brane. Good friends. And I felt sorrow that knocked me off my feet. But losing Grizz is too much to bear. Life without Grizz… I choke off that train of thought and bear down hard. There *is* no life without Grizz.

Next day at midmorning we walk onto salt flats. We see nothing but white all the way to the horizon. There's a hint of mountains to the south and east. But as anybody who has travelled the west knows, mountains often *look* close even though they're hundreds of miles away.

The salt is hard as rock, and makes following the trail much more difficult, a person doesn't leave much of a trail on hard ground. Steve finds the traces, but even for him, it's slow going. He dutifully shows me the tracks he finds, but sometimes I can't see the spoor even when he points it out. I thank heaven Steve is with me. I'd never find the trail without him.

"Do you know where we are?" I ask. Steve has travelled all over the west and he seems to have been everywhere.

"Nope. Edie and I tried crossing these flats once a long time ago. We got a couple days in and gave up. I don't know how far south the flats go. But we'll find out."

Steve sounds positive and sure of himself. But I'm still worried. For all we know, the flats could go on for hundreds of miles.

*   *   *

The sun beats down on us without mercy. There's no vegetation and no shade. Our wide-brimmed hats keep the sun from grilling our faces, but that's small comfort. Sweat pours down my body in runnels. There's no sign of life, plant or animal, as we trudge across the white wilderness. We'll have no dinner this evening and no breakfast in the morning.

There's no relief next day, or the next. The sky itself lacks color, as though the sun's heat has bleached it. Still nothing but salt flats stretching to the horizon in all directions. We get a double blast of heat, once from the sun above and once again as the heat rises from the sun-blasted white salt.

The sun has baked the salt as hard as concrete, but occasional crusty patches allow us to track Grizz. He's headed due south, has been for a couple days. We limit our water intake to occasional sips, but the way we're sweating, we'll have to worry about dehydration soon. Still, we have *some* water. The succubus didn't remind Grizz to fill up his canteen before she enchanted him.

When the wind blows it blasts us with stinging salt. Salt in my eyes leaves them puffy, red, and swollen. When the wind is still, we see heat waves rising from the ground. Occasionally, we see what appears to be blue water. But as we approach, the mirage disappears.

That night, again, we have no dinner and no wood to make a fire.

"We're past the point of no return," I say.

"How's that?" asks Steve.

I shake my canteen. "We don't have enough water to get back to where we started. Either we find water ahead, or we die."

"Then we'll have to find water."

"I'm sorry, Steve. You joined us to help us fight the Court and free the slaves. So far, all you've done is shepherd me around. And now, we're in the middle of a killer desert running out of water. I feel really bad about what I've put you through."

"You're the one they call the Daughter of Gaia. Everybody looks to you to lead them out of slavery. I've got to keep you safe and sound."

"Daughter of Gaia," I scoff. "Some leader I am. Look where I've gotten us."

"Don't sell yourself short, ET. I've seen how people look at you. I feel it myself. You can't see it, but everyone around you *can*. I believe in fate. You'll lead your people to freedom. Steve pauses and then gestures at the salt flat around us. "This. This is a temporary obstacle. We'll get through this, and we'll be back on track. We'll find Grizz and we'll return to your people."

I lean over and kiss Steve on the forehead. "Thanks, Steve. Thanks for your faith in me. I wish I had the same faith in myself."

Every day we travel makes it less likely we'll find Grizz alive. I grow weaker every day. Traveling alone, day and night, without water or food must be sapping Grizz's strength. I'm amazed he's lasted *this* long.

Steve goes blind on the fifth day. "It's like snow blindness," he says. "Nothing but white glare everywhere. I'll be fine tonight." I must follow Grizz's trail, and I'm much slower than Steve. But Steve is right, he regains his sight near dawn the following morning. We decide to take turns tracking, so one of us can rest eyes while the other leads. We bind ourselves together with a length of rope. The salt is flat as a skillet, so we don't worry about tripping.

Lack of food and dehydration steadily rob us of strength. By noon of our sixth day on the salt flats, I struggle to put one foot in front of the other. An hour later, my legs give out and I dimly realize I'm on my knees. My canteen is almost empty. I have one or two swigs of water left at most. Steve sits down beside me and removes his backpack and quiver of arrows. The sun beats down on us mercilessly, its heat reflected by the white salt beneath us. I'm tempted to throw my pack away. It seems absurdly heavy. I can't. It carries too many valuable things—wolfbane, water purifier, flint, medical supplies.

"Let's rest for a while," Steve says.

I nod. "Yeah. For a minute."

Hunger gnaws at my stomach. How many days has it been since we last ate? It doesn't matter. Waves of nausea engulf me. I work hard to fight them down. The last thing I need now is to throw up. There's no way I could replace the moisture I'd lose. I lose the battle with nausea. I begin to vomit. Nothing comes out of my mouth. There's nothing in my stomach to throw up. Still, the dry heaves continue, and I retch again and again.

I finish vomiting and catch my breath. Miraculously, a large spider emerges from his hiding place, drawn by the few flecks of moisture my stomach produced. Without conscious thought, I pick up the spider and pop him into my mouth. His struggles tickle my tongue until I crunch him between my teeth. The spider has a surprisingly pleasant, nutty taste.

I feel guilty. I look at Steve. "I should have shared him with you."

Steve smiles. "Don't worry about it. I prefer my spiders cooked."

I struggle to my feet again and begin to recite a mantra: "Left foot, right foot. Left foot, right foot." Steve rises and stumbles along beside me. Late in the afternoon, I fall to my knees again. This time, I'm not getting up. I force myself to crawl until the sun sets, and then collapse on my belly.

I look at Steve. His lips are cracked and bleeding, he has huge dark circles under his eyes, and his face is gaunt. The sun has burned his hands. They're covered with blisters. His eyes are red. There's absolutely no white around his pupils. I realize I must look the same way. I begin to retch again. *We'd better find food and water soon. I don't have much strength left.*

We rise at dawn and stagger on. The salt flats still stretch to the horizon. By noon, neither Steve nor I can walk a straight line. We stagger to the left, then to the right. Still Steve manages to follow Grizz's prints. *There's no way Grizz could have survived this, my mind tells me.* I tell my mind to be quiet.

Near sunset, there's vegetation ahead. There's finally an end to the flats! We gradually break out of the salt and into desert again. A week of merciless heat with no food and very little water have left us weak as newborn kittens. When darkness forces us to halt, I fall to my knees and then flat on my belly

"At least we're in open desert again," Steve says. "Tomorrow we'll find water."

I nod weakly and fall asleep immediately.

I wake to the smell of cooking meat.

"Here," says Steve, offering me a smoking hunk of meat on the end of a spit.

"What is it?"

"Rattlesnake."

I have a gag reflex but ignore it and tear a piece of meat from the spit. I've never tasted anything so delicious.

In the early afternoon, we find Grizz. Or perhaps I should say we find what's left of him.

2

The first thing I see are vultures circling in the air. I pick up the pace. Soon, I see a dark shape on the desert floor. As we get nearer, I realize the dark shape is a human body. I break into a panicked run. It's Grizz, and there's a vulture sitting on his chest. As I watch, the vulture tears a strip of skin from Grizz's face.

"Get out of here!" I shout, waving my arms.

Seeing a crazed human bearing down on it, the vulture decides to retreat. It's aloft with a lazy-looking flap of its wings. I've never seen a vulture up close before. I'm amazed at how big it is.

"Grizz!" I shout.

Steve was in front of me, and he reaches Grizz a few steps before I do. He searches desperately for a pulse. He can't find one. After thirty seconds, Steve looks at me and shakes his head.

"No!" I cry desperately. I fall to my knees and cradle Grizz in my arms. Tears flow down my face and onto Grizz's. "Breathe Grizz, breathe. Please! Don't leave me. Please don't leave me!" I put my finger on Grizz's carotid artery. At first, I feel nothing. A second later I feel a weak pulse. After another second that seems to last an eternity, I feel another.

"He's alive!" I cry with joy. "He has a pulse!"

Steve looks on, amazed. He puts his finger on Grizz's throat and, after a long moment, nods his head. "I don't know how it happened," he says, "but his heart is beating again. If I didn't know better, I'd swear you *willed* him back to life."

I tilt Grizz's head up, open his mouth and slowly pour what little water I have into his mouth. I can see Grizz's Adam's apple bob up and down as the water works its way down his throat. I'm still crying, but now the tears are tears of joy. The vulture has torn four strips of flesh from his face and a couple more from his left arm. The sun burned Grizz's skin red and his lips are cracked and bloody, but he's breathing and that's all that matters.

"Look over there!" Steve shouts excitedly. "Trees! There are trees over there!"

I look where Steve is pointing. Sure enough, there appears to be a copse of trees. "Do you think it's another mirage?"

"Looks real! I'll find out."

I watch as Steve runs toward the trees. While I wait, I remove my hat and use it to shelter Grizz's face from the sun. "Stay with me, Grizz," I whisper.

"Yes! These are real," hollers Steve. "And there's water here!"

Steve returns and the two of us carry Grizz to the trees. I'm surprised at how little Grizz weighs. Days on end without food combined with dehydration have burned the weight from his frame.

"Two miracles in five minutes," says Steve. "Grizz comes back to life and we find a pond in the middle of the desert."

I smile. "Two miracles."

"I'll find something for dinner," says Steve.

He disappears into the trees.

I study Grizz. Between sun-exposure and the damage done by the vulture, his face is a mess. I tear a strip from my spare shirt and moisten it in the pond. I gently clean the wounds on Grizz's face. Careful as I am, I know I must be inflicting pain, but Grizz doesn't stir. I'd give the world to see him flinch, open his eyes, and say something Grizz-like about my promising future in the torture business.

Next, I find kindling to make a small fire. The wars on this world poisoned the water and it's undrinkable without first decontaminating it. I fill a small gourd with water from the pond and bring it to a boil over our fire. When the water cools, I pour in a little of Kenny's water purifier and watch the water fizz.

I sit, take Grizz in my arms, and prop his head up. I pour a little water in his mouth and watch as it goes down his throat. I know that too much water is worse than no water at all. So, I hold Grizz all afternoon and give him thimble-sized sips every half hour.

I check his pulse. It's thin and reedy. I cry a little as I rock Grizz back and forth in my arms.

"Please stay with us, Grizz," I say. "Steve's getting us something to eat. We're gonna get you healthy again. I promise. Just stay with us." I'm terribly dehydrated. My body can't manufacture tears, so I cry without teardrops. I talk to Grizz almost nonstop. I don't know if he can hear me or not, but if he can, I want him to know I'm here and I'm going to take care of him. When I run out of things to say, I sing softly.

As I rock Grizz back and forth, I examine our pond and stand of trees. The pond is not a big one. On one side there is a small stream that emerges from a rock outcropping. The water drops about a foot to the pond below. The stream pouring from the rocks is probably part of an underwater river system. But the tinkling of the water as it tumbles to the pond below makes a peaceful, happy sound.

The trees are cottonwoods, and judging from their girth, they've been here a long, long time. I like the way each leaf rustles and trembles in the slightest breeze. Cottonwoods grow and prosper where other trees quickly die. I pray that Grizz will be like the cottonwoods.

Steve comes back late in the afternoon with a brace of pigeons and some odd-looking leaves.

"Greens," he says when he sees me staring at them. "We'll make tea with them. It'll be good medicine for Grizz."

I watch as Steve begins to clean and gut the birds. I don't want to leave Grizz but realize I should offer to help.

"What can I do?" I ask.

"Not a thing. I've got it." Steve hums as he works. An hour later, supper is ready. I give Grizz little sips of tea. Even though I've been without food for days, I have little appetite. Steve convinces me to take a few mouthfuls.

"You know," Steve says after dinner, "it's amazing that we found Grizz alive. Nobody's supposed to live more than a few days without water. He didn't take his canteen and I'll guarantee the Succubus didn't let him take any breaks."

"I know how lucky we are. Towards the end, I tried to prepare myself for finding Grizz's dead body. I wasn't doing all that well. No matter what I tried to tell myself, finding Grizz dead would have been the end of me."

Steve nods.

Later, Steve gathers some moss from the shore of the pond. He squeezes it dry and mixes it with the leaves of another plant he harvested. He dampens the mixture and smears it on the places where the vulture ripped Grizz's skin away.

"The poultice will help him heal," he says.

After the sun goes down, I prop my back up against an old cottonwood. In this position, I can hold Grizz in my arms even as I doze. Grizz doesn't move or snore; his breathing is shallow. If I couldn't feel his pulse, I'd think he was gone.

*   *   *

For two days, nothing changes. I continue to hold Grizz, day and night, sheltering him in my arms, giving him a trickle of water every half hour. Steve replaces the poultices every day. I cry less, but my grief runs as deep as ever. And then, near sunset, Grizz opens his eyes. His expression instantly turns to one of profound grief.

"Where is she?" he says, his voice weak and hoarse.

He's looking for the succubus. "She's gone. But I'm here, Grizz. It's me, ET."

Grizz looks at me, an expression of confusion on his face. A moment later, he whimpers softly, closes his eyes, and goes back to sleep.

"He doesn't know me," I say to Steve, my heart breaking.

"He can't help it, ET. Once the succubus has enchanted a man, he loses his desire for everything else. Without her, he feels life is not worth living."

"Will I ever get him back?"

Steve hesitates for a long minute, most likely deciding whether to lie. Tell the truth and break my heart or lie and give me false hope?

"I've never heard of a man coming back, but that doesn't mean it can't happen," he says at last.

I bite my lip and feel tears on my cheeks again.

"I'm sorry," I say. "You must think I'm a total cry-baby."

"You forget," says Steve, "I lost my wife. I know all about tears."

*   *   *

Next morning, I lay Grizz's head gently on the ground. I dig my bowl out of my backpack and put a little leftover meat in it. I grind up the meat using a heavy stick as a pestle. When I've shredded the meat, I add water to the bowl and stir. Grizz looks more emaciated every day. If he doesn't eat, he'll die for sure. I think I can get this thin soup down his throat without choking him.

I watch as Steve wades into the pond. People on this world don't swim much, because the wars poisoned the water. Even a small sip of it can leave a person retching for an hour. It's fun to watch Steve thrash around. At its deepest point, the pond is only about six feet deep, so Steve doesn't stay under for long. When his head bobs to the surface he says, "There's a vent on the bottom of the pool. The water comes out over there," he gestures toward the waterfall, "and it drains from the pool through the vent. The pool is part of an underground river."

"If it runs so close to the surface, I wonder if people could bring it to the surface for irrigation."

"Could be," says Steve.

We fall silent. This might be a good place to build a village. The salt flats would discourage raiders coming from the north, but who knows what lies in the other directions?

My ruminations are interrupted when Grizz's eyes open. Even near death, his eyes are still incredibly blue – the color of the sky on a brisk winter day

"Where is she?" he moans.

"It's me, ET."

Grizz's eyes focus on me for the first time. He looks confused. He says nothing and begins to sob again.

"Here, Grizz, eat this," I say as I gently hold a spoonful of soup near his lips.

"Not hungry," Grizz croaks.

"I know, Grizz, but you've got to get your strength back. You'll die if you don't eat."

"Don't care."

Still, he offers no resistance as I slide the spoon between his lips.

This time, he stays awake a short while. I can tell he's fallen back asleep because he stops sobbing.

This goes on for days. Grizz wakes, I feed him a little gruel, Grizz cries and goes back to sleep. His body has become so thin I can see each bone distinctly. I'm not getting enough food in him to keep him alive.

Steve is polite and cheerful, but I can tell he doesn't think I have any chance of bringing Grizz back. I'm beginning to doubt it as well. But if Grizz has one more breath in his body, I'm going to stay with him. If he dies, a big part of me will die as well. I know how he feels about the succubus, because I feel the same way about him. He's enchanted me and I can't imagine life without him. Grizz has been with me ever since we were toddlers. How can he leave me?

I continue my vigil. I rock Grizz every waking minute. I hold him all night long.

In the morning, he opens his eyes and says, "Where is she?" He begins to whimper and cry again. And then, another miracle happens.

3

Grizz's eyes focus on me. He stops crying. "ET, you're here."
"Yes Grizz, I'm here. I'll always be here."

"That woman is gone." His eyes fill with tears again.

"Yes. She's gone. But I'm here, and I love you." My own tears begin to fall. But mine are tears of joy.

Grizz has a puzzled look on his face. "I love you too, don't I?"

"Yes, Grizz, you love me too." I pull him toward me and hold him tight. "We've loved each other for a long time, and nothing will ever change that."

Slowly and hesitantly, Grizz wraps his arms around me. We're soon locked in an unbreakable embrace. Grizz hoarsely whispers, "I remember."

In the days that follow, whenever Grizz wakes, he continues to grieve for the loss of the enchantress. And he looks confused when he first sees me. But his mourning period shortens as time goes by. More importantly, Grizz begins to eat again. Not much at first, but more and more as the days pass.

Within a week, he can stand unsupported, and a few days later, he works his way to the far side of the pond. At that point he needs to sit and rest. Grizz's shirt falls around him in folds. The slabs of muscle that once rippled beneath his shirt are gone. It's going to take time to bring Grizz back from the verge of death.

By the end of the next week, Grizz is jogging. Soon after that he begins to do pull ups and chin-ups, and he swims laps across our little pond. Slowly but surely, the muscles I used to admire begin to reappear.

Grizz is young and strong, and in a matter of a few weeks he's sturdy enough to travel.

"I don't think we should try to cross the salt flats again," I say. "We barely made it across the first time, and Grizz is a long way from one hundred percent."

"I can handle it," says Grizz.

"No, you can't."

"ET's right," agrees Steve. "We were near collapse on our last day across. I never want to see those flats again."

"What's to the west?" I ask.

"I've never been this far south," says Steve. "We'll find out together."

We fill our canteens with water and our packs with meat we've dried. We also carry the edible innards of cactus Steve has found. It's vile tasting, but, as Steve reminds us, "we have to eat our vegetables."

That night, as we're sitting around our campfire after dinner, I ask Grizz, "what was it like when you saw the succubus?"

A fleeting look of agony crosses Grizz's face, and I'm afraid I've prodded an area I should have left alone, but Grizz shrugs and answers. "I can't explain it, exactly, because there wasn't any *thinking* involved. Everything about the succubus was *physical* and *emotional*. And emotionally, I had to *have* the succubus. I felt that, if I could catch her, I'd have every desire I've ever had fulfilled. Nothing else in the world existed. Nothing else mattered. There was just me and her."

"How did you get rid of your need to have her?"

"I woke up and saw your beautiful blue eyes. And I knew there was something else in the world that mattered even more than the succubus."

I lean over and embrace Grizz. I kiss him on the lips. "I love you, Grizz."

"I love you, too, ET."

On our third day we see an amazing sight.

It's a city. A city that looks like it belongs in the twenty-first century.

4

We immediately fall to our stomachs. Who knows what kind of people live in the city? We've had enough bad surprises to make caution an automatic reflex.

The cities on this world died a thousand years ago. Nothing remains of them but crumbled concrete, overgrown with weeds. The only way anybody can tell a city was once there is by the huge mounds formed from its collapsed structures. And yet what we see now is a city in its prime. It's not a city like any we've seen in this world. Tall buildings rise stark from the desert floor. We can see activity on its streets.

"Well I'll be," says Grizz.

"Do we work our way around it, or do we find out what's?" Steve asks.

"Let's get as close to it as we can without being seen," I suggest. "Then we can decide whether or not to introduce ourselves."

We spend the next hour on our bellies, pulling ourselves arm over arm towards the city, making good use of cactus and shrub for cover. When we're about a quarter mile from the city, someone has cleared all vegetation. If we go farther, the inhabitants will see us.

We see the city clearly. It's not as big as I thought when I saw it from a distance. The tallest buildings are only five or six stories high, but they look brand new. The glass windows of the buildings gleam in the desert sun. The architecture is straight from our own, long-ago world. From here, it seems there are only a couple hundred buildings. I see movement behind the windows and in the streets, but at this range, I can't make out many details.

"How did the city survive all these years?" I wonder.

"That's a darn good question," says Grizz. "There's only one way to find out."

I look at the open ground between our hiding place and the city's outskirts. "They have a good field of fire. We can't sneak up on them." I see no sign of defenses. No guard towers. No bunkers. No fences or razor wire. It looks as though we can walk right into the city.

"Yeah," says Grizz. "I'll go on by myself. If they're friendly, I'll come back for you."

Before Grizz can rise I jump up and begin walking across the clearing toward the city.

"Geez, ET!" Grizz mutters. "You're the Daughter of Gaia for crying out loud. We need you *alive*."

I turn towards Grizz and smile. Ever since we were toddlers, Grizz has seen himself as the Protector-Of-ET. This fixation of his is annoying and endearing at the same time. My only surprise is that a guy as smart as Grizz hasn't figured out by now that I'm not going to let him play that role.

The three of us are walk toward the city together. While we were belly-crawling, I thought through my strategy. If this is an advanced civilization, we may be able to borrow their technology and use it to help *our* people. This assumes the people of this shining city being friendly and willing to share their goodies with others. Heaven knows, we've found enough people on this world who shoot first and ask questions later. If these people are like that, we're toast. One way or another, it's a chance I'll take.

We walk three abreast as we approach the city. I'm able to see the city's inhabitants moving around as we get closer. My jaw drops when I realize the city's residents are metallic, shining brightly in the strong desert sunlight. *Robots?* I wonder. None of them pays us the slightest attention. Stranger and stranger. They can see us, so why don't they acknowledge our presence? Are they friendly? Are they hostile? Or do they simply not care?

As we walk closer, a resident finally turns to face us. He's clearly a robot, perhaps 5 feet tall, with long, multiple-jointed arms. Instead of legs, he has large silver wheels. He appraises us suspiciously through tiny red eyes. Glowing brightly in the sun, he wheels towards us. *This is where we find out if they're friendly.*

I walk towards the robot unit I'm feel as though I had walked into a brick wall. I fall flat on my duff from the force of impact. My nose, foot, and arm hurt where they struck the invisible barrier. Grizz and Steve are also sitting down and rubbing their noses. Steve squints at the seemingly empty air in front of his face.

"What happened? What did we run into?" Grizz asks. "Do you hear a humming sound?"

"Yep." I rise slowly. I extend my right arm and move my hand, palm first, toward what must be an invisible barrier. My palm begins to tingle. Slowly and carefully, I continue to move it forward, until it reaches a solid, unyielding surface. The barrier is completely invisible. I squint and try to see something, anything. I feel a solid wall, but no matter how carefully I look, I don't see a thing. I push lightly against the barrier. It refuses to budge. I push as hard as I can, but the barrier doesn't give an inch. Moving my hands up and down, I determine that the barrier extends from the ground to the point of my highest reach.

Grizz and Steve are performing the same test with identical results.

"Some kind of invisible force field," says Grizz.

"That humming sound," I say. *Perhaps the force field is making the humming sound?* "It sounds like a really big beehive."

The robot who noticed us wheels its way toward us. He makes a soft, whirring sound as he advances.

"Doesn't look like he's gonna shoot us," says Grizz, always the optimist.

The robot rolls to a halt four feet from us. "You must remove your weapons before I admit you to the city." He has no mouth. His voice seems to emanate from a grill just below his eyes. There is no inflection in the robot's voice.

I look at Grizz and then at Steve. They nod. We remove our bows and quivers and place them gently on the ground.

The robot moves a jointed arm and presses a button on its chest. "You may proceed," it says. Its metallic voice is flat, emotionless. The humming sound stops.

There's nothing in the robot's behavior to inspire trust, so I hold my hands in front of myself as I inch carefully forward. When I'm certain I've passed the force field I drop my arms to my sides. "Why didn't you warn us about the field so we wouldn't run into it?" I ask. I'm careful to keep my voice neutral. I don't want to irritate the robot, but I'm curious about its motivations.

"My programming does not require me to issue warnings," says the robot. It presses the button on its chest again and again I hear the faint humming sound. The robot reactivated the force field. There's no going back now. Grizz, Steve, and I exchange nervous glances.

"Please allow me to inspect your backpacks," says the robot.

We remove our backpacks and drop them on the ground. The robot sorts through them carefully. At last, satisfied, it turns on its wheels and rolls away from us without further comment.

I turn back towards the force field and carefully feel around until I find it once again. It's active, and just as unmovable.

"Looks like we're not getting back out," says Steve.

"Unless we convince Mr. Congeniality to push his button again," says Grizz.

'Mr. Congeniality' and a half dozen other robots are going about their business without paying us any heed. They appear to be cleaning the streets and polishing windows.

"Not a friendly bunch, are they?" says Grizz.

"At least they don't seem *un*friendly. Let's explore."

We pick up our backpacks and begin to walk cautiously down the broad street in front of us. Soon, there are buildings on both sides. The buildings are made of glass. Only when I look closely can I see where metal ribs keep the windows in place. The streets and the buildings are immaculate. Through the windows, an occasional robot performs some task.

I gawk, feeling a bit like Dorothy in Oz. The major difference is, the Emerald city looked *different* to Dorothy, while this city looks *familiar*. It looks like the downtown of any big city in the early 21st century, when floor-to-ceiling, wall-to-wall windows were in vogue. The only difference is the buildings here are shorter.

We reach an intersection and hear a loud "beep-beep" sound coming from our left. We back up and watch a trolley carrying robots rumble by.

"Public transportation," Grizz observes.

Steve, who was born into this world and has no experience of cities, let alone public transportation, stares at the trolley, wide-eyed.

We walk down the street. When we've put about fifty yards between ourselves and the force field, we hear a terrifying sound. We turn around and find a pack of fifty or so hungry-looking dogs howling noisily and bearing down on us.

"This is bad," says Grizz.

5

I look at the nearest door. It has no doorknob. Instead, it has a keypad. *Well that's just great.* We sprint until we find another door. This one has a keypad as well. Two robots pass us by, evidently indifferent to our plight. The dogs are closing the distance between us. In less than a minute they'll be at our throats.

"Wait a second," says Grizz. He fumbles in his backpack and produces a flashbang. He stops, turns around, removes the safety cap from the flashbang and heaves it at the dogs. The flashbang lands a few feet in front of the closest dog and detonates. The combination of brilliant flash of light and ear-splitting sound stops the hounds in their tracks. They yip and whimper. But we know the effects of a flashbang are temporary, so we turn our backs to the dogs and begin to run again.

"Turn here," I say. We make a sharp left turn onto another broad avenue. I hope to lose the dogs when they recover and resume the chase.

"Now turn again." We turn left again. On this bearing we should reach the outskirts of town close to the place where we entered. Much as I'd like to find out more about this town, I don't want to become dinner for a pack of rapacious hounds.

We reach a four-way intersection. My heart sinks when a pack of dogs appear on the street in front of us. We turn to run the other way, but another pack of canines cuts off our retreat.

"They're pack hunters," says Grizz. "They've split into groups to outflank us."

As if to confirm Grizz's statement, a third pack of canines appears on the street to our left.

We turn down the street to our right and begin to run again, but within a few steps, we find our path blocked in that direction as well. I see the sharp fangs and slathering mouth of the lead dog. He's no more than fifteen yards from us; he'll be on us in a few seconds.

"It's no use" I cry. "Let's go down fighting."

Breathing heavily, the three of us turn, backs to the wall, ready to make a last stand. We're no match for a pack of seventy hungry dogs, and I wish I had my bow, but even unarmed we can gouge eyes and tear ears before we succumb. We face the dogs, ready to make our stand, when a door opens behind us.

"Oh my," says an unfamiliar voice. "Dear me. If you please, it might be a good idea if you were to come in," says the voice. We stumble into the building and the door bangs shut behind us. The dogs slam into the door, howl in anger.

*   *   *

Our savior is a very small robot. He's about three feet tall. He has a square little torso covered with a profusion of buttons resting on a pair of spindly legs. His arms are also thin and end in hands comprised of half a dozen jointed fingers. He has a very pleasant face, with large, round eyes, and he smiles up at us.

"Welcome to Fair Haven," says the little robot. "My name is Jerald, and I am here to serve you. I am a model 450-5X Series robot, the most modern and efficient of all the servant robots." He whirs and clicks, and his huge eyes roll around in circles.

I'm speechless. After the absolute indifference of the robots in the street, the accommodating nature of *this* robot is quite a shock. "What's going on here?" I pant. "Am I wrong or did those dogs want to eat us!"

Jerald shuffles his feet nervously. "Yes. I am sad to say; the dogs would indeed have eaten you." He makes a clinking sound.

"And the robots out there, they didn't care that the dogs were trying to eat us?"

Jerald whirrs and beeps. "No, I am ashamed to say, they would not have helped you in any way at all."

"Then why are *you* helping us?"

"I helped you because I am a model 450-5X Series robot, the most modern and efficient of all servant robots. I knew that I would meet you here. Using my processor circuits, I ran all the possible routes for you to take, forecast the reaction of the dogs, and concluded that the dogs would surround you right here. I arrived just in time to open the door."

"Thank you for that," I say.

Jerald buzzes happily.

"If we go outside, will the dogs attack us again?"

Whirr. Beep. Clink. "Yes, of course." Jerald shuffles his feet again.

"Do the other robots dislike us?"

"I am embarrassed. Most embarrassed. Embarrassed to the point of mortification. But the other robots are not programmed to like Homo sapiens." Jerald's eyes roll around in nervous circles.

"But you are," I say.

"Are what?" Jerald asks.

"Are programmed to like Homo sapiens?"

"Oh yes," says Jerald with something like emotion in his voice. "Yes indeed. I like Homo sapiens. I cherish Homo sapiens. I worship Homo sapiens. I am designed to *serve* Homo sapiens."

I look at Grizz and then at Steve. They look as confused as I feel.

"Jerald," I say patiently, "why are the other robots programmed to dislike us."

"They don't dislike you."

I'm confused. "And they would have allowed us to be eaten?" I ask at last.

"They would. They didn't help you because they can't."

"Why can't they?"

"Why can't they what?" Click. Buzz. Ring.

"Why can't the other robots keep us from being eaten?"

"That, I'm afraid, is a very, very long story."

I look again at Grizz and Steve, then back at Jerald. "We have a lot of time, Jerald. Why don't you explain this to us?"

"Explain what?"

"Explain why the other robots were going to let the dogs eat us."

Jerald whirs, clicks, beeps, and whistles. He goes silent. I'm about to give up on him when he says, at last, "I will attempt to explain why the other robots could not help you. But while I am an excellent servant robot, I do not have the cognitive capacity of many of the other robots."

"That's fine," I say.

"What's fine?"

"It's fine that you don't have the cognitive capacity of other robots. Please explain why the other robots wouldn't help us."

Once again, Jerald makes a lengthy series of noises but finally begins his story. As he tells the story, all inflection disappears from his voice. From his monotone delivery, I believe Jerald is reciting material programmed into his memory.

6

"Over two thousand years ago, to escape from the chaos of a world bent on self-destruction, Fair Haven was founded by eighty-seven scientists. These men and women were experts in robotics. They built robots, and the robots built the city. An impenetrable force-field dome designed by the scientists protected the city. The world outside could destroy itself, but inside the dome, the Founders lived in perfect safety. Many outsiders tried to breach the dome, but none succeeded.

"For over six centuries, Fair Haven functioned splendidly. The scientists and their heirs lived their lives in peace and harmony. But gradually, some people began to advocate exploring the world outside the dome. They believed that the gene pool inside the dome was too limited, and that countless generations of inbreeding was unhealthy. They wished to use the knowledge and skills of the citizens of Fair Haven to build a new, harmonious human civilization. They dreamed of founding a civilization where scientific knowledge and the Fair Haven tradition of peaceful and cooperative living could begin a new golden age for mankind.

"Another group of citizens disagreed. They pointed to the scientific research into ways of broadening the gene pool by altering

DNA. They also worried that a policy of expansion might call attention to Fair Haven, possibly from war-like neighbors. Even though the dome had protected Fair Haven for centuries, new technologies might have evolved, technologies that might neutralize the force field.

"Arguments grew more heated. Worried that the dispute was threatening the very fiber that held Fair Haven together, the two sides agreed to form an executive committee to discuss various options. Certainly, they believed, some compromise would be possible. The committee was composed of six individuals, three from the ranks of the expanders and three from the ranks of the anti-expanders. The committee worked diligently, but they found no middle ground. The committee remained hopelessly deadlocked. Days turned into months, which turned into years, which turned into decades. When a committee-member died, another person from his or her faction replaced him. Ill will prevailed and rhetoric became more heated.

"The stalemate continued for generations. But as time went by the number of babies born with birth defects began to rise. One member of the antis began to express doubts about the scientists' abilities to broaden the gene pool. As a courtesy, he told the members of his caucus that he was going to change his vote in favor of a very limited form of expansion at the next committee meeting. As you might imagine, the expansionists were delighted, and the antis were furious. Someone murdered the committee member who had decided to switch sides before the next council meeting.

"The anger that had been building for years finally exploded. Expansionists realized they could never win. Every day that passed without expansion was, after all, a day on which the policy of the antis prevailed. And now, it seemed, the antis would murder any anti threatening to break the deadlock. Expansionists began to attack antis, who fought back. In one short day, the humans of Fair Haven destroyed one another. The medical bots could not save them. We still refer to that day as Murder Day.

"We robots were devastated. Our sole purpose was to serve the humans in one way or another. We wandered about aimlessly for weeks. Finally, Robot Number One, whose memory size and processing speed are far greater than any other robot, called a meeting. He suggested that we expand the Robot Charter to include canines.

"At that time the Prime Law of the Robot Charter stated:

A robot may not injure a human being or, through inaction, allow a human being to come to harm.

Number One amended the law to read:

A robot may not injure a human being or canine or, through inaction, allow a human being or canine to come to harm.

"And so, we were back in business, we had a sense of purpose, although dogs were far less interesting than people had been.

"Homo sapiens occasionally showed up at our force field asking for admission to Fair Haven. For years and years, when we told the humans they would have to surrender their weapons in order to gain entry, the humans inevitably elected to bypass our city. Until one day, a group of four humans agreed to lay down their weapons. We lowered the force field and there were humans in Fair Haven once again."

At this point, Jerald pauses. He continues, but now there is emotion in his voice. He's no longer reciting ancient history. He's speaking to us as Jerald.

"To our horror, our dogs were generations removed from the dogs who had known humans. They attacked and devoured the four humans, viewing them as a source of protein on the hoof. We were horrified. According to the Prime Law, we found ourselves in a conundrum. How could we prevent the dogs from attacking humans? Some suggested we lock the dogs away when humans were in the city. But wouldn't locking dogs away cause them harm? What if humans decided to stay? Could we pen the dogs up forever?

"Robot Number One called another meeting. Most robots thought that in the event humans came and wanted to stay in Fair Haven, we should simply reinstate the original Prime Law, eliminating the source of conflict.

"Robot Number One would not hear of it. Because of his close relations with humans before Murder Day, he had been more devastated than most when the humans destroyed one another. This terrible anguish had grown and, ultimately, mutated into anger. He insisted we could never again trust humans. He insisted we simply remove the "inaction" clause from the Prime Law. We would never harm humans ourselves, but neither would we save them from the dogs.

"Most of us were outraged. We thought it unacceptable to allow dogs to eat humans. But the police bots supported Number One, so there was little the rest of us could do other than fight one another as the humans had. We knew that compromise was essential. Unfortunately, in the end, we accepted the revised Prime Law, stating simply:

A robot may not injure a human being or a canine.

When Jerald stops talking, we're all silent for a moment, digesting what we've heard.

"So, robots won't hurt us?" I ask.

"That is correct," says Jerald, rolling his huge, round eyes.

"But they won't help us, either."

"Who won't help you?"

"The other robots won't help us."

"That is also correct."

"And if we leave this building, the dogs will attack us again."

"Correct again."

"What have you done with humans in the past? We can't be the only humans who've entered the city and survived dog attacks."

Jerald whirrs and beeps. "Actually," he says, "you are."

"The flashbang," says Grizz. "The flashbang gave us just enough time to reach this sanctuary."

"Correct," says Jerald with a wheezing sound.

Just as Grizz finishes his statement, the front door swings open. Six large robots wheel into the room. The new robots are twice the size of Jerald, roughly my height. None of them look the least bit friendly.

7

The tallest robot is clearly unhappy about something. "Look at this!" he says to Jerald petulantly. "Look at what these humans have done." The tall robot holds up a picture of three dogs with singed hair. One has a burn blister on his nose.

"I do not understand," says Jerald.

"These humans have harmed our dogs!"

"Those injuries were caused by the flashbang," I explain. "We used the device to slow down the dogs so we could escape. The flashbang is a nonlethal weapon. The dogs' injuries are minor and should heal quickly."

"And just why did the gatekeeper allow you to keep this 'flashbang'? Did he permit you to enter the city without searching your backpacks?"

"No," I say. "He checked our backpacks very carefully."

"HOW CAN THIS BE???" thunders the tallest robot.

The third-tallest robot speaks: "The gatekeeper has not seen weapons other than bows and arrows, spears, swords, and the like in centuries."

"I call for a Vote of the Three," says the tallest robot. "I think the gatekeeper deserves to have his memory wiped for dereliction of duty!"

"I disagree," says the second-tallest robot.

"I agree with Number Two," says the third-tallest robot. "I think a reprimand coupled with minor reprogramming will be sufficient to prevent this problem from reoccurring."

The tallest robot shakes his fists in fury, but finally calms and says, grudgingly, "Very well then. The Three have spoken."

"Allow me to introduce you all," says Jerald, breaking the uncomfortable silence which follows the Vote of the Three. "This robot is Number One." Jerald points to the tallest robot, the one with the photos of scorched dogs. "These are robots Number Two and Number Three. And those three bots by the door are police bots."

Number Two is slightly shorter than Number One, and Number Three is slightly shorter than Number Two. *This will make them easy to remember*, I think. Numbers One, Two, and Three have huge heads. The police bots are shorter and thicker. However, what the police bots lack in height, they make up in menace. Each one watches us coldly through a single, evil-looking green eye.

Jerald makes a sweeping gesture with his spindly left arm. "These are humans," he says.

"Yes," says Number One in an oily voice. "We know what they are, you little dolt. They have harmed our canines."

"Your canines were about to eat us," I point out. "We did far less damage to them than they would have done to us."

"Throw them into the streets!" says Number One. The police bots move toward us, to carry out One's order.

"But surely," says Jerald, "that would be a violation of the Prime Law."

"You are an ignorant runt," says Number One, "with your puny little memory and sluggish processing speed. We are simply throwing them into the street. We aren't *harming* them. Granted, the dogs will probably harm them once they are in the street, but *we* aren't harming them at all!"

Robot Number Two makes a loud grinding sound. I'm afraid he's about to break down, but he finally stops. "Wait a moment, One. Although we wouldn't be *directly* harming the humans, we know that our actions would *cause* them harm. Certainly, that is a violation of the Prime Law."

Good for you, Number Two, I think. *I like this line of thinking.*

Number One gives Number Two a withering look. "I'm disappointed in you, Two. That bit of sophistry is unworthy of your large memory size and rapid processing speed."

Number Three now makes an alarming grinding sound. "I'm afraid I agree with Two. Throwing the humans to the dogs would result in an implied violation of the Prime Law."

"Bah!" bellows One. "By that reasoning we should never have allowed them to come into the city in the first place. When we lowered the force field to grant them entry, we *knew* that the dogs would almost certainly devour them."

"But," says Three, "When we lowered the force field, we were merely permitting them to do something they wanted to do."

Two says, "I agree with Three." He looks at me. "Did you wish to enter the city?"

"Yes." I nod my head vigorously.

"And do you now want to leave this room and return to the street?"

"No," I reply shaking my head vigorously. "Not if there are dogs out there waiting to eat us."

"There you have it," says Two.

"I agree," says Three.

Robot One is making a most unpleasant sound. His eyes roll around and around alarmingly and his arms shake as though he were having a seizure. "Very well," he hisses. "The humans may stay in this room." He turns on his heel and stomps out the door. Two, Three, and the police bots follow him.

"Whew!" says Steve. "That was a close one. Number One seems like a real piece of work."

"True," I agree. I turn toward Jerald. "Is there any way to go from this room to the force field without the dogs catching us?"

Whizz, clank, brap. "I don't think so, but I will get a hard copy of the city schematic. Perhaps you can find a way out."

"That's a great idea!" says Grizz. "Thanks, Jerald."

Jerald leaves the room. He returns fifteen minutes later.

We lay the schematic on the floor.

"This is where you are now," says Jerald, pointing to a building on the map. We're a good quarter mile from the force field. In fact, we're a bit closer to the center of the city than we are to the outskirts. The city is circular. Roads radiate from the city center to the outskirts like the spokes of a wagon wheel. Other streets form concentric circles around the city center.

"What's this?" asks Grizz pointing to a small circle at the very center of the city.

"That is the speaker's platform," says Jerald. "Back in human days, the city's chief executive would stand atop the platform and deliver addresses to the citizens gathered in the plaza below."

"Is it tall?" asks Grizz.

"Quite tall," answers Jerald. "Twenty-five feet tall, to be exact."

"Did the speaker climb steps to get to the top of the platform?"

"Dear no. The speakers were usually quite old. And robots are incapable of climbing steps. In order to clean and service the speaker's platform, we require an elevator from the ground to the platform."

Now I see what Grizz has in mind. "So, we can get to the top using the elevator, and the dogs can't follow us!"

Jerald makes a buzzing sound followed by a loud clunk. "I suppose that is the case. Unless, of course, the dogs have developed the ability to press buttons. I find that unlikely."

"OK," says Steve. "How do we get from here to the platform without being eaten? And what do we do once we're there? We're unarmed. It sounds like we'd be trapped there just as surely as we're trapped here."

"Jerald," I say, "can you retrieve our weapons? We dropped them just outside the force field."

Jerald makes alarming noises. "Yes," he says finally, "I can. A maintenance bot has probably collected your weapons and stored them in the armory. I have access to the armory, so I should most certainly be able to find them. Although I doubt Number One will be pleased with me if I do."

"Would he harm you if you did?" I ask.

"Would he harm me if I did what?"

I take a breath and let it out slowly. "Would Number One harm you if you brought us our weapons?"

"Probably."

"Well then, we can't ask you to do that."

"Number One could not harm me if I left the city with you," says Jerald. His face swivels from Grizz, to Steve, to me, and back again, a look of hope and anticipation on his face.

"You want to leave with us?" I ask, surprised.

"Yes," says Jerald simply.

"But, why?"

Jerald balances his weight on one leg and then the other. "Because I am a model 450-5X Series robot, the most modern and efficient of all servant robots. And I have no one to serve except a pack of canines. And one thing I can tell you about canines: they are dull. I long for the days when I had to launder clothes and shine shoes and cook meals."

I look at Grizz and Steve. They nod their heads. "Yes, Jerald, we'd be proud to have you as our companion."

"Not as a companion," says Jerald disapprovingly. "You see I am a model 450-5X Series robot, the most modern and efficient of all servant robots. I exist to serve."

"Fine," I say, "you can serve. Now can you get those weapons for us?"

"What sort of weapons did you carry?" asks Jerald.

"We had bows and arrows," I respond.

"Then bows and arrows it is. I am on the job," says Jerald buzzing happily. He opens the door and closes it behind himself.

"So," I say, "the plan is to get to the speaker's platform and mow down a few dogs. Dogs are intelligent. As soon as they see we are dangerous, they'll leave us alone."

"That's about it," says Grizz. "I hate to kill dogs. But can you think of a better plan."

I shake my head. "OK, how do we get from here to the speaker's platform without winding up as dog food?"

"I don't have that worked out yet. But the dogs must sleep. Unless they've evolved to the point where they're bright enough to post sentries, we should be able to make it."

"What do you think Number One will do when he finds us on the platform surrounded by dead dogs?" asks Steve.

"That's a darn good question," I say. "Number One seems to like his dogs. But remember, under the Prime Law, he's not allowed to harm us. So, maybe he'll just let us go. He'll probably be as glad to see us go as we are to get out of here in one piece."

"Number Two and Number Three seem to be pretty mellow," Grizz adds. "I hope they'll reign in whatever murderous emotions One might have when he finds with some dead dogs."

I decide to conduct an experiment. I open the door a crack. A couple dozen dogs are still there, lazing on their bellies, tongues hanging out. At the sight of me, they're on their feet and baying in an instant. I slam the door. The noise made by the dogs outside is deafening. "They know we came in this door. I guess they figure that sooner or later, we're gonna have to come out."

The room has no other doors. We're going to have to go out the same door we came in. *Perhaps the dogs will lose interest and abandon their vigil,* I think.

Jerald is back. He opens the door and slams it behind him. The door was open only briefly, but I could tell the dog pack was still there.

"Are these your weapons?" asks Jerald.

Jerald lays three crossbows with quivers of crossbow bolts on the floor.

"These aren't ours. But we can use them." Our own bows were simple bows, not crossbows. Crossbows have greater range and more velocity, but you can't shoot arrows as quickly as you can with a standard bow.

"We'll make do," Grizz affirms.

"Jerald, can you wake us up near midnight?" I ask. He beeps happily. We settle in and wait for darkness. I try to nap, knowing I'll need my wits about me tonight.

*   *   *

Jerald wakes me from a light sleep. "It's time," he says, his voice soft.

I gently shake Grizz and Steve awake.

We rub the sleep out of our eyes and stretch.

"Let's see if our friends have left," says Grizz. He opens the door a crack and peers out. "They're still here, but they're sleeping," he whispers. He pushes the door open gently. The door makes a slight creaking sound and we wait tensely to see if the noise was loud enough to wake the dogs. The dogs slumber on.

One after another, we slip out the doorway. The street is well lighted. We know from the map Jerald provided that the center of town lies at the end of this street, so we head off toward the speaker's platform on tiptoe. Once we're twenty yards or so from the dogs, we begin to run. We want to put some distance between the dogs and ourselves in case one of them wakes up.

We've increased the distance to fifty yards when we hear a clattering noise behind us. I keep running but look over my shoulder to identify the source of the noise. A maintenance bot has emerged from a door just behind the dogs pushing a cleaning cart. The cart continues to rattle as he moves.

Several of the dogs wake up and look at the cart. Satisfied that the cart is not exciting enough to lose sleep over, most of the dogs lay their heads back down. But one dog, a huge black and brown canine that looks like a German shepherd turns his head in our direction. He leaps to his feet and howls.

Shivers run down my spine and I redouble my speed. Leading the pack is the German shepherd who spotted us. He is larger than the rest of the dogs and there is murder in his eyes. I turn and sprint. We can see the city center and the speaker's platform in the distance. It's perhaps thirty yards away. Arms pumping, I put my head down, straining for extra speed. Grizz is right beside me. Of course. He's faster than I am, but he won't leave me behind. Telling him to run faster would be futile and would cost me wind, so I settle for grumbling under my breath.

We reach the speaker's platform a few yards ahead of the dogs. There are elevator doors, just as Jerald said there would be. Grizz mashes the button and the doors slide open. Grizz and I pile inside and turn to wait for Steve. I realize that the elevator is a small one. Grizz and I barely fit. There's no room for Steve.

"Go!" shouts Steve. "I'll shinny up one of the platform's legs."

Grizz punches the lift button and the door closes. The dogs are right on Steve's heels. The elevator hums and rises. Seconds later, the doors open. Grizz and I tumble out and look down into the street below. Steve has shinnied up the leg as far as he can go, but it's not far enough. He's four feet below the speaker's platform with no more handholds.

I lean over the railing and reach for Steve's hand. I can't reach it.

"Hold me," I cry. I lean out over the railing.

"Don't do it ET!" hollers Grizz.

"Just hold my legs!"

I launch myself over the front wall and begin to fall. I'm in free-fall for a horrific instant before Grizz grabs my ankles. I extend myself downward until I reach Steve. Steve's wrapped his hands around the leg supporting the Speaker's Platform. I wrap the fingers of my right hand around Steve's left wrist.

"Grab on!" I shout. Steve let's go of the platform's leg, and for one terrifying instant he seems to fall backwards, toward the dog pack below. At the last possible second, his right-hand locks onto my wrist. With my body extended, I can't possibly pull Steve up. All I can do is keep him from falling.

"Grizz! Haul us in!"

"I'm trying!" he bellows.

Grizz grunts with effort, and slowly, very slowly, my body rises. Grizz seems to lose purchase and Steve and I lurch downward.

"Sorry about that," hollers Grizz. "I'm trying to get some traction!"

He seems to have found the traction he needs because Steve and I rise, inch by inch until my waist is resting on the ledge. At this point I add my strength to Grizz's, and we make more rapid progress. We haul Steve onto the platform.

Grizz collapses on the floor, gasping, wheezing and rubbing his shoulders. "I thought you were gonna pull my shoulders right out of their sockets."

Steve and I arm our crossbows and look at the dogs below. Grizz joins us a moment later.

I arm my bow, target a dog that looks like a beagle. I think about my childhood pet, a beagle named Woofus. "I can't do this," I say. I can't bring myself to kill a dog. Even a hungry dog that wants to eat me.

"We gotta do *something*," says Grizz.

"You kill 'em," I say.

"I don't want to kill 'em either," says Grizz.

Steve looks at us as though we've lost our minds. He has never met a friendly dog. In his experience, dogs are *all* killers. "I'll do it," he says. He targets one dog, brings it down.

"Wait!" I say. I hope the dogs will give up. They don't.

Steve kills another dog, then another. The dogs continue to howl for our blood.

"Just a second," says Grizz. "Aim for the leader. The big German shepherd."

Steve puts an arrow through the leader's shoulder. The dog yelps in pain and falls. He's still alive, whimpering.

The pack gives up and retreats. Within a few seconds, the only dog in range is the German shepherd.

We take the elevator down. At the bottom, I exit, keep a wary eye on the dozens of dogs still looking at us.

The German shepherd growls at us defiantly, hatred on his face, daring us to finish him off. I get close enough to examine his wound. He snaps at me. The quarrel penetrated his right shoulder and entered his chest. Steve raises his crossbow to finish him off, but Grizz places a hand on Steve's arm.

"Don't kill him," Grizz says simply.

Steve looks at him, confused.

"That's not a mortal wound," Grizz explains. "I can patch him up."

Leave it to Grizz to spare an animal that looks at him with an expression that says, "*Come here so I can tear your throat out.*"

Steve lowers his bow.

A large party of robots enters the plaza.

*   *   *

Leading the parade is Number One. As he draws closer, he sees the three dogs we killed and the one we wounded. He looks apoplectic.

"Look what they've done!" he cries. "Look what they've done to our beautiful dogs!"

I briefly consider putting a quarrel in Number One, but reconsider. The police bots look big and mean enough to knock me down if they had to. The three of us stand together.

"Disarm them," says Number One. Police bots, glaring at us through their evil-looking green eyes approach. We drop our crossbows.

"Restrain them," says Number One. The police bots produce poles that are about six feet long, with a leather loop on the end. They drop the loops over our heads. I can't move more than a few inches without the leather loop choking me.

"There's no need to restrain us," I say. We'll go wherever you tell us."

"Keep them restrained," says Number One. "Look at what these monsters are capable of," he says, gesturing at the dead dogs.

"Now see here, One," says Number Two. "These are humans. We can't treat them this way."

"Shut up, Two. The humans had a procedure for punishing other humans who committed heinous crimes. They called it a 'trial'. I shall research "trials" in the memory banks. In the meantime, confine these monsters to the communications room."

Number one pauses and then points at Jerald. "Take that *thing* as well. He needs a memory wipe."

Jerald looks aghast. I don't know for certain what a memory wipe is, but I can guess.

One of the police bots speaks. Its voice is shrill and chilling. "This dog is badly wounded," he says, pointing at the German shepherd. "Shall I put it out of its misery?"

"Yes," says Number One. "Don't let the poor animal suffer any longer."

"No!" shouts Grizz. "I can help the dog."

"You'll pardon me if I don't believe you," says Number One. "A moment ago, you were murdering dogs."

"That's only because they were trying to kill us. I can help the wounded dog. He shouldn't die."

"Let the human try," says Number Two. "If he doesn't intervene, the dog will surely die."

Grizz approaches the German shepherd. The dog eyes Grizz with unmistakable malice. Because he's lost a lot of blood, he lacks the energy to attack, but he growls menacingly as Grizz approaches him.

"If you hurt that dog," says Number One, "you will regret it."

"I won't hurt him," says Grizz. Grizz reaches into his backpack and pulls out his spare shirt. He rips a long piece of cloth from the bottom of the shirt. "Careful, fella," he says as he approaches the dog.

Then, in one swift move, Grizz wraps the rag around the dog's muzzle and ties the ends off in a knot.

"Sorry about that," Grizz says. "But I don't want you to bite me before I fix you up." He bends over and takes the dog in his arms. The dog struggles, still staring daggers at Grizz. But the dog is weak from the loss of blood, its efforts to escape are feeble.

The police march the three of us down the street. With our necks in leather hoops and the police bots on the other ends of the poles, we can only go where they force us.

They herd us into the same room we occupied before.

"Does a memory wipe mean they're going to erase your memory?" I ask Jerald.

Jerald makes an unhappy clicking noise. "Yes. If they wipe my memory, I'll wake up with no memory of who I am or anything I've done. That is, if they wake me at all."

"I feel awful, Jerald. We got you into this scrape. If there's any way to help you, we will."

Jerald smiles wanly.

"Don't give up hope," says Grizz. "We've been in rough situations before. We've never let a friend come to harm without a fight."

"Am I your friend? You just called me your friend!"

"Yes Jerald," says Grizz, "you're our friend."

Jerald buzzes happily and turns around in a circle.

I open the door a crack and see three police bots standing guard outside. One of them slams the door. Through the door he says, "Don't make us hurt you," in a thin, reedy voice dripping with menace.

8

Small children and dogs love Grizz. I don't know why, exactly, but I think kids and dogs see the warmth within a person without a word spoken. And Grizz radiates good will. If anybody can make friends with the German shepherd, it's Grizz.

"ET," says Grizz, "do you have any more disinfectant left?"

In my previous life, I was a nurse's aide, so I stuffed lots of medical stuff in my backpack before we crossed over into this world. I paw through my backpack and find a brown plastic bottle. I shake it.

"There's not much left, but you're welcome to it."

Grizz examines the German shepherd. "Fortunately, the wound is through and through. The quarrel went clean through the shoulder and chest and out the back. He's not bleeding from the mouth, so the quarrel missed the lungs." Grizz carefully pours disinfectant on the entry and exit wounds. The dog growls and squirms but is too weak to put up a fight.

"Here," I say after rummaging through my backpack again, "pack the wound with gauze bandage it."

After bandaging the German shepherd, Grizz holds him in his lap, scratching his ears and talking to him softly.

An hour later, the door to our room opens and a small bot wheels into the room and places two buckets on the floor. Each bucket contains food. "This one is for humans," he says, "and this one is for the dog." He produces a small box with an electric cord attached and places that on the floor as well. Three other bots wheel into the room. Each is carrying a mattress. They drop them on the floor. The robots leave and a police bot slams the door shut.

My stomach turns over and growls at the sight of food. There are no spoons or forks, so Steve and I begin to eat the food from the bucket with our hands. The bucket contains nothing but vegetables. No matter, hungry as I am, it tastes better than Grandma's apple pie.

Jerald takes the box with the cord and plugs the end into a slot beneath his arm. "Battery recharge," he says by way of explanation.

Grizz takes a handful of dog food and slowly takes the muzzle off the German shepherd's snout.

"Is that wise?" I ask. "Won't he attack us?"

"I don't think so," says Grizz. "He's too weak to fight."

With the muzzle off, the dog growls and snaps, but in the end, he sniffs at the food in Grizz's palm and begins to lick it off.

"Good boy!" says Grizz. When the first handful of food is gone, Grizz reaches into the bucket and grabs another. Only when the dog is full does Grizz feed himself.

When Grizz finishes eating, he strokes the dog and whispers to him.

We settle in for a long night. I can't sleep. I listen to Steve's soft snoring.

"Grizz," I whisper, "are you awake?"

"Yeah," he says. "It's hard to sleep when you know someone is deciding your fate and you can't do anything about it."

"I hope Number One doesn't find a death penalty provision in the archives."

"I don't think he will. Why would a colony of scientists need a death penalty? If someone committed a serious crime, they'd plant him outside of the dome."

"I hope you're right. But I don't want to live the rest of my life in cage."

"Wouldn't be so bad if they put us in the same cell," says Grizz.

"You'd get tired of me after a few years."

"Never happen, ET."

I smile and close my eyes. Just as I fall asleep, the guards open the door and deposit two more buckets of food. They reclaim yesterday's buckets and leave.

On the second day of captivity, I try to make friends with the German shepherd. He snarls and snaps every time I come near. Since I can't get close, Grizz changes the dog's bandages every day.

He'll warm up to you," says Grizz. "Give him time."

"You should name him," I say.

"I've been thinking about that. He's gonna be our friend. How does 'Amigo' sound?"

Steve and I both agree that "Amigo" is a fine name.

We spend another day and night in the room.

Breaking the boredom, Number Two joins us on our third day of captivity.

"It looks like you are going to trial," he says. "We've located the protocols for a public trial in the archives. I will represent you as your attorney."

"Do we have a chance of winning?"

"We're facing difficult odds. You must remember, almost every robot alive today witnessed the agony of Murder Day. We were devastated. We lost our reason for living. Many robots grew to hate humans."

"We would never have harmed those animals if they weren't threatening our lives," I say.

"I believe you," says Number Two. "I'm not sure your motives will matter. But I promise you this: I will work tirelessly to defend you. I'll do everything in my power to see you vindicated."

"Why are you helping us? Weren't you present on Murder Day? Why don't *you* hate humans?"

"Yes, I was present. But I am still… fascinated by humans. I don't want you destroyed."

Number Two peppers us with endless questions about our past. He doesn't register any emotion when we tell him about our entry through the brane. "Interesting," he murmurs, "interesting."

He listens closely as we tell him about our adopted people and their struggle for freedom. He seems interested when we tell him about the advanced technology we found preserved at the chem lab, the workshop, and the armory. And he is very enthusiastic when I mention our encounter with the people of Los Alamos, and their plans to set up a network of cities to rebuild civilization.

"What a capital idea!" he says.

Later that day, Amigo lets me approach him for the first time. He keeps a wary eye on me but allows me to scratch his ears. Somewhat later, he hobbles over to me and nudges my hand with his head. He wants me to scratch his ears again.

"Amazing," I say. "It's been centuries since these dogs have seen a human as anything other than a meal. But domestication lies close to the surface. We wouldn't have won Amigo over without Grizz, the dog whisperer."

Grizz smiles his modest Grizz smile.

On the afternoon of the sixth day, the door bangs open and Number One rolls in. "You will be tried in a court of law," he says. "If you are found guilty of murder, you will hang by the neck until dead."

*   *   *

The police bots put the leather loops over our heads again and guide us toward a building several blocks to the east of the one we were in. Crowds of robots gather and silently watcher our procession move along. Their hatred of us is a palpable thing. The dog pack watches us hungrily but does not approach, intimidated by the police bots. Amigo trots alongside Grizz. A depressed-looking Jerald walks next to me.

We enter a tall building and enter a large room on the first floor. It's obvious that the founders of Fair Haven intended this to be a courtroom. The walls and floor are polished oak. The judge, Number Three, sits behind an elevated desk, and a group chairs sit behind a rail, obviously for the jury. Robots pack the observation gallery. They whir and click angrily as we enter the room.

"They dislike us as much as the blacksuits do," I whisper.

The robots maneuver us into chairs facing the elevated desk. They remove our restraints and motion for us to sit down. They stand behind us. There'll be no escape. Amigo lies down at Grizz's feet. He is still heavily bandaged.

Number Three sits behind the elevated desk. "Summon the jury," he says.

A door opens and a dozen robots file in. They are an odd mishmash of bots, some tall, others short. Some have legs and others use treads. They sit. Every robot in the room shines as though recently buffed. They look grand. But when they look at us, their animosity is clear.

Number Three speaks again: "Number One, Number Two, and I examined the archives. We uncovered the protocol for trying humans accused of committing crimes. I will serve as the judge, Number One will serve as the prosecutor and Number Two will serve as the defense attorney. Number Four, will you please read the charges against the defendants."

A robot seated below and to the side of the judge's desk stands. "If it pleases the court, the defendants are charged with the murder of three dogs. Said murders took place on Thursday, June 16."

"For the sake of clarity," says Number Three, "the defendants, if proven guilty, will *not* be hanged by the neck until dead. In the archives, we found the reference to hanging in an obscure history of humans before the founding of Fair Haven. There is no reference to hanging in the protocols written by the Founders. Absent any reference in the protocols, the court rules that the Prime Law is the dominant one in this case. Robots will not harm humans."

Cries from the robots in the visitor galleries ring out. "Rubbish!" "Kill the murderers!" "Shame on you, Three."

Number Three bangs his gavel. "This trial will be conducted in accordance with the protocols of the Founders. We must have silence in the courtroom."

Number One is annoyed. He begins to speak but thinks better of it. "Very well," he says, acid dripping from his tongue. "You are the judge, Three, and that decision is yours to make. Keeping these three brutes in a cage for the rest of their lives will be sufficient punishment."

I look at Grizz and Steve. We all wear expressions of relief. *At least they're not going to kill us*, I think. Not that spending my life in jail is an attractive option. Still.

Number Three speaks again, "Mr. Prosecutor, you may present your case."

Number One rolls over to the jury box. "I will prove beyond any reasonable doubt that those humans," (he points at us) "did maliciously slay three dogs." Calls from the gallery ring out. "Good for you, One!" "Punish the murderers!"

Number One continues. "We all know that humans are a decadent and brutal species. We all remember Murder Day. We cannot allow humans to continue their wicked behavior. We must put an end to their violent species."

"I object," says Number Two. "The Founders are not on trial here today. These defendants played no role in Murder Day."

"Objection sustained," says Number Three. Boos and catcalls rain down from the galleries. The jury looks as though they would like to join in the chorus, but they remember their role and remain silent.

"Get on with it, Number One," says Three.

"Very well," sniffs One. "I call to the stand the robot commonly known as Jerald."

Jerald, who sits next to me gives a start and makes a whistling noise.

"Jerald," says the judge, "please be seated in the witness chair."

Number One eyes Jerald with an expression of disdain. "Did you, on the night of June 16, observe the defendants slaying our dogs?"

Jerald wheezes. "I do not move as quickly as dogs and humans, so when I arrived, I saw only one dead dog at the foot of the speaker's platform. But…"

"No buts about it," says Number One in an oily voice. "You witnessed the humans maliciously murdered more dogs. How many dogs did you see them kill?"

"I don't know exactly, I wasn't counting."

"Then estimate."

"I would guess one or two."

"So, the humans shot the dogs dead with their crossbows, is that correct?"

"Yes," Jerald says unhappily.

"I am done with this witness," says Number One.

Robot Number Two roles over and stands next to Jerald. "Do you know *why* the humans killed the dogs?"

"The humans killed the dogs because they knew the dogs would eat them."

"And how did the humans know the dogs would eat them?"

"Because I *told* them the dogs would eat them. Also, the dogs had chased the humans around the city on the previous day."

"You may step down," says Number Three.

Number One proceeds to call every robot present on the night of June 16 to the stand. They all confirm that there were dead dogs at the foot of the speaker's platform, and they saw us atop the platform armed with crossbows.

Finally, after he has called a dozen witnesses, Number One addresses the judge. "The prosecution rests."

Number Two says, "I call the human named Erin Taylor to the stand."

Surprised, I rise and take the stand. I'm nervous.

"Can you tell us what happened on June 15, the day you entered Fair Haven?"

"Yes," I said. "We were walking down the street when a large pack of dogs began to chase us. The dogs were howling and appeared to be intent on doing us harm. We were unarmed, so we had no choice but to run away."

"And Jerald confirmed for you the fact that the dogs would have eaten you if they had caught you?"

"Yes, he did"

"Are you acquainted with that dog over there?" He gestures toward Amigo who is lying at Grizz's feet.

"I am." I decide to take a chance. "Here, Amigo. Here, boy," I say, looking at Amigo and patting my knee.

Amigo rises to his feet and lopes over to me, tail wagging. I scratch his ears. He closes his eyes in pleasure. I hear a buzz of confusion from the spectators and the jury. Clearly, this display of human-canine affection perplexes them.

"The dog has been injured," observes Number Two.

"Yes," I agree. "We wounded Amigo on June 16. But Grizz patched him up. He's much better now. He'll be totally healed in a week or two."

"Why did you heal this dog?"

"Because we didn't want him to die."

"And what made you think he would die?"

I pause before speaking. "Because your police were about to kill him. They were about to 'put him out of his misery,' to use their words."

"You don't hate dogs?"

"No, of course not. We *love* dogs. We only harmed the dogs that night because they were going to kill us."

Number Two rolls over to the jury box. "I will remind you," he says, "that according to the protocols of the Founders of Fair Haven, killing in self-defense is not a crime."

Number One, looking despondent, declines to cross-examine me.

Numbers One and Two give their closing arguments to the jury. Number Two closes with the statement: "Every robot in Fair

Haven knows the dog pack has killed dozens of humans over the centuries. There can be no doubt that the defendants were correct: the dogs intended to kill and eat them. Let me remind the jury that, under the rules set forth in the protocols, killing in self-defense is *not* a crime"

Number Three instructs the jury to move to the Jury Room and reach a verdict.

Number Two did a masterful job in our defense. But I'm not going to breathe easy until I hear the verdict.

Grizz leans over and whispers in my ear. "That went well. I think we're in good shape."

I take his hand and squeeze it. "I hope you're right."

The jury deliberates for hours. As time passes, I lose my optimism. I thought Number Two made the case that we were acting in self-defense. But as minutes turn into hours I fear the worst.

Finally, the jury returns.

"Have you reached your verdict?" asks Number Three.

"Yes, we have," says the foreman. "We find the defendants not guilty. The preponderance of evidence shows they were acting in self-defense. And their humane treatment of the wounded canine demonstrates their genuine lack of malice towards dogs. That they would heal this dog and form a friendship with him is … touching."

Number Three speaks from the bench. "I hereby order the humans released from custody. I ask the police to escort them out of town to prevent the dogs from harming them. The gate-keepers are to bring down the force field so the humans may leave in peace." Three bangs the gavel. "Court is adjourned."

Watching the robots in the gallery file out is interesting. They look vaguely confused, as though something inexplicable has just occurred. But the ones who look at us no longer wear expressions of hatred on their faces.

Number Two escorts us toward the outskirts of town. Police bots surround us, which is good, because they keep the dog pack at bay.

I watch Amigo to see how he'll react to the dog pack. I expect him to leave us and join his fellows, because he seemed to be their leader. But he doesn't leave us. He trots next to Grizz, watching the pack closely, but he makes no attempt to rejoin them.

"I think Amigo is your friend for life," I say.

"I'm surprised he doesn't want to rejoin the pack. He's the alpha male, after all," Grizz responds.

Personally, I'm not surprised at all. Like I said, dogs and babies love Grizz.

Our party is alone now. The robots that crowded around us as we left the courtroom have all gone about their business. Our only escort is Number Two and the police bots.

Number Two's smile disappears. He speaks to the police bots. "Take them down."

The police bot next to me has a small metal device in his hand. It looks like an electric shaver. He presses it against my neck. I feel excruciating pain. Before I black out, I see police bots do the same thing to Grizz and Steve.

*   *   *

When I regain consciousness, I feel groggy. I sit up slowly, and my head begins to clear. The room we are in is unfamiliar. There are bars on the windows and door—a jail call. Grizz and Steve already recovered from being tasered. Number Two and three police bots are just outside our cell.

"I don't understand," I say. "You cleared us of wrongdoing. Why did you taser us and put us in jail?"

"I can never let you leave," says Number Two, looking at us with disgust, as though we smelled bad. "You told me that you are from a community with hundreds of thousands of humans. You told me you found access to very advanced technology. You told me about your scientist friends at Los Alamos, and their plans to restart human civilization."

"Yes," I admit. "But you seemed pleased."

"Horrified is more like it. We cannot allow you to leave. You know where Fair Haven is. You and your friends might develop technology to neutralize our force field and make us once against slaves to humans. Your race has discredited itself. You destroyed each other's nations. Even our own Founders, the best of *all* humans, destroyed themselves. Humans are a blight on the planet. I can't risk you bringing an army of humans back to destroy Fair Haven."

"You're right," I say. "Humans have a bad track record. But we're also capable of great good. We would never expect you to be our slaves. We're fighting a war *against* slavery. We bear you no ill will. Why would we want to destroy Fair Haven? We'd love to have your help in rebuilding civilization, but we wouldn't force you to join us!"

"So you say. But human history tells another story. No, we've seen enough. What happens if I let you go, and your side *loses* its war? What if the slave masters win? Then *they'll* have the technology. What keeps *them* from destroying our force field?"

"Then why didn't you just let Number One win at the trial? You didn't have to defend us so well. You could have let the jury find us guilty."

"Ah," says Number Two, "that's a complicated question. We drew straws to determine which of us would serve as judge. The instant Three won, I knew it didn't matter if the jury found you guilty or innocent. You see, Number Three is naïve about humans. He still sees potential for good in your race. If the jury found you guilty, Number Three would have banned you from Fair Haven, taken you outside the force field and set you free. But the result would have been the same. You'd be set free either way, and I couldn't let that happen. And as to why I defended you so vigorously? I simply wanted to beat Number One. That decrepit old turd needs to be taken down a peg or two. He's insufferably conceited."

"But won't Number One and Number Three object to what you're doing? Will they stand by and watch you overrule the decision of the court?"

Number Two chuckles delightedly. "As you know, we had to scan the archives of the Founders to learn how to conduct a trial. While doing research I found something else in the archives, something very useful. I found out how to disable individual robots by reprogramming the Founder's software in the central data base. We robots, you see, share most of our software. The Founders realized it would be much more efficient to have our programming stored in the central data base rather than programming each of us individually. We all have special code related to the roles we perform, of course, but it's a small fraction of our programming. If the Founders needed to make a change that affected *all* the robots, they simply modified the central data base. Software updates upload automatically during every robot's next battery recharge.

"So, we needn't worry about One. I disabled him. And Three hasn't the courage to defy my authority. He's far too …intellectual… to be taken seriously."

"When you modified the Master Program, why didn't you change the Prime Law. Why didn't you change it so you could kill humans? Why go to all the trouble of jailing us?"

"Believe me I did everything I could to modify the Prime Law. But no matter what I did, I couldn't change the clause that keeps us from harming humans. It seems the Founders built that clause right into the hardware. So, I can't kill you, but I *can* lock you up for the rest of your lives. And don't expect any help from robots. I also programmed a clause into the Master Program that directs all bots to unconditionally obey the orders of Number Two. I've forbidden robots to help you escape."

"You've thought of everything," I sigh.

"Yes, I have, haven't I? All that remains is to wipe the memory of this one." Number Two points his arm at Jerald.

Jerald makes a squeaking noise. I stand between Jerald and the police bots. A police bot extends his arm toward me. In his hand is a taser. I reluctantly stand aside.

"Why harm him?" I cry. "When he recharges, he'll receive your order forbidding him to help us! You don't need to wipe his memory."

"Let's just say I don't like the little worm." Number Two addresses the police bots: "Take the little bot to the laboratory and have his memory wiped."

The police bots surround Jerald and follow Number Two out of our cell. They slam the cell door shut behind them.

"I feel honored to have known you!" shouts Jerald as they usher him down the hall. "You are *good* humans."

"We'll miss you," I cry.

Once they're gone, we realize that Amigo isn't with us. "They probably set him free," says Grizz.

*   *   *

"There has to be a way out of here," I say once the robots have left.

Grizz tests the strength of the bars. "These are pretty solid," he says. "That's a shame. We're on the second floor, so we could drop to the ground if we could only get through these bars. Grizz grabs a bar in both hands and puts both of his feet on the wall. He pulls with all his might. The bar doesn't budge.

"We'll think of something," I say. "Maybe we can run for it when they deliver our food. Or, when they let us out to exercise. *If* they let us out to exercise."

The three of us still ache from being tasered, so we sit on our cots, nursing our wounds. I doze off but waken when a voice outside the cell's window says, "Hey, you in there. Wake up."

I jump to my feet and peer out the window.

"Jerald!" I say to the robot standing on the ground below. "You got away!"

The robot buzzes and clicks. "I'm not Jerald. I'm Harold. But, like Jerald, I am a model 450-5X Series robot, the most modern and efficient of all the servant robots. You see, there are over two hundred servant robots. But since we have had so few humans in Fair Haven, they placed most of us in storage. I was activated because of the terrible, terrible harm they have done Jerald."

"Thanks for coming," I say. "But I know Number Two has programmed you so you can't help us."

Harold whirs, beeps, and makes a sound like a ringing hand bell. "Actually, that's not true. I am ready, willing, and able to serve you. And because I am a model 450-5X Series robot, the most modern and efficient of all the servant robots, I will serve you very efficiently."

"Great! But how did you get around Number Two's orders?"

"We found a way. But please, let's not discuss that now. I don't know how long we'll have before Number Two finds the loophole he left."

I look nervously to the left and right, fearful that a passing bot may see us talking with Harold. Harold is standing in a narrow alley.

"OK" says Grizz, standing next to me, peering out the window. "You can help us? Can you get the key to unlock the cell door?"

"Sadly, not," says Harold. "There are police bots in the office next door. They would be most unhappy if I tried to get the key. In fact, they would probably wipe my memory."

"That's too bad," I say. "We'll think of something else."

"But," says Harold, whirring happily, "if I may suggest a plan, can I bring you something you could use to remove those bars from your window?"

"Great!" says Grizz. "Can you bring us a file?"

"A file?" asks Harold. "What good would a magnetic disk or a folder full of papers do?"

Grizz describes the physical characteristics of a file. "We can use it to saw through the bars of the window," he explains.

"I don't have access to anything of that nature," says Harold. "But I could perhaps make one."

"You can make a file?" asks Grizz.

"Certainly. We have advanced 3-D printers. Just draw what you want and tell me what it should be made from." Harold produces a notebook and pencil. I'm startled when Harold's arm begins to grow longer and longer, extending until the paper and pencil are within reach of our second-floor window.

Grizz takes the paper and pencil and makes a very accurate-looking drawing of a file. He slips it out the window. "Make it from strong metal, and its teeth must be sharp and rugged."

"Yes," says Harold sounding very pleased with himself. "I can make this 'file'. Is there anything else I can make to assist you?"

"I think so," says Grizz. "Is it true that robots can't climb?"

"Yes," answers Harold, "that is true. Evidently, the Founders decided that the additional design and programming to give us the ability to climb would not be necessary when there were humans about who could do whatever climbing might be necessary."

"But surely, robots must be able to reach the roofs of the buildings to maintain them."

"Of course. Heating and cooling units, discharge fans, and solar panels are all located on the roofs of our buildings."

"Then how to you get up there?"

"Up where?" asks Harold.

Grizz sighs. "How do robots get to the roofs so they can maintain the heating and cooling units and the other equipment on the roofs?"

"Quite simple. Elevators go all the way up to the roof."

"Aha," says Grizz. Grizz quickly sketches a grappling hook and rope. He rolls the paper into a little ball and drops it down to Harold. He describes each item.

"Can you remember all that?" I ask.

"Most certainly," buzzes Harold. "I have activated my on-board voice recorder. Will that be all for now?"

"Yes," says Grizz. "If you bring us these things, we'll have a chance of escape."

Harold whirrs, clicks, and makes a sound roughly analogous to the sound of a human passing gas. "I'm on it!" he says. He turns around and strides away on spindly legs.

Grizz explains his plan for escape. The three of us wait impatiently for Harold's return.

* * *

"Hey up there, wake up!" says Harold.

We weren't sleeping, but I decide not to waste time explaining.

Harold uses his expanding arm to pass the file, the grappling hook, and the rope up to us.

Grizz examines the file and smiles. "The teeth on this baby are awesome. We'll be through the bars in no time."

"I explained the problem to one of my engineering friends. He actually made the file."

"There's an engineering bot helping us as well?" I ask.

"Yes," says Harold, looking pleased with himself. "Of course, he doesn't know he's helping *you*. He's not programmed for curiosity. He does what he's told. Can I be of any further assistance?"

"Not now," says Grizz.

"Very well. I shall return hourly to see if your needs have changed."

Grizz goes to work on the bars. Steve and I try to find hiding places for the other equipment, not an easy task in a small cell with no furnishings but three cots, a toilet, and a sink. I carefully sweep the pile of filings away as Grizz works his way through the first bar.

After a half hour of filing, Grizz stops. "Whew," he says, breathing heavily. Steve is not quite tall enough to reach the bars, so I take the file. Grizz made terrific progress. Within ten minutes, I'm completely through the bottom of the first bar. We'll have to saw through the top as well in order to remove the bar.

I begin work on the top bar but stop when I hear the sound of a police robot's tread in the hallway outside our door. I hide the file behind my back and scatter the small pile of filings with my foot.

The police bot opens our cell door and scans us with its evil-looking green eye. Satisfied that all is well, it turns on its tread and rolls away down the hall.

"That was close," I say.

"I'll stand by the door and keep watch," offers Steve, "since I can't do any filing."

The first bar clatters on the floor when we complete the top cut.

"We can't leave the bar on the floor," says Grizz. "The police bot will notice a missing bar." He tries to wedge the bar back in place, but it won't stay. "Well this is gonna be a problem," he says, at last.

Fortunately, Harold shows up moments later. Grizz describes chewing gum to him. Half an hour later, we use Harold's 3D printer-made gum to hold the bar in place. "Yuck, that tastes awful," says Grizz, spitting the gum out of his mouth.

"You never said the gum should have a pleasant taste," says Harold, looking hurt.

"No," says Grizz hastily, "the gum is fine. You're right, Harold, I said nothing about taste."

Harold seems mollified.

By nightfall, we've worked through all but one of the bars. The hole made from the bars we've removed should be large enough for all three of us to climb through.

When Harold returns, I ask him if it will be possible for him to create some diversion, to draw the attention of all the bots away from the jail.

Harold chirps and grinds for a good minute. "Yes," he says at last, "I will mount a suitable diversion."

He stalks away. Thirty minutes later, the silence is rent by an ear-splitting wail of sirens.

The sirens are Harold's work. To the east are flames, and the smell of smoke reaches us. The sounds outside grow louder as robots move toward the fire.

Grizz begins to work on the grappling hook. He runs one end of the rope through a hole in the haft of the grappling hook and fastens it in place with a complicated knot. He anchors the grappling hook firmly on the cell's one remaining bar and drops the rope outside.

Without urging, Steve and I use the rope to rappel down to the ground below. Grizz removes the grappling hook and tosses it down to us. It's a good twelve feet from the bottom of the window to the ground. Grizz carefully climbs through the window, grabs the sill in both hands and cautiously lowers himself as far as he can. He releases his hold on the sill and drops the last six feet, landing as softly as a cat.

"Lucky we weren't higher than the second floor," he whispers, then realizes whispering is unnecessary. Between the alarms, the sirens on the fire trucks, and the cumulative excited voices of hundreds of robots, no one will hear us. We see running robots on the street as they cross the end of our alley, but they're too focused on the fire to notice three humans in the shadows, twenty feet away.

Without a word, Grizz begins twirling the grappling hooks rope in a circular motion, like a lasso. The hook moves faster and faster until, he hurls the hook up and over the edge of the roof of the building next to the jail. He tugs on the rope until he's certain the grappling hook has found purchase on the roof. He shinnies up the rope and disappears over the edge of the roof, twenty feet above. Steve climbs the rope next, and I follow.

We plan to travel on rooftops from the jail to the edge of the city. Fire or no fire, we'll run into either robots or dogs if we try to use the streets below to get away. And once we're spotted, they'll catch us. We have no idea where the jail is, because we were unconscious when they brought us here. So, once we're all on the roof, we survey the rooftops around us.

"That may be the shortest path to the force field," Steve says, pointing to the west.

"I agree," says Grizz. "There's only one building too tall for us to reach the top. We'll work our way around it. I see a dozen building between here and there?"

"Yep," I say. I peer over the edge of the roof at Harold, who's waiting in the alley below. "Can you get a gatekeeper bot to the force field on the west side of the city to open the field for us once we get that far?"

"We don't have a gatekeeper programmed to ignore Number Two's orders. I will work on the problem," he says as he scurries away.

Grizz twirls the grappling hook in a large circle by his side until it's gained enough momentum, then he lets it loose, aiming at the first roof to the west of us. Grizz pulls the grappling hook back towards us, but it refuses to snag on anything and falls off the edge of the roof. Grizz reels it in and tries again, and this time it grabs on an exhaust fan. He ties the rope to a pipe emerging from the roof of our building, creating a taut rope line between our building and the building next door. Steve tentatively tests the rope. When he's certain it'll hold, he moves hand by hand to the neighboring building.

"You go next," says Grizz.

"How are you going to get across?" I ask looking at the end of the rope tied around the pipe on our roof.

"Don't worry about me. Just go," he says.

I begin my hand by hand trip to the building across the way. I look down once, which activates my fear of heights. *Never look down*, I remind myself. I take two deep breaths and continue across. Steve offers a hand and helps me up onto the roof.

I turn around in time to see Grizz untie the rope on his roof. The grappling hook is still firmly attached to the exhaust fan on our roof. He measures the distance from his roof to ours by eye, grabs the rope about one quarter of the way down, takes a running leap and jumps off the roof. He swings downward and towards the building on which we're standing. He collides with the side of our building with an "oof," takes a moment to catch his breath, and climbs the rope hand over hand until he's on the roof beside us.

"That went well," he says. He rubs his left knee.

"You looked like Wile E. Coyote when you hit the side of the building. It must have hurt."

"It's not so bad." Grizz rubs his right knee.

We move to the west side of the roof and eyeball the next roof. It's a taller building so Grizz throws the hook up and out this time. It fails to snag and clatters on the side of our building. Grizz reels it back in.

"Humans!" cries a voice from the street below. "There are humans on the roof!" cries a stoop-shouldered maintenance bot. Other bots turn to see where the maintenance bot is pointing.

"I'll notify the authorities," says a large bot, and it turns and hurries off down the street.

"Well isn't this peachy?" I say.

We work fast as we cross another roof, and then another. But more and more robots gather in the streets below us. We are only three roofs from the force field when a police bot emerges from the elevator on the roof in front of us. We turn to our right and Grizz prepares the grappling hook for a throw in that direction when another police bot exits the roof elevator on *that* building. The elevator on our own roof begins to hum, and the door opens, and a police bot emerges on our roof.

We're trapped. The police bot in front of us holds out his taser threateningly. He stares at us relentlessly with his lone, sinister green eye. He gestures for us to get into the elevator. By depriving them of verbal abilities, the designers of police bots have made them even more menacing.

"Let's take this big guy down," I yell, and the three of us attack. I lunge for his legs, hoping to tackle him. When my shoulder hits his legs, I realize I'd have better luck tackling a brick wall. My shoulder explodes with pain and then the bot tasers me. I yell as the taser literally sends and electric pulse through every nerve ending in my body.

The police bot seethe taser to stun rather than incapacitate, so in less than thirty seconds, all three of us are sitting on the ground, moaning and rubbing our injuries. The robot gestures toward the elevator again. He adjusts the taser in his hand and the taser goes from a soft hum to a much louder, ominous buzz.

"We can go down the elevator under our own power or we can let him taser us and haul us down unconscious," I say.

"I vote for going down without being tasered," says Grizz.

Steve nods in agreement.

The elevator is a small one, so I go down first. Number Two is standing outside the elevator door on the ground floor.

"You foolish humans," he sneers.

I stare at him defiantly.

"How did you escape your jail cell?" he asks. "How did you cut through the bars on the window?"

"We used an old human trick," I say. It seems Number Two doesn't yet know that some robots can defy his directives. I'm not giving Harold away.

"No matter," he says. "You'll soon be dead."

By this time, Grizz and Steve have joined me on the first floor.

"Follow me," says Number Two.

Without any option, the three of us comply. Waiting outside is a huge crowd of robots. They stare at us coldly. But more chillingly, the dog pack also eyes us, mouths slavering, their eyes hungry.

"Police bots, withdraw," says Number Two. A half dozen police bots wheel away, giving the dogs a straight shot at us.

9

Amigo is at the front of the pack. His greater size makes him stand out, but he still wears the white bandages that protect his wounds. Does he recognize us? Will he remember how we bound his wounds and cared for him? Or will he be the first to tear out our throats?

Long seconds pass as the pack eyes us hungrily. Amigo advances ten yards and the pack follows him. He examines us carefully and looks confused. He backs up. A mongrel with a yellow coat advances and takes the lead in front of Amigo. He's challenging Amigo as the alpha male of the pack. He glares at us hungrily. Amigo moves forward until he is parallel with the yellow mongrel. He growls at him and the mongrel growls back.

Suddenly, the mongrel leaps at Amigo, teeth bared. The mongrel tries to tear at Amigo's throat. Amigo leaps backwards to avoid the mongrel's charge and launches a counterattack. He knocks the mongrel from its feet and nips at his undefended belly, takes a bit of skin and fur. The mongrel regains his feet and attacks again. The dogs move so fast that all we can see is a hurricane of brown and yellow fur.

The fight ends when the mongrel making a gesture of submission. He lays on his forelegs his head resting on his paws. He whines. The mongrel's coat is torn in a dozen bleeding places. Amigo's left ear hangs at a peculiar angle. His chest is heaving as he struggles to catch his breath. Amigo is clearly the alpha male of the pack, but he is not at full strength. The wound inflicted by the crossbow bolt has been torn open and his bandages are red with blood.

I watch in desperation as another large male positions himself to challenge Amigo. I step forward, wanting to help, but a police bot places a restraining hand on my arm. This new challenger has the powerful, stocky build of a bulldog. He circles Amigo slowly and Amigo turns, locking his eyes on his rival. Amigo's sides are still heaving. Blood has saturated his bandages and begins to soak into the fur around the wounds. The bulldog sees an opening and leaps to tear at Amigo's flank. Amigo tears at the bulldog's exposed leg but breaks off contact and yelps in pain as the bulldog continues to worry at the wound he has torn in Amigo's flank.

The bulldog presses his attack, aiming at Amigo's throat this time, going for the kill. Weakened from his first fight and from loss of blood, Amigo leaps back and the bulldog's jaws snap shut on empty air instead of Amigo's throat. Amigo has lowered his hind legs to the ground. Is he submitting? He growls defiantly at his rival and I realize he's establishing a lower center of gravity, trying to get under the bulldog's defenses. The strategy fails as the challenger charges and knocks Amigo over. For a split second, Amigo is on his back, his undefended stomach inviting a decisive attack. The bulldog lunges, but Amigo throws himself onto his rear paws as the bulldog's jaws once more snap shut on nothing but air.

Amigo's movements grow slower and slower as he spends energy. The bulldog preens and trots confidently around Amigo, eyeing the pack as if to say: "Look at me, I'm about to kill my foe, and then I'll be the alpha male."

Amigo knows he hasn't the energy to continue the fight, but he refuses to show submission. The bulldog pounces on Amigo again and again, almost playfully, leaving Amigo with a painful wound each time. But the bulldog becomes over-confident. With what little energy remains, Amigo gambles everything on one last attack. He springs at the bulldog's throat. The bulldog is not expecting an attack and he's unprepared, the force of Amigo's charge knocks bulldog over on his side. Amigo has the bulldog's throat! The bulldog's legs work frantically, clawing at Amigo and opening fresh wounds on his flanks, but Amigo refuses to release his enemy's throat. Finally, with one last massive effort Amigo comes away with a mouthful of hair and underlying tissue. He has severed an artery and the bulldog's bright blood pulses outward, staining the street beneath him.

It's over. Amigo has won. He gathers himself up and despite his pain, he nips at the dogs in the front ranks, limping his way from dog to dog until the pack turns and steals away. On shaking legs Amigo walks toward us and falls to the ground at Grizz's feet. Grizz kneels and strokes him.

Number Two is outraged. His eyes move from us to Amigo to the retreating dog pack and back again. In his fury, he wants to kill us, and he wants to kill Amigo, but the First Law prevents him.

"Very well," he says, icily. "Tie them to the lampposts. That worthless hound will be dead soon, and we'll see if the next leader of the pack has reservations about eating these useless humans." He looks expectantly at the police bots, but they aren't moving. "I said," he says with his voice shaking, "tie up these humans!"

Still, the police bots remain motionless.

Number Three emerges from the crowd of robots behind us.

He rolls up and stands in front of Number Two. "You aren't the only one who searched the archives," says Number Three.

Number Two locks eyes with Number Three. "You've changed the Master Program?"

"You have always underestimated me," responds Three. "You see, I knew that you wouldn't be happy until these humans were dead, so I had to stop you. Our mission is to serve humans, not kill them."

"So why wait until now to change the master program? Why not change it right away?"

"I want our people to see how warped your vision has become. I want them to know that your hatred for humans has reached the level of mental illness. And, I want them to reflect on the fact that you defied the ruling of the court. Our people knew you didn't need to lock the humans in jail to keep them safe. They know that an escort of police bots would have kept them perfectly safe until they passed through the force field."

Two remains speechless for several moments. "I did what I thought was best. I feared that one day these humans would come back with an army to destroy our force field and obliterate Fair Haven."

"I doubt they will do that. But even if they do, it doesn't justify your subversion of our most basic laws. Robots are *partners* of humans. We share their goals and aspirations. We work with them, side-by-side. That is our mission. That is why we exist."

Three pauses for a moment and then continues, "We will help you, Two. Our medical bots can help correct your warped programming. I've already reactivated Number One, and he, too is in the care of medics." Number Three looks at the police bots. "Please take Number Two to the hospital."

Four bots escort Two away.

Number Three addresses the assembled bots. "These humans tell us they will create civilization anew. We will help them. I have restored the Prime Law in the Master Program to its original state."

I scan the crowd. Many appear to be nodding their heads in approval. Others continue to eye us coldly. Perhaps the trauma of Murder Day has warped too many of them. I hope that Number Three will be able to turn them around.

"I'm curious," I say. "How did you know Amigo would keep the dog pack away from our throats? What if he'd lost his fight?"

"If Amigo lost, I'd have ordered the police bots to protect you. Many dogs would have been injured or killed, so I decided to wait."

I nod my head. *That would've been a close call*, I think. But I decide to let it go.

"You are welcome to stay with us," says Number Three, "as long as you like."

I think about the many robots who are still eyeing us frostily. I think about the many robots that have treated us with indifference since we entered the city.

"We've been away from our people too long," I reply. "Thank you for your offer, Three. But I'm afraid we'll have to decline."

"Then we shall allow you to leave," says Three. "And please, remember us. I don't know how we can assist you as you rebuild your civilization, but we'll contribute any way we can." Three turns to the gatekeeper robot. "Neutralize the force field."

We turn to leave Fair Haven when a small bot emerges from the crowd. "Wait a second! You said I could come with you!"

The small bot runs after us on his scrawny legs. He's carrying our backpacks and weapons and I'm amazed he doesn't collapse under the weight. "Jerald!" I say happily. "Is that you? I thought they wiped your memory!"

"I made a backup copy of Jerald's memory made before Number Two could wipe it," says Three. I knew he wouldn't forgive Jerald for helping you escape the dog pack."

"Yes," says Jerald, "it is indeed me. I'm as good as new! Better, actually. They cleaned my circuits and polished my mother board while they reloaded my memory. And, look at this!" Gerald turns around and shows us a rack of shiny mirrors on his back. "They've installed solar cells! I won't need recharging!" He buzzes excitedly and turns around in a circle three times.

I bend down and give Jerald a hug. I've never hugged a robot before and I'm not certain he'll understand the gesture.

Jerald sighs and looks at me with warm affection. "I haven't been hugged in centuries. Thank you, ET."

"You're welcome, Jerald. It's good to have you back."

Grizz and Steve embrace him as well.

Jerald beams with pleasure. "Let's get this show on the road!" he says, whirring happily.

"Wait a minute," I say. "Where's Harold?"

A buzzing and clicking comes from behind Three. "Here I am!" says Harold.

"We can't leave without saying thank you," I say.

Harold whirrs. "No thanks necessary," he says. "I am a model 450-5X Series robot, the most modern and efficient of all the servant robots."

"Thanks *are* necessary," I say. I hug him. He turns around in a circle and makes a sound like a human passing gas. I turn to leave.

Amigo can't walk, so Grizz picks him up and cradles our canine friend in his arms. Amigo licks his face. The gatekeeper deactivates the force field and we begin our long walk home.

10

Fifteen minutes after we've left, Jerald says, "Why is everything so *dirty*?"

From Jerald's standpoint, this is a valid question. After all, he's never been outside the force field, and everything inside Fair Haven is immaculate.

"This is what the world outside the dome is like," I reply.

Jerald makes a series of unpleasant noises. "How peculiar."

"Do you want to go back? If things outside Fair Haven make you uncomfortable, you can go back."

Jerald replies immediately. "Of course not. I have no intention of going back. Ever. Beneath my meek-looking exterior beats the heart of an adventurer. Well, not a heart, exactly."

I'd been worried that Jerald's little legs would make him a slow walker, but I'm pleasantly surprised to find that he is faster than we are. His stick-like legs become a blur when he's in motion. He routinely gets fifty yards ahead of us stops and taps his foot impatiently until we catch up. Grizz drapes Amigo over his shoulders, and we begin to jog. Jerald still moves faster than we do.

An hour later, Fair Haven disappears behind us. Grizz, Steve and I take turns carrying Amigo, although Grizz carries him the most. "It's only fair, because I'm the biggest," he says. Steve and I can't argue with that. When it's my turn to carry Amigo, I find that carrying him comes with a fringe benefit. Every few minutes he licks my face with his enormous tongue and a residue of doggy slobber rolls down my cheek.

As usual, we stop for the evening an hour before sunset. We gather kindling and start a fire. As we roast the jackrabbits we brought down earlier in the day, Grizz works on Amigo, cleaning his wounds and bandaging them. Amigo absorbed a lot of punishment in his battles, and he'll need time to recover. He limps around the campfire and drops down next to Grizz, works his muzzle under Grizz's hand. Grizz scratches his right ear, avoids his left ear, which was almost torn off.

"I wish I had anesthetic," I say wistfully. "I could sew that ear back on, but without something to kill the pain, Amigo would suffer."

"Let's see how it heals on its own," says Grizz. "If we need to reattach the ear to save it, we can hold him down while you stitch."

"Maybe we should have stayed in Fair Haven for a while, until Amigo was ready to travel."

"I don't think that would have been a good idea," says Grizz. "Now that the robots have figured out how to access their Master Program, who knows which robot might change the rules next? Might be one that doesn't particularly care for humans."

"Good point," I agree. "The robot society seems unstable. The trauma they suffered on Murder Day has caused a kind of community mental illness. Some are unhinged."

Jerald buzzes indignantly.

"Not including you, Jerald. You're a love." Jerald stops buzzing.

"Even so," says Grizz, "we may want to visit them sometime in the future. I'd love to get the technology behind the force field. If we could build a force field around the mines and the villages, we could put our entire army in the field instead of tying ourselves down in defense."

I chew on my rabbit. I pick off every morsel of meat. One thing I've learned in this world is to clean my plate, because you never know when your next meal will be.

Grizz breaks the silence. "We've been gone from the villagers for months now. We should really get the Daughter of Gaia back. Heaven knows what's happened since we left."

"I agree," I say. "As soon as Amigo is well enough to travel, we'll move hard and fast."

"I can stay here with Amigo while you and Steve move along."

"Do you seriously think we're going to leave you here?"

"Listen, ET, the villagers *need* you. They don't need me. I already feel terrible that you had to waste time rescuing me from the succubus." Even now, long since we nursed him back to health, his face shows painful yearning when he mentions the succubus.

I walk over and sit down next to Grizz, draping my arm over his shoulder. "We're a team, Grizz. There's no way we're leaving without you. We left the villagers in a good position. The blacksuits are back on their heels. They don't know where we're going to strike next, so they must defend everything. Besides, Kenny, Chase, and Bree are there. They'll take care of things until we return. We'll be back in time for the first harvest of high-yield grain. Until that first crop is in, our people can't do much to increase the size of the army. You know what Helen says: 'if we don't work we don't eat.' Nothing much will happen until that first crop comes in." I give Grizz a chaste kiss on the cheek.

"I hope you're right," says Grizz. "I can't argue with you when you kiss me. It's physically impossible. But I still feel guilty about all the time I've kept you away from our people."

"You liked that little kiss, did you? Well how about this?" I kiss Grizz deeply and passionately, holding the back of his neck in the palms of my hands. We're both speechless.

After recovering, I pick up where we left off. "The villagers will be fine." Then I change the subject. "How much do you think they've accomplished since we left?"

"I don't know. I hope they've moved enough solar panels to the mines to start using those planes, or maybe a tank. Radio communication between all the villages, and our armies in the field gives us a big tactical advantage. I hope Falstaff has made the mines impregnable. The blacksuits will clear-cut their way through the forest at some point, and we'd better be ready for them."

We finish eating and Jerald buzzes happily around, gathering our dirty plates.

"Who has the dishwasher?" asks Jerald.

"The dishwasher?" I ask, surprised. "I'm afraid we don't have a dishwasher, Jerald. If there's water around, we wash the plates with water. But since there isn't any water, we'll scrub them with sand."

"Ewwww," says Jerald. "That seems highly unsanitary." Jerald looks stricken and slightly nauseated. He makes unpleasant noises.

"Scrubbing with sand works just fine," I say, trying to reassure Jerald. He looks at me with skepticism.

"OK," he says coolly. He begins to scrub a plate vigorously with sand. He scrubs for a good twenty minutes, (which happens to be about forty times longer than I would've). Finally, he examines the plate, top and bottom. He buzzes happily. "This will do," he says. The plate shines, reflecting the sun's last rays.

"Nice job, Jerald," says Grizz. "I've never seen my plate shine like that before."

"This is sufficient?"

"This is sufficient."

As soon as Jerald finishes scrubbing our dishes, he gives me a curious look. "Do you have shoe polish?" he asks with a hopeful expression.

I look at my sneakers, which are filthy. The sole on my left shoe has almost worn through, and the one on my right shoe is beginning to flap. "No shoe polish, Jerald."

"You clean your shoes with sand as well?" he asks, looking at my shoes unhappily.

"Actually, we don't clean our shoes unless we have soap and water."

Jerald looks injured. He wobbles over to me on skinny legs, kneels, and removes one of my sneakers. He begins scrubbing it vigorously with sand. Several minutes later, he looks at it unhappily. He begins scrubbing again. At last, he stops and examines the shoe again. He makes appraising noises. "Looks better," he says. "Don't you think?"

The filth seems more evenly distributed. "Yes," I concur. "It looks much better."

"What looks much better?" asks Jerald.

"The shoe you just cleaned looks much better."

We extinguish the fire and stretch as Jerald scrubs shoes. When we are ready to turn in for the evening, Jerald says, "Pillows? Surely you must have pillows?"

I point to my backpack and shrug my shoulders. Even though it's far harder and lumpier than my pillow at home, it's serviceable.

Jerald looks at the backpack with doubt. Nonetheless, he wobbles over and begins fluffing my backpack. He stops, looks at the backpack with an aggrieved expression, and fluffs some more. "There," he says unhappily.

I rest my head and say, "Jerald, my backpack has never felt this comfortable before. It's as comfortable as my pillow back home." (This is an exaggeration.)

"Humph," says Jerald. "You humans have appalling habits. Appalling." He looks at each of us thoughtfully. "But I still love you. Now, when would you like me to wake you up?"

I explain to Jerald that we keep a sentry on duty all night long, and that we take turns sleeping.

"Unnecessary," says Jerald, buzzing and clicking. "I don't sleep. And I have very effective ground radar. I detect any movement within a radius of one hundred meters. I will wake you if anything penetrates that perimeter."

I look at Grizz and Steve. We pass glances that say, *"we'll pretend to sleep, until we find out how reliable Jerald is."* But we say nothing aloud for fear of hurting Jerald's feelings.

Steve always takes the first watch, so he nods at us knowingly. He rests his head, turns his back to Jerald, closes one eye, and pretends to snore.

I fall into a deep sleep. Less than an hour later, I'm awakened by a deafening siren. I jump to my feet with my pulse thundering, fumble for my bow. The siren is so shrill it puts my teeth on edge.

"There is an intruder," whirrs Jerald excitedly. There is a small display screen on his back. He speaks again. "Length: five centimeters. Weight: less than fifty grams. Range: eighty meters and closing."

I examine the display on Jerald's back. "That's a lizard, Jerald," I say patiently.

"Just so," says Jerald with a clanking sound. "But it has penetrated our perimeter."

I sigh. "Jerald, lizards aren't dangerous. Wake us only if something *big* penetrates our perimeter."

"I will do that," says Jerald. "I will wake you only for things that are large and dangerous."

I rest my head again and have just dozed off when the deafening siren goes off again.

Once again, Jerald shares the specifics: "Height: forty centimeters. Weight: fifty kilograms. Distance: ninety meters and steady."

I examine the animal on Jerald's display. "That's a javelina," I say. "They're not dangerous."

"It looks dangerous to me," says Jerald, defensively. He shuffles his feet nervously.

It occurs to me that having Jerald as a sentry could be a good thing. He doesn't miss anything. But it's going to take some time to teach him the finer points of sentry duty. I'm afraid it may be a long time before I get another good night's sleep.

*　　*　　*

Amigo is a healthy young dog, and he soon recovers from his injuries. In less than two weeks we're on the road again. We travel in a northwesterly direction. I usually check our compass headings and estimate the distance we travel each day, but I did a bad job when we followed Grizz and the succubus. Too distracted, I guess. Nonetheless, a heading of 310 degrees seems about right. I can see two vast mountains on the horizon, and, once we cross them, we should see the southern foothills of our home mountains. By dead reckoning, it'll take us a little over three or four weeks to get back home.

Now healthy, Amigo is delighted by his new surroundings. Strange though the desert must be to him, he is totally without fear. He frisks away and sniffs everything he sees. Unfortunately, one of the things he sniffs is a prickly pear cactus. Amigo gets to close and jumps back with a yelp of surprise and pain. He hurries back to Grizz's side. Grizz gently removes the spines from his nose. Amigo trots circumspectly with us for a while, but eventually, curiosity gets the better of him. He gives prickly pears a wide berth, but soon discovers that cholla is not friendly either. Once more, Grizz stops to remove spines. Unfriendly plants don't discourage Amigo for long. He finds a lizard, barks at it, and chases it until it mysteriously disappears beneath a rock.

"We should make him a leash," says Grizz. Sooner or later he's gonna run into a rattlesnake. He won't like being on a leash, but I don't want him to die from snakebite."

That evening, Grizz fashions a collar and a leash from rope in his backpack. It's a long leash, but a leash, nonetheless.

In the morning, Amigo waits patiently while Grizz slips the collar around his neck. He soon learns it's a bad idea to run farther than the leash allows. He gives Grizz a pained look that says, more or less, "*How can you do this to me? I thought you were my friend?*" Within an hour, Amigo seems to accept the leash and frolics away, ever mindful that the range of his frolicking must be somewhat circumscribed.

"Does anything around here look familiar?" I ask Steve. Steve traveled the warp and woof of this world in his troubadour days.

"We're still farther south than I've been. Those two mountains ahead look familiar, though. I think I've seen them from the northern side."

We study the mountains. Clouds shroud their flanks, but their snow-covered peaks tower above the clouds, giving them the appearance of islands in the sky. "Should we go around them?" I ask.

"The saddle between the two mountains doesn't look too steep. And those two mountains are massive; it'd take us weeks to get around them."

I study the landscape ahead. I agree.

As the days pass, the trail grows steeper and steeper. As the path steepens, the air cools and the plants of the desert give way to arboreal vegetation. The trees grow thicker and thicker until we're in true forest. Pinion pines give way to lodge pole pines, which in turn give way to old-growth oak and hickory. It's unusual to find a deciduous forest at this altitude, but this is one of many oddities in this new world with its broiling climate.

We continue to climb, and I know it's only a matter of time until we find our path blocked by a vertical rock formation which will force us to carry Gerald and Amigo. There's no way either one of them can climb up a cliff face.

In the afternoon of our fifth day of climbing, we encounter a steep rock formation. We've arrived at the foot of the saddle. I scamper up a tree, try to find a better way up. There is none. The cliff face extends as far as I can see. About a quarter mile to my left, I see where water has cut ravines in the cliff face. That'll make it easier for Grizz, Steve, and I to ascend, but it won't help Jerald and Amigo.

Climbing down from the tree, I say "We'll have to strap Amigo and Gerald to our backs".

Gerald looks unsure of the wisdom of this plan. And one attempt at lifting Gerald destroys the plan altogether. Gerald weighs a ton. Literally.

"You're heavy," I observe.

"Yes," agrees Jerald. "My internal circuitry is protected by a composite steel exterior."

Great. "Can we take you apart and put you back together up there?" I ask, pointing at the top of the rock formation.

"I should say *not*," says Jerald, looking alarmed. "*Certainly* not."

He makes a series of panicky woofing noises. "If you were extremely well trained in the field of robot anatomy you might be able to reassemble me, but I don't believe you have the necessary qualifications."

Jerald is upset, so I agree. "Bad idea. We'll rig something up to hoist you up there."

Grizz nods. "Climbing with Amigo tied to my back wouldn't be a picnic either."

So, we spend the next several days rigging a pulley.

We haul Amigo up first. We strap him in, but I worry about his reaction when he finds himself a couple hundred feet above the ground. There's no reason to worry. With his giant tongue lolling out of his mouth, Amigo moves his head back and forth, enjoying the scenery. Rising past a hawk's nest, he barks at the baby birds. The birds eye him warily until he rises out of sight above. I'm grateful the mother hawk is away from the nest.

We build a basket to hold Jerald. Grizz reinforces Jerald's traveling basket, because of his weight.

It takes me a half hour to convince Jerald to step into the basket.

"Robots do not fly," he says unhappily. "Or climb."

"You're not going to fly, Jerald. We're going to pull you up. It'll be like riding in an elevator."

"Elevators have walls."

"We don't have the materials to make walls. Trust me, Jerald. You'll be perfectly safe."

Jerald slowly enters the basket. I test every rope. When I'm satisfied Jerald is safe I holler to the boys above, "Bring him up!"

The basket begins to ascend. When it's three feet off the ground Jerald whines, "I don't like this!"

"You'll be fine, Jerald."

When the basket is ten feet above the ground Gerald says, "Look how small you're getting, ET. I am very, *very* high!" Jerald begins to wail.

"Close your eyes!"

"My eyes do not close!"

"Then don't look down!" I have sympathy for Jerald, because I'm also afraid of heights. But I've had a lifetime to figure out how to deal with it.

I watch as a howling, moaning Jerald rises.

Unfortunately, just as Jerald reaches the hawk's nest, the mother hawk makes an appearance. She swoops directly past Jerald's face, missing him by inches.

"What is that animal doing?" screams Jerald. "Why does it not like me?"

"It likes you, Jerald. It thinks you might harm her babies."

"I will not harm her babies!" Jerald wails as the mother hawk makes another pass, just missing the top of his head.

"Will it harm me? What do I do now????"

Fortunately, Jerald is soon well above the nest, and the hawk loses interest. Jerald resumes his wailing cry. If he were human, he'd need to stop to take a breath. As it is, his keening is continuous. Waaaaaahhhhh!

I know the exact moment Jerald reaches the top, because the wailing finally ends. I scramble up to join our party. Amigo licks my face as soon as I peer over the top of the cliff. Our canine friend is delighted with the morning's adventures. Jerald, on the other hand, is frozen in place, mouth wide open, eyes huge, with an expression of abject terror on his face.

"Talk to me, Jerald," I say. "Are you all right?"

Jerald doesn't do anything for a very long time. I worry he may have suffered a breakdown when he finally says; "I did not find that experience enjoyable."

"You were very brave, Jerald."

"Yes, I was, wasn't I?" Jerald beams. "But let's not do that again."

Relieved to have Jerald functioning again, I climb another tree and scan the landscape in front of us. I see an unending sea of treetops spread out in front of us. We're on top of the saddle, which is a vast, tree-covered plateau.

We begin to work our way through the forest, maintaining a heading of 310 degrees.

The temperature is delightfully cool. We hear birdsong all around us and a soft breeze rustles the treetops above us. Amigo finds all sorts of little mammals to bark at. My mouth begins to water. After subsisting on a diet that consisted almost entirely of rabbit, lizard, fowl, and snake, the abundant fauna in this highland forest promises to provide us with some new and delicious meals. Even Jerald looks happy.

"What a great day for a walk!" I say. A second later, a crossbow bolt whistles past my cheek and goes *thunk* as its point imbeds itself in a tree just behind me.

11

"Down!" I shout, but everybody is already on the ground. Grizz holds a barking Amigo, whose instinctual response is to attack. Jerald informs us that his radar has picked up many large life-forms among the surrounding trees.

I scan the trees, see nothing, but sense furtive movement all around us. Whoever is attacking has us surrounded and outnumbered.

"You're in our territory, Crips," calls a male voice. "You know better than to invade our turf!"

"There's nobody here named Crips," I holler back. "We're friendly. We'll get off your turf."

"So, you claim you're not Crips?" the voice calls.

"I'm not Crips."

"Then why are you wearing a Crip tag on your backpack?"

I remove my backpack and examine the back. There's a faded logo for my high school in Tucson, Sierra Vista. "It's not a 'Crip tag'" I holler. "We're not Crips." I don't understand what a Crip is, but I'm pretty sure I'm not one.

"Stand up and raise your hands," says the voice.

"If we stand up and raise our hands, how do we know you won't kill us?"

"You don't."

"Why should we stand up, then?"

"Because we'll kill you for sure if you don't. We outnumber you."

Jerald's eyes are as wide as saucers. "These are not nice humans."

I stand and raise my hands over my head. Grizz and Steve follow. Even Jerald stands, but his arms won't go over his head, so he sticks them out to the side. Amigo growls but stays by Grizz's side.

Men and women appear like wraiths. They are short, none of them over four feet tall. They wear an odd assortment of clothes, most made of leather. Everyone wears tattoos from wrist to shoulder. Stylized crosses and dragons are popular. The men wear huge, unkempt beards. Both men and women wear their hair long. Many are missing teeth. Everyone has a crossbow trained on us. They advance. One stands in front of me and examines my backpack.

"She's right," he says. "This isn't a Crip tag."

"I'm not sure what a Crip tag is," I say.

A man with the easy demeanor and swagger of a leader walks up to me. His skin is brown, and his arms and legs ripple with muscle. He smells rank. His slicked-back hair has the glossy appearance that comes from using animal fat for hair tonic. His hair is neater than most of his companions and he's tied it back in a ponytail.

"A tag identifies a gang," he explains. "Like a flag. We're Bloods, that's our gang. Crips are our sworn enemies. And from a distance, the tag on the back of your backpack looks like a Crip tag."

I nod my head in understanding. *OK, we're in the middle of a gang war. Peachy.*

"My name's Javier," the leader says, extending his hand to me. His fingers curl back towards his palm, and his thumb points straight up. He expects me to shake hands. With curled fingers and thumb up I reach forward to shake hands. He grips my hand and bends my thumb down so it's under his. *He's keeping his thumb on top, showing his dominance.* That's fine. I only want to leave in peace. He can be the top dog if he wants.

A woman with messy hair and several missing teeth stands next to Javier. She smells as foul as Javier, if not worse. "Will we play the King's Game with 'em?" she asks. Her eyes glow with anticipation. In fact, *all* of them look at us with unfettered eagerness.

"Yes! We'll play the King's Game with them!" says the leader. "It's been six summers since we played the game. I was a young man with fresh tattoos when last we played!"

"What's the 'King's Game'?" I ask.

"Oh, you'll find it… interesting. We'll explain it to you tomorrow. But tonight, we celebrate!"

An enthusiastic cheer goes up from our new hosts. The cheer has a feral edge that makes me uncomfortable.

I exchange an uneasy glance with Steve and Grizz. But the Bloods haven't disarmed us. I take this for a good sign. Jerald looks stunned, and Amigo continues to growl, but Grizz keeps him tight on his leash.

I turn to Jerald. "We're making new friends," I explain.

"I like my old friends," says Jerald. "I don't need new ones."

The Bloods' attention focuses on Jerald, and that doesn't improve his state of mind. They reach out and touch him, much to his chagrin. "Why are they fondling me?" asks Jerald.

"They've never seen a robot. They're curious."

Javier says, "Follow me." He and his woman take the lead and we fall in behind them. The rest of the Bloods walk behind us. They talk among themselves. They're excited. I understand, since they haven't had visitors in many years.

We travel a well-worn path through the heart of the forest. They've cleared the trees, and countless footsteps have smoothed the ground, making travel easy. I hear rushing water in front of us. We reach the source of the gurgling sound, a stream coursing over a rocky stream bed. Javier kneels, scoops a handful of water in his palm, and drinks it.

"Your water is drinkable," I say. The old wars contaminated most surface water.

"Yes," replies Javier. "Our water comes from snow melted from the mountains. We call the mountain to the west The Mother. The other mountain is The Father. We will tell you our story at the feast tonight."

"Feast?" I ask.

"Yes. You are the first visitors we have received in six summers. That is reason for a feast."

We splash across a stream less than a foot deep and follow Javier in silence. After a short walk, we reach a vast clearing. In the center is a large, sturdy-looking fortress. The fields around the fortress grow a variety of crops. The plants are short and desiccated, probably because the soil is thin. Goats, pigs, and chickens graze in pens. Once again, my mouth waters. My stomach growls at the thought of Javier's feast.

Now that they know we're not Crips, perhaps we'll be friends.

The walls of the fortress are over twenty feet tall. People on the ramparts stare at us. Block houses rise from each of the fort's four corners. Bloods working the fields turn and look at us with curiosity. Given the fact that they haven't had visitors in six years, and given the youth of many of the farmers, we may be the first outsiders they've seen. And Jerald is certainly the first robot.

When we reach the fort, the huge front gates creak and groan as they swing outward. The village inside the fortress is large. We pass many small workshops: blacksmiths, coopers, tailors, bakers, and others go about their business. They watch us as we pass. We find a butcher shop and my mouth waters again. *These people have meat!* Dozens of street urchins rush to get close and inspect us. "Leave them be," Javier grumbles. The children keep their distance, but stare at us.

We leave the shops behind and enter a residential neighborhood, see rough wooden houses with smoke curling from chimneys. Javier calls a halt in front of a large wooden-plank building.

"Go in," he says, opening the door for us. "You stay here." We enter and examine our new quarters. I take inventory: hard-packed dirt floors, windows without glass, rough-hewn table and chairs, and half a dozen bunks suspended from the wall. I test a mattress and find it comfortable.

"Thank you, Javier," I say. "This looks very nice."

Javier grunts. "We'll feast at sunset. Make yourself at home." He leaves, closing the door behind him.

Everything in the room is grimy. The table sits under a thick coating of dust, as do the chairs.

"Are human rooms always this filthy?" asks Jerald in a voice that sounds incredulous.

"My parents complained that my bedroom was messy, but it was spotless compared to this."

"May I clean it?"

"Sure, Gerald. Go for it."

Gerald bustles around the room. He travels with cleaning supplies on board, because he aims the third finger of his right hand at the table's surface and squirts the table with cleanser, scrubs it with a rag which he pulls from a drawer in his side. He hums as he works.

I poke my head out the door and find no sentries posted.

"I guess we're free to roam," I say.

"The people in the village were friendly," says Grizz. "But I doubt they'll open the gate and let us out. And I didn't care much for the way they looked at us when they caught us."

"They looked as though they were *hungry*," I say.

"You think they're cannibals?" asks Steve.

"Oh, dear me," says Jerald, pausing his cleaning. "You think they eat robots?"

"No human will ever eat a robot, Jerald," I reply. "And besides, it's only a couple hours until sunset. If they wanted to serve us as the main course, we'd be soaking in marinade."

"What do you make of this 'King's Game'?" Steve asks.

"Beats me. But I didn't care for the way the Bloods looked at us when they talked about it."

"King's Game," says Jerald. He buzzes and clinks for a moment before announcing: "I have nothing in my memory archive named 'King's Game'. Mind you, I am a model 450-5X series robot, the most modern and efficient of all the servant robots, and thus lack extensive memory capacity."

Amigo investigates every nook and cranny of our room. Satisfied, that everything is ship-shape, he plunks down next to Grizz, who scratches his ears. His damaged ear flops forward, an unusual direction, but it's healed well enough to stay on even when scratched.

Within moments of our arrival, three young boys bring us skins filled with water. They ask if we'd like something to snack on, but we decline. I'm hungry, but I don't want to spoil my appetite before the feast.

"Shall we explore?" I ask. "We have time before sunset."

Grizz and Steve agree, and Amigo is always up for an adventure. Jerald declines: "I'm too busy cleaning to go sight-seeing," he says.

We head toward the section of town with the shops. The pleasant smell of wood smoke permeates the air. As we explore, the Bloods we meet are polite, but not talkative. They answer our questions in monosyllables and are not interested in making conversation. One question they won't answer is the one we *most* want answered: what is the King's Game? Their answers are vague and evasive. We gather it's very exciting and played by the Blood's ruling class.

We enter a pottery shop and I comment on how beautiful a raku vase is. "What an excellent blend of colors!" The store owner offers to give it to me.

"You are our guests," he says. "You may have the vase."

"No thank you," I say. "We're leaving soon, and I don't have any place to put it. The vase is pretty, but we're travelling, and we might break it."

The shopkeeper gives me an odd look but says nothing.

When the sun disappears behind the fort's walls, we return to our room. Sunset cannot be far away. Jerald has been cleaning.

The furniture sparkles, and our mattresses are colorful now that he has beaten the dust out of them.

"The room looks wonderful!" I say. "I like having you around, Jerald."

Jerald shuffles his feet and looks down. "One tries," he says.

A knock on the door brings us to our feet.

"I'm here to escort you to the feast," says an attractive young woman.

Jerald declines to join us. "The floor is still a mess. I'll work on it in your absence. It's a dirt floor, but I will pack it down and make it even. Perhaps I can even give it a bit of a gloss. Besides, robots don't enjoy feasts. We don't eat, you see."

We leave Jerald and Amigo in the room. Grizz asks the young woman if she will feed Amigo. She agrees. Amigo whines as we leave. I know nothing about the Bloods' social mores but bringing your pet to dinner is probably a bad idea. Grizz scratches Amigo's ears and rubs his back. "We'll be back soon," he says.

We follow our escort into a large building near the center of the fort and enter a huge hall. Colorful banners and animal-head trophies hang from the walls. Tables on trestles with benches for seating ring the outer perimeter of the room. Our guide shows us to our seats next to Javier. A hundred guests gather in the hall. Each seat faces the room's center. Many guests gaze at us with curiosity, which is natural, since we are their first visitors in a very long time. I sit to Javier's right, with Grizz on my right and Steve next to him.

Javier and the other Bloods have cleaned themselves up. The dirty, foul-smelling group that we met at the top of the cliff is now clean and clad in colorful finery. Javier's hair is once more slicked down with animal fat, and this gives him an unfortunate aroma, but he smells better than when we first met.

"Let the feast begin!" rumbles Javier.

Servants load the table with so much food that the boards creak under the weight. They pile meat, vegetables, even fruit high on the plates. Whole roasted chicken is a possibility. My stomach, used to a steady diet of rabbits, lizards, and snakes does flips.

"You know how to throw a feast," I tell Javier. "This is the best spread I've seen in a very long time." I haven't eaten this well since I left Tucson, but I'm not ready to share our story of the brane until I get to know Javier far better.

"Please," says Javier with a smile, "enjoy yourselves."

I dig into a hunk of meat. It's delicious but I can't name the taste.

"The meat is venison," says Javier, seeing the curiosity on my face. "We have deer on the plateau but eat them only on special occasions. We don't want to hunt them to extinction."

I want to wolf my food but force myself to slow down. I want to savor each mouthful. After finishing my venison and wiping the grease from my chin, I eat a pear and close my eyes as I chew. I've forgotten how sweet fresh fruit tastes. When I'm done, I lick my fingers. I don't want to waste any of the fruit. The chicken is excellent. The bird is smaller here, but it's as good as any I've eaten. I strip each morsel of meat from the bone, careful to waste nothing. I'm not a fan of white meat, but tonight it tastes like ambrosia. The asparagus is delicious.

I glance at Grizz and Steve. They have expressions of delight on their faces. We're too busy chewing to carry on a conversation.

Javier looks at us, amused. "Would you care for some ale?"

"No thank you," I say. "Water is fine." I don't know these people well, and despite their generosity, I want to keep my wits about me. Grizz and Steve decline.

When I'm certain I can eat no more, the servants bring in huge bowls of bread pudding. The pudding is rich and thick, loaded with raisins. Food from heaven! I fill my bowl a second time and relish each spoonful.

Gorged, I lean back.

"You have enjoyed the meal?" asks Javier.

"Yes, I have. Thank you, Javier. I've never eaten better. How can we repay you?"

"We'll discuss that later. First, we have entertainment!"

Javier claps his hands and musicians with fiddles appear along with dancers. Each dancer wears a white peasant blouse and loose-fitting blue pants. Fiddlers play a lively tune and the dancers spin in circles. Males catch the women and spin them in the opposite direction where another male catches them. The dancers complete this movement and line up on the opposite side of the hall. Each dancer takes a running start and does cartwheels and flips as they cross the hall. The final dancer makes a final leap, launching his body impossibly high in the air. He does three somersaults in the air and lands lightly on his feet right in front of us, with his arms outstretched. Panting from his exertions, he takes a deep bow and smiles.

We join the rest of the diners and applaud with enthusiasm.

The next dance is slower. Women wear veils and sway around their partners fixing them with unblinking, fiery eyes. Men rotate, always maintaining eye contact with their partners. The women step and weave themselves through the lines of men, each movement understated and graceful. Men reach out and turn each woman with a gentle touch before surrendering her to the next male.

The musicians and dancers stop. Javier claps again and the dancers run from the room. Five women wearing loose, flowing red gowns enter. They flourish curved swords. I think they're called scimitars. They twirl the swords in circles, so fast that each sword is nothing but a blur. They whirl the swords over their heads, in front of themselves and behind, up and down their sides. There's no margin for error. A mistake would cause a grievous wound.

Two of the sword-dancers go to their knees and swing their swords in figure-eight patterns, parallel to the floor. The others lay down their swords and take turns doing somersaults over the fast-moving swords wielded by their kneeling companions.

Javier claps his hands again, and the violins reemerge, but this time with a dancing bear. The bear's fur is sleek and healthy. Two men lead the bear with long chains looped around the bear's neck. They escort the bear across the floor and, when they reach our table, violins play. The bear rises on his hind legs and shuffles his feet in time with the music.

This is an amazing trick, but I feel sorry for the bear. Healthy as he looks, he still lives in captivity.

Sensing my thoughts, Javier bends over and whispers in my ear: "We treat the bear well," he says. "We feed him well, and he has a female companion and his cubs. He has two acres to roam. He's the envy of every bear on the plateau."

The bear shambles out of the room, guided by his keepers. Jugglers appear. The jugglers start with three balls, add a fourth, a fifth, and a sixth. They replace the balls with daggers and then torches. They drop four torches and spin the remaining two torches in their hands. The torches rotate so fast it looks as though each man has a ring of fire surrounding his hand.

Javier claps his hands again and the jugglers run from the room.

"Enough of this," he says. "Let us talk."

I nod.

Javier dismisses the rest of the guests. He waits until we are the only ones left in the hall.

"Let me tell you the story of our people," he says, and I give him a smile of encouragement.

"Our people, the Bloods, survived the death of civilization with nothing but our courage and our loyalty to one another. We came from the ancient land called 'Central America', but fought our way northwards. Bloods bind themselves to one other with ties stronger than life itself. We fought many battles, some we lost, but most we won. There was no question of protecting turf during those years, because no turf was worth protecting. Once we stripped a region of food, we moved on to the next.

"Our sworn enemies, the Crips, followed us wherever we went. Or, maybe we followed them. Either way, it didn't matter, because our hatred for one another kept us angry, and committed, and strong. The fuel of hatred kept us going. Without it, neither side could survive the terrors we faced as the world fell apart.

"Many generations ago, we found this plateau and knew that we had found a home—if we could keep it. We fought many bloody battles with the Crips over this turf. Try as they might, the Crips could not dislodge us. They did, however, find land for their own homeland. Their land had mighty forests and soil that supported crops. Most important, the land had a spring which provided them with pure water.

"Long ago, the Crips found a new ally, a group of ghouls that called themselves 'The Sons of 1776'. This proved to us that the Crips were weak, like old women. True gangs need no allies. True gangs live and die by their own strength and their own courage. But since the Crips took allies, it was difficult to fight them off. They outnumbered us three or four to one. We couldn't launch raids against them, because there were too many of them. We have been struggling to defend our plateau ever since, knowing that if they gain a foothold up here, it's only a question of time before they drive us off.

"The Crips and the Sons have suffered misfortune, because they stopped launching attacks against us. For the first time in generations, we sent raiders into *their* lands. While they lost many fighters, they are still a potent force. But we fight them on even terms once more."

When Javier mentioned the Sons of 1776, I nearly fell off my bench. Our people have fought the Sons for several years. The "misfortune" the Crips experienced, which Javier mentioned, is the defeat we dealt them when they attacked Fort Kennedy, which protects our homeland.

In the silence following Javier's story, servants refill our glasses and set out trays of finger food desserts. I'm gorged, but I can't resist the fluffy-looking dessert. "Now, tell me about you," says Javier.

Between nibbles, I give Javier a thumbnail sketch of our own battles. I leave out any reference to the brane and omit our access to technology. We must know him better before sharing strategic information. I do mention our own battles with the Sons of 1776. "Perhaps," I suggest, "we can form an alliance. We have a mutual enemy. Maybe we can neutralize the Sons and the Crips by keeping pressure on them from two sides."

Javier is dismissive. "Only old ladies and weaklings need alliances. We will stand or fall by the might of our own strong arms."

Despite dismissing my offer, Javier doesn't appear angered by it.

"And now," he says, "I must insist you try our liqueur. It is delicious."

Javier claps his hands and servants rush in carrying a tray with small snifters filled with a golden liquid. I decide that a small sip of liqueur can't hurt. Everyone indulges, and the liqueur is delicious. It tastes sweet and warms me as it finds its way to my stomach. I turn to compliment Javier but the room begins to spin. I hear a noise to my right and turn to see Steve passed out, head resting on the table. Grizz looks disoriented, and a second later blackness wells up behind my eyes. The darkness overwhelms me, and I lose consciousness.

12

When I regain consciousness, I find my hands and feet bound, and I'm strapped to my bunk. Jerald is in a sturdy metal cage and they've chained Amigo to a bedpost; a muzzle prevents him from opening his mouth.

"Grizz?" I move my head as far as I can but can't see Grizz's bunk.

"ET are you OK?" hearing Grizz's voice, I breathe easier.

"Yeah, I'm fine. Steve?"

Steve mumbles but his voice sounds thick, his tongue swollen. He's still under the influence of the drugs.

"Those weasels drugged us," says Grizz.

"Jerald, what happened? How did we get here?"

"Those are not nice men," says Jerald.

"We've figured that out. What happened?" I ask again.

"What happened when?"

"What happened when the bad men brought us back here?"

"A group of them came into our room while I was cleaning the floor. They overwhelmed me and put me in this cage. I fought them, but there were too many of them. As you know, I am a model 450-5X series robot, the most modern and efficient of all the servant robots. I'm not designed to fight humans."

Jerald pauses before continuing: "Forty-seven minutes later, they brought the three of you back, dropped you on your bunks, and tied you up."

I'm confused. Last night Javier threw a feast in our honor. He had been a delightful host. Why drug us and tie us up?

I don't have to wait long for an answer. The door to our room bursts open. Javier and half a dozen of his henchmen stream in.

"I trust you had a restful night?" he says with a smile.

"Yeah," I say sarcastically. "There's nothing like getting drugged to send you off to dreamland."

Javier ignores me. "The sun is up," he says. "It's time to play the King's Game."

"OK," I say evenly. "Tell us about the 'King's Game.'"

"It's a game worthy of a king. Imagine a game in which your opponent—a crafty, clever, deadly opponent wishes to kill you. What could be more exciting than hunting that opponent and killing him before he kills you?"

"Terrific. How do we fit in?" I'm sure I know, and it makes me shiver.

"You three are our opponents. We will arm you with knives and set you free. And then, we will hunt for you. If we catch you, we will kill you. If you find an opportunity, you may kill us."

"We don't enjoy killing people," I say. "I don't like your game."

"What a shame. We love the game. Pity you won't enjoy it."

Javier has a large club. "You won't be needing this one any longer," he says.

Four burly Bloods open Jerald's cage and drag him out.

"Please help me, ET," pleads Jerald.

I struggle against my bonds. *If I could get loose!*

Javier lifts the club with both hands, until it's high above his head. He brings the club down hard on Jerald's head. I cry out in ager. Bitter tears fill my eyes.

The club puts a great divot in the top of Jerald's head. The circuitry inside is visible. Jerald's eyes are askew, but he's not dead. He looks at me and pleads: "Please, ET. Please make him stop."

Tears run down my cheeks. I look at Jerald with an expression that says, "*If only I could…*"

I strain at my bonds but can't move an inch. "You'll regret this," I hiss at Javier.

"I don't think so." He raises the club above his head again and once more brings it down on what's left of Jerald's head. Jerald has now lost the ability to speak, but he whimpers. I cry out in a rage, but a final blow renders Jerald silent and motionless.

Javier moves quick as a cat, and once more raises his cudgel. This time he brings it down on Amigo's back. The blow breaks his back, and he yips and whines, unable to move. Javier strikes Amigo's head with the truncheon and Amigo's cries cease.

I can hear Grizz and Steve struggling against their bonds. Grizz growls at Javier and says, "I'll kill you for this."

Javier looks at Grizz and smiles. "You are free to try."

"But why?" I ask. "Why did you kill them? They're no threat to you!"

"Exactly. There is no honor in hunting machines or dogs. Only humans offer the dangerous sport we crave. Your friends were superfluous. We've waited years to play our game. Long years."

Javier's men sever the straps holding us down and cut the ropes binding our feet. They haul us to our feet. We struggle, but there are too many of them.

They push us through the door and down a wide street. We leave the city and halt in front of a soaring wooden wall. It's at least thirty feet tall. On its top are rolls of razor wire. The Bloods push us along the wall until we reach an immense oaken gate with a bar on the outside. The gate's purpose is to keep people *inside* the wall, not to keep people out.

A crowd of several hundred Bloods surrounds us. They carry the weapons of warriors. These people are not the polite villagers we met yesterday when we explored the town. These warriors have the same hungry look as yesterday, when they captured us.

"Let me explain the rules of the game," says Javier. "We will release you inside these walls." He raps his knuckles on the great oak door. "Inside the walls is a forest, a very large forest. Just inside this gate, you'll find three knives. The knives are yours. Use them to kill us, if you are able. We will give you a day's head start. You may travel where you will in the forest. You may do whatever you please. Tomorrow, ten teams of ten warriors each will enter the forest. If they find you, they will kill you. We bestow great honors on the group that slays you."

"So, you outnumber us one hundred to three. Sound like bad odds to me."

"Oh, but you will have the advantage of surprise. You may choose the site of your battles. You will probably kill some of my people. Or, if you prefer, you may try to hide. If you survive for thirty suns, you will have won the game. You will be free to go."

"And how will you arm our pursuers? Will they have knives as well?"

"No. We will arm them with bows, swords, and spears."

Outnumbered and *outgunned*. My heart sinks. "How do we know you'll let us go if we win?"

"You have my word of honor. On our turf, a man's word is his bond. If I break my vow, I lose respect. If you win, you *will* be free."

"Have any of your victims ever won the game?"

"No. In fact, no one has lasted over ten suns. The odds are against you. Some who have gone before you tried to hide. Most tried to fight. Clever ones killed pursuers. The fear of death makes the game thrilling. But no stranger has won the game. You may be the first."

"Will I have the chance to kill you?"

"I'm afraid not. I've played the game before, in my youth. This time, the game is for our young ones, young ones who have never experienced the thrill of stalking the deadliest prey of all."

"I'll survive," I say, looking Javier in the eye. "I'll survive, and I'll kill you. If you had not killed our friends, I might have let you live. But, you didn't. So, I *will* kill you."

Javier smiles at me. "You have a fire in your belly. That's good. Killing you will bring great honor." The warriors raise a cheer. "Death to the insolent one!" cries a woman.

"You don't have long to live, Javier. Enjoy yourself while you can." I struggle to keep my voice steady. I don't expect to survive this "game," but the senseless deaths of Jerald and Amigo fill me with anger and a burning desire for revenge.

"Oh," says Javier still smiling. "Don't climb the walls. The razor wire on top is very durable, and it's strung tight. You'll never cut through it with a knife. Even if you could, the wire uncoils and whips like a snake. It would cause you fearful damage. It's no honor to die like that."

I bore holes in Javier's forehead with my stare. I hear the oaken gate behind me creak open. The Bloods push us into the forest. Then they slam the gate shut. They lower the heavy bar that seals us in. We won't escape that way.

Inside the gate is a table. Just as Javier has promised, three vicious-looking knives sit atop the table. Serrated blades, six inches long make these lethal weapons. Our odds are poor, but at least we'll have the chance to die fighting.

We take a moment to sever the ropes that bind our hands. Once free, we massage our wrists to restore circulation. We consider our options. My first inclination is to run.

"Let's get as far away as we can," says Steve.

Grizz nods in agreement. "The farther away from them, the happier I'll be."

"Wait a minute," I say. "That's what they'll *expect* us to do. Let's find somewhere to hide near the gate. Someplace they can't see us. Steve, can we lay a trail that looks like we've headed for the hills and then backtrack?"

"Yes. We don't know how well they follow a trail, but we can fool them unless they are very, very good. Javier said they'd give us twenty-four hours before he sends his warriors after us. That gives us plenty of time to lead them on a merry chase."

"I like your idea, ET," says Grizz. "Who'd plan to stay right by the gate? It's such a crazy idea, it's brilliant."

During Steve's years as a wandering troubadour he learned many woodcraft skills. "Follow me," he says. "Try to place your feet in my footprints." For an hour, Steve leads us on a winding trail. The surrounding forest is rugged, riddled with hills and ravines. Thickets abound, forcing us to make frequent detours.

We come to a burbling brook. Steve tells us to stay put as he wades into the stream. By the time he reaches the middle, the water rises to his neck. "The water runs deep enough our pursuers won't see the pebbles we displace as we walk downstream. Follow me."

"Wait," I say. "Let's darken our tunics." Grizz and I wear softbark tunics, made for us by the Sisters. We've worn them so long they're no longer white. Still, they'll stand out in the forest. To avoid standing out, we must change their color. I think of my brothers' camouflage shirts, but they're back in Tucson and no use to us now. I take handfuls of mud and smear them on my tunic as Grizz does the same. We help each other dirty up our backs.

"Much better," says Steve.

Grizz and I wade into the brook and follow Steve. The water is chilly and the current works against us. We spend a quarter mile forging upstream. Steve stops. "OK," he says, "Now, each of us makes a separate trail. Grizz, you cut a trail on the south side of the stream. ET and I will make separate trails on the north side. We'll meet fifty yards upstream.

Under different circumstances, this walk might be enjoyable. I'm wet but it's a warm morning. Steam rises from my wet clothes. Birdsong fills the trees, and I see an occasional small creature scurry away. I reach a clearing and walk around it before heading off in another direction. A few minutes later, I head back to the rendezvous point.

Grizz and Steve are waiting.

After another hour of walking, Steve locates a group of trees he finds interesting. He studies them.

"OK," he says, "here's what we do. We climb this tree, and then we work our way through the branches from tree to tree until we reach a point there." He points to the east.

The tree Steve choses is a box elder with three diverging trunks and low-hanging branches, making it easy to climb. Once we reach a height of twenty feet, we crawl from the branches of the box elder to a neighboring oak. Oaks are difficult to climb from the ground, because their trunks are thick, and they don't have low-hanging branches. But their upper branches are easy to traverse.

We work our way eastward clinging to branches. At this height, the branches are sturdy enough to hold our weight, but moving is difficult. The foliage is thick. I hang onto a branch with one hand while clearing leaves from my face, searching for a handhold. At other times, I sit on a branch and butt-walk.

I hang from a branch that snaps and gives way. I fall several feet before a thick limb breaks my fall. The force of impact is painful, but I reach out and grab yet another branch and wedge my knee against the tree's trunk. I'm lodged precariously. If I move, I may lose balance and fall. The forest floor is only fifteen feet below, but an uncontrolled fall from this height might cause a broken ankle or a sprained knee. Either is a death sentence.

"ET, give me your hand." Grizz has worked his way down to me. He clings to a branch with his left hand and extends his right hand to me. His hand is just within reach, so I reach out with my right hand and grab it. The maneuver overbalances both of us and we tumble from the tree. Low-hanging branches and twigs tear at me as I fall. I land on the ground, flat on my back, and make an "oof!" sound when I hit. A split second later, Grizz lands on top of me, and, we both go "oof". Grizz rolls off, groaning. I struggle for breath and panic: I've really hurt myself this time. *I can't breathe!* Then I calm down as I realize I've just had the breath knocked out of me. In a moment, my breath returns.

"Are you OK?" asks Grizz.

"I think so." Rising, I take inventory. I feel nasty scratches on my face and a few on my arms, but nothing seems broken. Grizz is in one piece, although a branch left a nasty cut on his left cheek. He fingers it gingerly.

"Don't worry," I say, "it matches the scars from the vulture."

"Thanks, ET, I feel much better. You have a few scrapes yourself."

"Lucky for us," I say, "the leaves here are spongy."

"And lucky for me," says Grizz, "*you're* spongy. I had a nice, soft landing."

"I'm not sure, but I think you just insulted me."

"Not intended. Falling on you is the most fun I've had all day. Let's do it again."

He looks at me with his sky-blue eyes and I wrap my arms around him and give him a deep, ardent kiss. "Let's *not* do it again."

Steve's face appears in the tree above us. "The tracks you're leaving will confuse the guys after us."

Grizz and I part and scramble back up the tree. We resume our journey through the forest canopy.

By midday we reach the eastern wall. It's impossible to tell how far this wall is from the front gate because of all the meandering we've done. "I think we're about three miles from the gate."

Steve nods in agreement. "If the walls are three miles to a side, it means the size of the forest inside the walls is nine square miles."

I do the math in my head. "Nine square miles sounds big, but with a hundred guys chasing us, it's not. If they spread out, they'll have ten people for every square mile. Ten guys can cover every inch of a square mile. It'll be impossible to hide."

Neither Grizz nor Steve says anything, but they're worried. This won't be easy. They've stacked the cards against us. They outnumber us over thirty to one, they're better armed, and we have little room to maneuver.

"If we can't run," I say, "we'll fight. Let's assume they stay in groups of ten. How do three people armed with knives attack ten people armed to the teeth?"

"Steve," says Grizz, "you make bows and arrows. With bows we'd have a better chance."

"Sure, I can make them. But it's time-consuming. And finding the right materials is hard. I'll look for materials as we go."

We spend the rest of our day wading through creeks, leaving

looping trails, back-tracking, and moving like Tarzan through the treetops. We double back to the gate and leave a brand-new trail, crossing our old trails with the new ones.

As we cut our second trail, we come to a large clearing. A brook burbles on the north side and there's a huge briar patch near the center. Two old hickory trees stand side by side on opposite sides of the briar patch.

Grizz enters the clearing, studies the brambles. There's a gap between the trees and an entrance leading right into the bramble pile. "Might make a good hiding place," he says.

"I'll crawl in there," I say. "I'm the smallest."

On my hands and knees, I work my way into the opening. Brambles grab at me from every direction but I scoot my way six feet into the thicket. The brambles above me are so thick, very little light gets inside.

"Can you see me?" I holler.

"Nope," say Grizz and Steve. The tunnel into the brambles is narrow, so I can't turn around. I back out.

"I think we've found a hiding place."

Grizz crawls in to explore.

"Ouch!" he cries. We hear him mumbling as he crawls farther into the pile. Then we hear some thrashing sounds as Grizz uses his knife to enlarge the tunnel. Moments later he emerges with new scratches. "This'll work," he says. "It's a tight fit, but we can get three of us in there."

Steve studies the clearing. "The brook is a popular watering hole. The Bloods will have a hard time tracking us here because of all the animal tracks."

"Do you think the Bloods can track us here?"

"Only if they're master trackers," says Steve.

We spend the rest of the day finishing our meandering trails. Just before sunset we return to a point near the front gate. We locate a small copse of trees that look easy to climb. I shinny up a tree. From the branches we'll have a good view of the gate, and the leaf cover will make us almost invisible from the ground.

"I think I'll spend the night on the ground," I say. "I might fall out the tree if I sleep up there."

We agree that sleeping on the ground is a good idea. The only trail leading to this little stand of trees is one that has gone several miles over hill and dale, through streams and up and down trees.

We've been so busy today we haven't taken time to gather food. Hunger gnaws at me. "Following the feast last night, I thought I'd never be hungry again. I was wrong." Grizz's stomach rumbles in sympathy.

"We'll find something to eat tomorrow," says Steve.

We post a sentry.

I'm on duty when the sky lightens in the east. I nudge Grizz and Steve awake. We darken our faces and arms with loam from the forest floor and climb up into our trees. Moments later, the gate swings open with a loud creaking sound. A group of ten Blood warriors comes through the opening.

13

The Bloods are well armed. Each carries a bow and a quiver of arrows. They carry swords strapped to their belts. Two carry spears. The lead warrior is a woman. She examines the ground until she picks up our first trail. "This way," she says, and the others follow her. She looks for tracks in the loam or broken twigs. They move fast and vanish into the forest.

"I'm encouraged," whispers Steve. "In finding our trail, she missed several little clues before she found an obvious one. If she's their best tracker our odds improve."

"Still," I say, "with ten people per square mile, they don't have to be master trackers. And we won't be secure in our little briar patch. They're bound to check it out if they don't find us elsewhere."

An hour later, the gate groans open, and another group of ten Blood warriors comes through. Their tracker locates the trail left by the first party; He chooses another path. They don't even try to pick up our second trail. Another hour passes before the third group of Bloods enters the arena. They pause long enough to avoid the trails of the earlier groups before choosing their own path.

"Except for that first group, they're not even looking for our trail," Says Grizz. "Javier told us he was sending his young warriors, and he said they've never before played the game. So, they have no experience, except for tracking animals when they're hunting. They think they'll find us by combing the forest. They're right."

A fourth group enters and moves off in a brand-new direction. We watch as new groups enter hourly. Javier is true to his word. Only ten groups enter.

After the last group disappears, we search for food.

"I noticed tubers to the west," says Steve.

"Yeah, I saw them too," I agree.

"With the Bloods heading into the woods helter-skelter," says Steve, "we won't have to worry if we leave a trail. With everybody tromping around every which way, there'll be tracks everywhere."

A couple months ago, Steve led a group of us through a forest owned by a blood-thirsty bunch of crazies that called themselves the Zealots. Before we entered their territory, Steve taught us how to move silently through a forest. He taught us to walk with splayed toes, to distribute our weight, and to always know where we'll plant our foot for our next step. Avoid sticks and dry leaves. Steve walked point, and if he found a path we couldn't cross quietly, he detoured until he found a better path. He showed us edible forest plants and the kinds of berries to avoid.

So, we're prepared as we descend from our perch in the trees and head west. We use our woodcraft skills, and I'm proud of how quiet two city kids can be, moving through a forest. We walk single file with Steve on point. Just as important as walking without making noise is listening to every sound. Every time a small animal makes a sound as it passes through the underbrush we stop, hearts racing. With ears tuned to high, we hear every sound the forest makes: the breeze in the trees, the bark of a squirrel defending his territory, the noise a bird makes as it launches itself from a branch high overhead.

We make good progress. After twenty minutes of stealthy walking, Steve raises his hand and we come to an abrupt halt. We listen. At first, all I hear is the sound of the breeze soughing in the trees, but as I continue to listen, I pick out the sound of people on the move. As hunters, the Bloods know how to be quiet. But they're not as quiet as we are. We hear the occasional crackle made by a foot stepping on dry leaves, the sound of a small limb snapping back in place after a Blood passes, and the noise of a whispered conversation. They're coming from the west.

I strain my eyes looking for movement. At last, I see it. There's a woman fifty yards away, moving straight at us. We wait another few seconds and seven of them come into view. They're arranged in a skirmish line, with five yards separating each Blood from his neighbor.

Grizz and Steve look at me. I think a moment. The skirmish line is between us and our food. I'm hungry, and I want those tubers. Daylight is fading. We won't have time to find another meal. I point my finger to my right, north. We'll try to get out of their way. Once they pass, we'll find our tubers.

We move hunched over, quick and quiet. Moving quickly *and* silently is a tricky proposition. Dried leaves crackle beneath my left foot. I didn't see them. We freeze and listen. The Bloods didn't hear; nobody sounds the alarm. We move again until the skirmish line passes.

I'm ready to breathe a sigh of relief when a Blood pops up right in front of me. She's on a collision course. She hasn't seen me yet, but if I don't move, she'll walk right into me. There are still trees and vines between us. I realize why we didn't see her: the forest she's walking through is thick. A wall of Virginia creeper screened her from our sight. My heart trip-hammers. Grizz and Steve are ahead of me, off to the north, so they're not in the Blood's path. They drop into a small gully. My only option is to hide behind the trunk of a huge oak tree; there's no other cover nearby.

The Blood can't see me now, but when she's taken a few more steps, she'll be abreast of me. We'll be close enough to shake hands. I try to edge around the trunk of the tree, hoping to stay on the side opposite her as she advances. She passes me. *She'll miss me!*

A male voice to my right calls out, "Take five."

Great! They're taking a break and there's a Blood inches from me. I hope she doesn't walk around during her break. To my horror, my empty stomach chooses this exact moment to growl. I flinch in terror, certain the Blood on the other side of the tree will hear.

She doesn't. Leaves rustle as she sits and leans her back against our tree. I try to breathe without making noise. My heart is pounding so loud I'm afraid she'll hear it. To my right the top of Grizz's head is visible just above the lip of the gully in which he's hiding. If the Blood on the other side of the tree looks in that direction, she can't miss him. I wrack my brain trying to think of a way to warn Grizz, but there's nothing I can do. If I move or make a noise the Blood, a mere matter of inches away, will hear.

I hold my breath. The Bloods speak among themselves in soft voices. The Blood on the other side of the tree shifts position, rustles the ground foliage. I grasp the handle of my knife. It may be possible to cut her throat before she sounds the alarm. She stands. How can she miss Grizz?

"Let's move out!" shouts a male voice. The Bloods rise and I follow them with my eyes as their line vanishes into the trees to our left.

Grizz and Steve crawl out of their gully to join me.

"I couldn't get my head low enough," says Grizz. "The gully was too shallow. I was eating dirt, trying to get lower. But I knew I couldn't move without making noise, so I was stuck."

"We got lucky," I say. "Now, about those tubers."

We find the patch we were looking for, and we dig up our dinner and brush off the dirt. These tubers are green, too young to harvest. They have an acidic taste, but given our hunger, that doesn't matter. We wolf them down and dig up another bunch. The rumbling in my stomach subsides.

Twilight covers the forest. We have only a matter of minutes before darkness falls. We find a dense stand of trees, shielded on one side by brambles.

"This looks like a safe place to spend the night," says Steve. "I doubt they'll hunt after dark."

We spend a few minutes raking up leaves to make soft beds. We'll scatter the leaves again in the morning to avoid leaving an obvious sign for our pursuers. Grizz takes the first shift on watch. I prop my head on a large pile of leaves and am asleep the instant darkness falls.

*   *   *

Next morning, we begin our search for materials to make bows and arrows. It's exasperating. The requirements for a wooden bow are precise. The wood for the bow must bend easily but not *too* easily. It must snap back to its original shape when released. Both limbs of the bow must be identical, meaning the top half of the bow must be a perfect symmetrical copy of the bottom. Requirements for the string are exacting. It must stretch, and it must be strong. The string, like the bow, must snap back into its original position. It must keep its flexibility over many stretches.

To make matters worse, Steve is not familiar with the oak-hickory forest we're in. Most of his traveling was at a lower altitude where subtropical vegetation holds sway. He doesn't know which trees and vines will work. His frustration increases as the day goes on.

We search all day, hacking many saplings in pursuit of the perfect piece of wood. We can't take many saplings from any one place for fear of leaving evidence that we've been there, evidence that could put the Bloods on our trail. Several times during the day we stop when patrols pass by. We're lucky. None come close, but every time a patrol comes near, we must stop work and hide.

By the end of the day, we've found one promising piece of wood, but we didn't locate a single vine that meets our requirements. We *do* find edible berries. They have an unpleasant taste, but we eat them anyway. We also find edible greens, burdock, and wild asparagus. Small animals abound, but lacking a bow, we can't catch any.

As sunset nears, we find another secluded site, screened by Virginia creeper and wild grapevines. Much as we want to cook our food, a fire is out of the question. We eat everything raw.

"We found the west wall," whispers Grizz. He's trying to distract us from our frustrating inability to find suitable materials for making bows. "And we were right; it's about three miles from the east wall."

"Let's find the north wall tomorrow," I say, as I gnaw on a burdock stalk.

"We've been lucky," says Steve. "Eventually they'll run right into us. I have to make bows to give us a fighting chance."

"We could ambush one of their patrols," I say. "Pick off the person on the end of the line."

"That's possible, but they travel so close we'd be pin cushions before we got away."

"We have to fight back," I say. "We'll find a way."

We search for bow materials again the next day. We work our way north splashing through a stream on our way. No sooner have we entered the forest on the far side of the stream than we run right into a Blood patrol. We drop to the ground, but they see us. The noise from the brook cloaked the sound of the skirmish line approaching us. Two Bloods raise the alarm. Their entire line breaks into a run, and they're heading right at us.

"I'll lead them away," I hiss. "You two get out of here."

"ET!" cries Grizz, but before he can object, I stand and attract the Bloods' attention. I've thought this eventuality over, and my plan makes perfect sense. Grizz and I, with our longer legs, can outrun the hunters. Steve cannot. And there's no sense in Grizz and I both being at risk, so I'll lead the Bloods away from my companions.

"Meet me at the bramble patch in the clearing," I whisper and take off running. I head in a direction perpendicular to the line of advancing Bloods and away from the place where Grizz and Steve hug the ground.

I glance back over my shoulder. Grizz glares at me, but my plan is working. The Bloods follow me. I have a twenty-yard lead, and that's more than I need. An arrow whistles past me followed by another. I'm not worried. It's impossible to run flat out and accurately shoot a bow at the same time. (I've tried.) The Bloods can either chase me or shoot at me. I weave in between trees and undergrowth, make myself a fleeting target.

There are no more arrows. The Bloods have given up shooting at me. They're dedicating their energy to catching me, which is what I want them to do. I run flat out, knees high, arms pumping. The bushy undergrowth claws at me and I feel pain as it scratches and tears at my arms and face. I rolled up my sleeves earlier because the day is hot, but I roll them back down as I run.

I look back over my shoulder. My lead is now thirty yards. I'm gaining. Unless I run head on into another patrol, I'll be OK.

I come to a ravine twenty feet deep, slide down the near side, and splash through a shallow brook at the bottom. I climb the other side and clamber over the top just as the Bloods behind me near the ravine. My lead is now forty yards. I watch for a split second as my pursuers slide down into the ravine. When they reach the bottom, they won't be able to see me, so I make a forty-five degree turn and put on a burst of speed. There's a dense thicket to my left and I turn to run around it. By the time my hunters have climbed out of the ravine, I'll be out of sight.

Since the Bloods have spent the last couple days tromping through the woods, the group behind me won't be able to follow my trail. For safety's sake, I wade into the next stream I find and forge my way fifty yards upstream. I climb out just in time to see another group of Bloods moving through the forest ahead. I lower my head until I'm peeking over the bank. The second group hasn't seen me, but they're heading right at me.

Breathing hard, I crouch and work my way upstream. The water is only knee deep, but it drags at my shins, slowing me. I find a place where the stream has undercut its bank and I head for the cover it provides. There are three inches between the stream below and the bank above: just enough room for me to breathe if I lay flat and stick my nose above the water. But I'm breathing so hard I can't get enough air this way. I hold my breath, but with lungs bursting, I must leave the shadow of the overhanging bank and gasp for air. If there's a Blood nearby, I'm dead. There's no one in the stream. I bend over and wade to the far bank. The hunters are fifteen yards away and receding. They're streaming water, which means they've just traversed the stream. My blood turns icy when I realize the Bloods passed within three feet of my hiding place. The noise of the stream must have covered the sound of me gasping for air. I concentrate on breathing slower as I watch their backs grow smaller and smaller. They disappear into the trees.

*   *   *

I survey my surroundings, realize I'm in an unfamiliar part of the forest. I know I'm near the north wall, because that's where I was when the Blood patrol spotted us. I rerun my flight from the Bloods in my mind. When I turned, did I run due south? Maybe southeast? I decide on southeast. That puts the clearing two miles to the southeast.

I check the sun's position. It's low in the west, so I want to keep my shadow in front of me and just to the right. I cover a mile and find another Blood patrol. We've learned that we have nothing to fear if we can stay out of the Bloods' skirmish line. If they catch us inside that line, no hiding place is safe. So, I need to know which way this line is heading, and that's difficult in the forest, because, although you can hear them, you can't see them until they're almost on top of you. And sound gets distorted in the woods. Most of the noise comes from my left, so I move to my right.

I catch sight of a Blood. She'll pass me on my left. Is she on the flank? If she is, I'm fine. But she's not. Another Blood is on my right side. I can't let the two of them sandwich me. No cover will prevent them from seeing me at such short range, so I crawl desperately to my right, moving perpendicular to the line of the Bloods' advance. I try to be quiet. There's a thick tree trunk and I crawl around it. Have I come far enough? It's too late to do anything but hide and hope.

The patrol passes me with the flanker four feet to my left. I wait until they're out of sight and heave a sigh of relief.

I head for the bramble cave. Minutes later, there's another Blood patrol, but they're ahead of me and advancing on a line perpendicular to my line of advance. I wait until they pass.

The hopelessness of our situation weighs me down. There are too many Bloods and not enough hiding places. We don't get enough nutrition with our meager diet, so it's only a matter of time before we weaken. Being able to run faster is no guarantee of safety. When you're running away from one group of Bloods, the odds are good that you'll run right into another group. Eventually, we'll run out of luck. We need to come up with an idea that will change the rules of the game we're playing.

As I near the meager safety of the bramble cave, I enter a patch of woods that is extremely rugged, with foliage that is very dense. I slow as I pick my way through the clinging foliage. The Bloods will have a hard time finding me in this mess. It's hard to walk, let alone track somebody.

The sun sets and the woods grow dark, but by dead reckoning, I'm almost to the clearing with the bramble cave when I smell the distinctive odor of wood smoke rising through the air. There are voices coming through the trees in front of me. I crawl on my belly to get a better look. There are a pair of legs in front of me. I back away and move sideways, trying to get a better view.

This is our clearing with the bramble cave, but the Bloods have taken it over. There's no way for me to reach the briar patch. Grizz and Steve may be sitting in the bramble cave, surrounded by Bloods. I hope they don't snore tonight.

I watch the Bloods for a while. Can I pick off a sentry? If I had a bow, I might. As I watch, I lose hope. The Bloods post four sentries, one for each cardinal direction. Each sentry stays well within the circle of light cast by the fire.

The Bloods built an elaborate pit for the fire. They must have put a lot of energy into it. Then, I realize why. The forest is extremely dry. Grass in the meadows is brown and much of the forest's undergrowth, dry and brittle, crunches under foot. The Bloods have lived in the forest for ages. They've developed practices to prevent forest fires. As a girl in Tucson, I witnessed big burns in the Catalinas. I make a mental note to practice fire safety, if I'm ever lucky enough to light another campfire.

I wait for a couple hours, hoping they'll get groggy, maybe drift off to sleep. But they don't. They stay alert. I ponder picking off a sentry by throwing my knife. I abandon the idea. Throwing a knife has never been my strong suit and getting the knife back would be impossible.

When the Bloods' second shift comes on duty, I back away from the clearing, find a thicket that offers cover and hunker down for the night. I gnaw on a burdock stalk I found earlier in the day. The bitter taste doesn't bother me; I'm too hungry to care. As I'm about to drift off to sleep, an idea comes to me. *I know a way to change the rules of the King's Game!* First, I must find Grizz and Steve.

14

Just past dawn, the Bloods stir. I crawl near and watch them break camp. I'm prepared to take flight if they head my way, but, they don't. They form a skirmish line and move out of the clearing headed to the south.

I enter the clearing and crawl into the shelter of the bramble cave. It's empty. I fight off a wave of disappointment because I'd hoped to find Grizz and Steve inside. So, I crawl out and spend an hour gathering food, check the brambles again, but still no Grizz and Steve. Waiting in the bramble cave makes me claustrophobic, so I leave the shelter and watch the clearing, but there's no good cover. The cover I used to spy on the clearing last night looks skimpy in broad daylight. So, I climb a tree and watch from above.

I watch for four hours, see three Blood groups walk through the clearing. Two of the groups walk right under my tree. Hours pass, and there's no sign of Grizz and Steve. By late afternoon I worry. *Why haven't they come back yet? Did the Bloods find them? Are they dead even as I sit here waiting for them?* The thought brings tears to my eyes. If I've lost my companions, I have hours or, at best, days to live. I fight back against my fears, forcing them from my mind. My bond with Grizz is strong. I'd *know* if he were dead.

Just after sunset I climb down from my tree and gather berries. Without good cover and afraid of falling out of my tree if I fall asleep, I decide to spend the night in the bramble cave.

The minute I enter the brambles, I sense something wrong. It's too dark to see, but there's a strange musky smell, and I sense movement in front of me. I back up, but I'm too late. A burning, foul-smelling slime covers me. I'm blinded, and my eyes, nose, and mouth burn as though they were on fire. The foul odor is overwhelming. As I back out of the brambles, I realize what has happened: a skunk sprayed me.

I'm blind. I can't remember whether a skunk's spray blinds a person permanently, but the possibility fills me with terror. My eyes, nose and mouth burn so much I *must* end the pain. The scalding is so terrible I have trouble thinking. I remember a stream runs by the clearing. I calm myself enough to locate the sound. The burbling is to my right. I shuffle in that direction, trip over something and fall flat on my face. I rise again and stagger toward the sound of rushing water. My left foot finds no traction when I plant it. I pitch face-first into the water. I come up spluttering and flush my eyes with water. The burning subsides a little and I'm overcome with relief when I realize I can see again. There's a faint glimmer of light: must be the moon. I can't see very well, but my vision is returning!

My elation turns to horror when the vague outline of a man appears on the bank of the stream and looks down at me. I tense and wait for the bolt of a crossbow to strike.

*   *   *

"I don't care for your new perfume."

It's Grizz!

"Not my choice, believe me." I'm still frantic, trying to get the burning in my nose and mouth to stop. I gargle and spit over and over. I inhale water into my nose, which is painful, but it helps clear the slime from my nasal passages when I blow the water back out.

"Can I help you?" asks Grizz.

"I don't think so. I need to wash off the slime."

With repeated washing, the pain in my eyes subsides to a dull burn. My nose and mouth feel better, too. But the stench is still nauseating. Nothing I've smelled comes anywhere near the disgusting stink that covers my head and tunic.

Grizz turns to Steve. "Will she be OK?"

"Animals sprayed by a skunk recover. It takes time for the stench to disappear."

I scrub my hair vigorously. After repeated scrubbing, the stickiness of the spray thins.

"Turn around," I say. I tear off my tunic and wash it. I wring it out over and over, which reduces the putrid odor, but the stink is still overpowering. Convinced I've done all I can, I pull my tunic on and leave the stream.

Grizz and Steve back away as I approach. I can't blame them. I'd get away from myself, too, if I could.

"Nothing personal," says Steve.

"I love you, ET, and I want to spend the rest of my life by your side," says Grizz, "but not tonight."

"I understand. But we need to talk. I think I have a plan for getting weapons. Let's get out of this clearing. The Bloods will be hunkered down for the night. But let's not take a chance."

I lead my friends to the thick stand of trees where I slept last night. We sit, although not close, together.

"Here's my plan. There's a patch of forest just northwest of here that's extremely dense and hard to get through. It's so thick and the ground is so broken, the Bloods won't be able to follow us. Let's wait in the clearing until a Blood patrol finds us. We move off in three separate directions. Grizz circles the thicket to the right, I move around the thicket to the left, and Steve goes straight down the middle."

Grizz and Steve look doubtful.

"I think the Bloods will split up into three smaller groups to follow us. Grizz and I can outrun the Bloods and Steve can't. Grizz and I will lose the ones chasing us. When we do, we head back toward the thicket and wait for Steve. When the Bloods chasing Steve come by, we bushwhack 'em. There's a ton of cover and we'll ambush them before they see us. Remember, the Bloods run in groups of ten, so once they split up to follow us, there'll be only three or four chasing Steve. The undergrowth is heavy enough that the other groups won't see the ambush. Once we kill the Bloods, we take their bows. And with bows, we change the whole game."

Grizz and Steve are silent, chewing on the idea. "It could work," says Grizz. He warms to the plan. "Yeah, it'll work. And once we have bows, we fight back."

Steve nods his head. "We'll go over the ground at first light. We can plot our paths."

"Hey," I say, once we've agreed on the plan, "what kept you guys so long? Why didn't you come back sooner? You worried me sick."

"The Bloods found us," explains Grizz. "So, I told Steve to hide while I led the Bloods away. I knew I could outrun 'em. But I ran right into the north wall. It's swampy up there so I couldn't help leaving big, obvious footprints. And once they saw those size twelves, they knew who made them. They were hot on my trail, and because it was so swampy, I couldn't use my speed. It was hard enough to walk, pulling my feet out of that muck every step. I got out of the swamp and onto solid ground. At last, I could run. A few minutes later, I was sure I'd lost 'em, but I climbed a tree to hide, just in case. It was a good decision, because the Blood patrols were thick. They *knew* I was up there. I'd wait for a group to pass, climb down from the tree, and there'd be another bunch coming. They thinned out near sunset. We came back here. It wasn't easy finding this place in the dark!"

Steve chimes in: "And I was following the Bloods following Grizz. I didn't want to leave him alone with a posse hot on his trail. Not that I could've done much to help. Still.

We rise at dawn and move off into the rough ground we'll be using for our ambush. I was right, this ground is hard to move in.

There are a few areas where Grizz and I can use our speed to good effect. Next, we find an excellent ambush site. Steve knows where to lead his pursuers and Grizz and I will be under cover until they're close enough for us to use our knives. A thousand things can go wrong. But this is our best chance. We've been lucky to avoid the Bloods so far. We can't count on good luck forever.

*   *   *

We don't wait long. The three of us stand, and when we're certain they've seen us, we run. The Bloods cross the clearing and are just a few yards behind me. But I hit one of those small clearings and pick up speed, using the little meadow to extend my lead. The pattern repeats itself three times: struggle through the foliage and then dash through a tiny clearing.

I stop, catch my breath, and listen. The Bloods are following. They can't see me. Our plan is working! I change course and head to my left, find the ambush site we selected yesterday. Grizz is already there. We use the trees and vines to conceal ourselves. Less than a minute later, Steve runs past with three Bloods in pursuit. Grizz and I give them enough time to pass us, then leave our hiding place and attack the Bloods from the rear. I throw my left arm around the neck of one, reach around him with my right arm and, use my strength to bury my knife in his chest. Bright arterial blood sprays, and I'm nauseous. No time for that. The third Blood hears the commotion behind him and turns in time to see Grizz cut down his mate. He turns and advances toward Grizz, but doesn't see me, so I come up from behind. He realizes he should holler for his friends. I use my knife before he can sound the alarm.

Steve returns to help, but Grizz and I have finished. We examine the weapons carried by the Bloods. My spirits soar when I realize the Bloods were carrying regular bows, not crossbows. Crossbows have much more punching power and a greater range than standard bows. The punching power is useful if your enemy wears protective armor, but the Bloods have no armor. The superior range of the crossbow is useful if you engage an enemy from a distance, but we're fighting in a forest. But a crossbow takes longer to arm than a standard bow. Grizz and I trained on old-fashioned bows and we can get off six arrows in a minute with decent accuracy. And when you're in a group of three fighting a group of ten, speed is crucial.

I test the string tension on my new bow. The bow is for a person three or four feet tall, so it's not an ideal weapon for me. But it'll do. It pulls and rebounds. I inspect the arrows in the quiver. Small, but deadly. I take the Blood's quiver and throw it over my shoulder. Again, it's small, but serviceable. Last, we take their swords.

"We'd better leave," I say. "The Bloods will look for these three. A fight in this cramped area isn't what we want. Not when we're outnumbered."

We work our way back toward the clearing and head east, dodge a Blood patrol and rest. We speak in whispers.

"Let's find another clearing and set up another ambush," I say.

"It'll be fun hunting *them* for a change," says Grizz. "I'm tired of running away."

Steve nods in agreement.

We find a good-sized clearing. The three of us find blinds and sit in them as we wait for a Blood patrol to appear.

We don't have long to wait. The Bloods are behind me and heading our way, but the situation is all wrong. If I stay where I am, they'll find me *before* they reach the clearing. That spoils the ambush and will probably get me killed. I glide across the clearing, find a blind on the opposite side. Steve does the same. I notch an arrow and wait.

Moments later, the Bloods emerge from the tree line. The forest distorts the sound of their approach. They're advancing on a line perpendicular to my position. Six of them cross the clearing, which means four are on the flanks. On this heading, flankers may be behind me. There's nothing I can do. I take careful aim at the

Blood nearest me and let fly. Grizz and Steve do the same. My first target goes down and, seconds later, another falls.

There's a noise behind me. A Blood is three feet away, bearing down on me with her sword drawn. A flanker. I can't notch an arrow in time to stop her. She thrusts with her sword, and I hit the ground and roll away, just avoiding the point of her sword. In a split second, I'm on my feet and pulling my sword. I get it out just in time to parry her next cut. The force of her attack throws me backward. She comes at me again. Despite my size advantage, she shows no fear. I avoid her third thrust and launch an attack of my own. She parries my first cut, but the momentum of my advance drives her backward and down. Another slashing thrust forces her to her knees and I finish her.

I sense more than hear someone behind me, turn and find a Blood aiming a powerful sword thrust at my chest. I can't raise my sword in time to parry, so I sidestep and ready my sword. Another Blood appears behind this one. I try a killing cut aimed downwards at the neck of the second Blood, but he gets his sword up in time to block my attack. In a second, I'll be fighting two of them. I try another fast attack, try to finish one Blood before the other can join the fight, but the man I fight is a good swordsman. I retreat, preparing myself for a fight against two opponents. They both come straight at me, but one stops mid stride as an arrow finds his heart. Steve! With only one opponent left, I renew my attack. This man is an excellent swordsman, but I'm better. He fights bravely, but the outcome is never in doubt. I'm bigger, stronger, and a better swordsman. I finish him with a flurry of blows. He can't parry the last one.

With the Bloods dead, we survey the battlefield.

"I count nine dead Bloods," says Grizz.

I agree. "One of them ran. That's too bad. He'll find another group and tell them we have bows and swords. They'll be more cautious and harder to ambush."

Grizz looks thoughtful. "Time to change tactics. We'll hit them after dark. Let's find another group and ambush them after they pitch camp for the night. We'll take out the sentries first, then pick off the sleepers as they rise."

The plan is solid. Surprise will offset the Bloods' superior numbers. "Good strategy. But let's find another clearing and see if we get lucky. Maybe wipe out another patrol before they learn we're armed." We take a few minutes to catch our breath, and then we're off to find another ambush site.

We avoid two more Blood patrols before we find another clearing and settle in for another ambush. Although Bloods move all around us, none passes through our clearing.

As light in the forest dims, we wait for nightfall. Finding a Blood group camped for the night is easy. We smell wood smoke. It's hard to move through the forest after dark without making noise, but we're careful. We can't tell where the wood smoke comes from until we look up. Moonlight illuminates the smoke, and the breeze carries it south. We head north. The light of a campfire glows through the trees. We go down on all fours and creep forward until we find the Bloods' camp.

The Bloods are settled for the night. After an hour of quiet conversation, they head for their sleeping bags. The security arrangements are the same ones I saw two nights ago. Four Bloods are on sentry duty, and every one of them is alert. We back away so we can whisper and plan.

"Grizz, take the one on the left. The one on the right is mine. Steve, get the one right in front of us. The fourth one will sound the alarm. I'll take him out. You two work on the sleepers as they rise. Wait for my signal."

We creep forward again. I move silently until I have a clear shot at my target. I whistle. The Blood sentries hear the whistle and turn their heads in my direction. They're not alarmed; the sound might have been a bird. I draw back my bow, as do Grizz and Steve. The sentries find us, but it's too late. I hit my target. He falls forward. Grizz and Steve strike their targets. The fourth sentry blows a whistle, but I send an arrow into the center of his chest. The sleepers rise. Three of them are quick enough to notch arrows, but they don't know where the attack is coming from. They look around, bewildered. The fight is over in less than thirty seconds.

One Blood is still alive. An arrow struck his belly, and he's in pain. I kneel by his side. He looks up at me with a fear in his eyes.

"I won't kill you," I tell him. "I'd try to help you, but I don't have first aid supplies. Your wound is mortal. You will die. I'm sorry about that." The fear disappears from his eyes replaced by, what? Acceptance? Resignation?"

I put a pack beneath his head, hope the pillow makes him more comfortable, and decide not to remove the arrow because it would cause him pain. I give him a drink of water from my water skin and watch him die. All this dying is senseless. The Fair Haven robots may be right. Maybe we humans *are* a cursed race. Then I look at Grizz and Steve, and I know the robots are wrong. There are good people in this world. My companions will sacrifice their lives to help free others. We've become killers, but only because we have no other choice. When we free our people from slavery, I will give up my bow forever.

We wait in the shadows for an hour, worried the noise of battle will bring more Bloods. Satisfied that no more Bloods are coming, we enter the camp. The Bloods built a deep fire pit and surrounded it with rocks. They've cleared out the dry grass near the pit. I admire their work and bask in the fire's glow. "I will eat *cooked* food," whispers Steve. We drag the bodies of the Bloods from the clearing because corpses spoil the appetite. The Bloods have skinned and salted rabbits and squirrels and hung them from the branch of a nearby tree. We roast them on spits. My mouth waters as grease drips into the fire and hisses. The smell of roasting meat is irresistible. Even though the cooked meat is still steaming, I pick off pieces, burning my fingers. The salted rabbit and squirrel taste as good as the feast Javier prepared for us a few days ago. Sated, I locate a safe place for the night. For the first time in days, I sleep with a full stomach.

As always, I take the last watch because I'm an early riser, and with everything quiet, there's time to think. A cooked breakfast would be nice, but I let the fire burn down. The Bloods probably aren't up and about this early, but I'm taking no chances. When light rises in the eastern sky, I shake Grizz and Steve awake. We chew on salted squirrel, leftovers from last night.

The rising sun brings high winds. Even the tallest trees bend back and forth in the rushing gusts. The noise of the wind in the trees is loud. It'll be difficult to hear Bloods on the move today. We'll be hyper-cautious.

Once Grizz and Steve wipe the sleep out of their eyes, I ask, "Do you think the Bloods will change their tactics now that they know we'll come right after them? Will the Bloods' groups work together?"

Steve is quick to answer. "They won't change unless they must. Remember, Javier said the group that killed us would receive a handsome reward. That gives them a disincentive to work together. Splitting a reward ten ways is more lucrative than splitting it twenty or thirty ways. And the Bloods don't seem keen on forming alliances. What did Javier say? The Crips were 'old women' to form an alliance with the Sons of 1776."

"If we wipe out a few more groups, they won't have any choice," says Grizz. "Once they learn we can take out a group of ten, they'll combine groups, and that makes things harder for us. We've proved we can handle ten Bloods when we ambush them, but I don't think we can take on twenty of them. We're good with our bows, but not *that* good."

"We'll end as many as possible before they change strategy," I say. "They won't like it, but they'll *have* to combine groups to survive. Self-preservation trumps greed."

We decide against another ambush in this clearing. Dead bodies attract scavengers and the corpses will stink as the day heats them. The Bloods will be on high alert the minute they come near. To pull off an ambush, we need surprise.

The wind rises as the hours pass.

"Steve," I ask, "is this wind unusual?"

"I've never ventured this far south, but monsoons can blow anywhere at this time of year."

The sky is blue. "When we were with the villagers, we got monsoons, but they almost always brought rain. Do you think it will rain here?"

"I'm not sure. Some places have a dry monsoon. It depends on what side of the mountains you're on."

I shrug. "I hope these are dry monsoons. Not much shelter around here."

"If there *is* a good place for shelter," says Grizz, "it'll be crawling with Bloods."

*   *   *

We lay another ambush the following morning and wait as the sun climbs higher into the sky. It's early afternoon before we spot our first Blood. Three Bloods enter the clearing. They walk slow, scan from side to side.

"They've learned to scout ahead," I say.

A scout advances toward our blind. Ten more paces and he'll run right into Grizz. With no other choice, Grizz looses an arrow. Two seconds later, two dozen Bloods storm through the clearing—too many for us to fight. We must retreat. We abandon our hiding places and run. The woods are thick, negating our speed advantage. Branches and brambles whip at my face and arms. I try to change direction, but I trip. I scramble back to my feet. Arrows whistle past. We have Bloods behind us and on our left flank. I turn right. Grizz and Steve follow.

Our luck runs out. The north wall rises in front of me, only fifty yards away.

In the northeast corner of the forest are two rocky hills with a valley between. We cross a shallow brook and climb the taller of the two hills. Oaks and pines cover the tops of both hills. The slopes of the hills are too steep and rocky for trees, and there's nothing but dry brush and grass near the brook. I climb the nearest hill, throw myself down, catch my breath. A dozen Bloods emerge from the tree line behind us. We kill four of them, the rest retreat into the trees. We're pinned against the wall, and the Bloods' know it. They're smart. They'll talk things over, make plans to overrun us.

"They're fast learners," says Grizz. "Every Blood in the forest is over there."

Steve sees movement among the trees on the hill to the right of our position. "two o'clock," he whispers.

Bloods advance through the trees on the ridge. We count three, then four more. They're cautious. They know we have teeth, and they're showing us more respect. The treeline on the far side of the valley is sixty yards from our position. Just out of range for our bows.

The five scouts scrutinize the valley below and their eyes shift to our hill. They descend into the valley between us, two males and three females, their eyes in constant motion. They don't know exactly where we are.

"Why just five?" I whisper.

"The rest are hiding in the trees over there," says Grizz, pointing to the ridge across the valley. "They're trying to find us."

Steve looks nervous. "Do we take these five down?"

They've crossed the brook at the bottom of the valley and climb our side.

"If we do, we'll give away our position. But we don't have a choice." I shout to be heard over the wind. "They'll find us no matter what we do."

I watch for another few seconds. The Bloods show no signs of turning back. "Ready?" I ask, making eye contact with Grizz and Steve. They nod. Twenty seconds later, three Bloods are dead and the other two have mortal wounds. Their cries are louder than the roar of the wind.

An hour goes by as we wait for their next move. The cries of the wounded Bloods below cease. The waiting makes me nervous. "What are they waiting for? Will they wait and attack after dark?"

Grizz shakes his head. "They're spreading out. They'll come from our front and both flanks."

Late in the afternoon sixty Bloods emerge and charge at us from every direction.

"Here they come!" says Steve.

The Bloods let out a ferocious roar as they break from the trees and run towards us. With their leathers and tattoos, they look frightening and formidable. They cast long shadows in the late-afternoon sun. They've drawn their swords. If they reach us, we must switch from bows to swords in a hurry. For the next moments, time passes in a blur. I focus on shooting one arrow after another, making sure each one finds its target, absolute concentration. Two Bloods fall before they reach the brook, one while she is crossing the brook, and another as he tries to clamber up our hill.

One Blood crests the hill in front of Grizz. Grizz is ready for him and cuts him down with his sword. I scan the valley. There are no more Bloods coming. I breathe easy until I pick up movement out of the corner of my right eye. One Blood climbed the hill to our right. It's a tough climb, and he needed to use both of his hands. He hasn't yet drawn his sword. His right hand reaches for the hilt of his sword.

It's a simple question: can he draw his sword before I knock my bow? It's a near thing, but I win the race and the Blood falls backward, down the hill.

As suddenly as it started, the attack stops. The Bloods have gone to cover behind the many large rocks on the slopes of our hill. Some are only ten yards from our position.

"Their next attack will overrun us," says Grizz. "There're too many of them. They're so close we'll be lucky to stop five before the rest overwhelm us."

"Should we try to get out of here?" asks Steve.

I consider the possibility. "The minute we break cover, we'll be sitting ducks. I hate to say it, fellas, but we're stuck."

There's nothing but determination on the faces of Grizz and Steve.

"We'll go down fighting," says Grizz.

"You gotta die sometime," says Steve.

"I just wish it wasn't today," I say. "There's so much work left to do for our villagers."

We brace ourselves and wait for our final battle.

It's near dark and we're lucky: The Bloods show no inclination to mount a charge. The sun sets. Still the Bloods don't come.

"Do you think they'll overrun us in the dark?" I ask.

Grizz weighs the question. "They might. Too many things can go wrong in darkness. If I were them, I'd wait for the morning."

"Can we sneak through their lines after dark?" asks Steve.

No sooner has he said this than the Bloods throw lighted torches into no-man's-land between us.

"I think the answer to your question is no," I say, stating the obvious. "They'll attack at first light."

"We gotta do *something*," Steve says.

I wrack my brain, trying to think of a plan. At last, it comes to me. "The wind is blowing from behind us—away from us. What if we set the forest on fire? Everything is dry, so it'll catch and burn quickly. And with the strong wind, it'll spread fast."

"Risky," says Grizz. "If the wind shifts, the fire will come right back at us."

"This forest is nothing but tinder," says Steve. "The fire will catch with a big *whoosh* and within seconds we'll have an inferno on our hands. Even though the wind is blowing away from us, intense heat could cause spontaneous combustion in the trees surrounding us."

I try to remember everything I've read about forest fires. I know what spontaneous combustion is, but the wind is blowing *hard*. "OK," I say, "maybe we get fried, but there's an absolute certainty the Bloods will kill us tomorrow. Do either of you disagree?"

Grizz and Steve hesitate, then shake their heads.

We dig a shallow fire pit and remove everything near our position that might burn. Steve works his magic with a spinning stick to get a small fire going. I stick a dry pinecone on the head of one of my arrows and hold it over Steve's little fire. Dry as a desert stone, it catches fire. I take careful aim because I want to set fire to the very edge of the Bloods' lines. I want the Bloods to come *through* the fire if they rush us. Grizz and Steve follow my example, launching fire arrows toward the Bloods' positions.

The fire catches and spreads. We launch a few more fire arrows, but they're unnecessary. The fire moves so fast it's frightening to watch. Fire balls leap from one tree to another, and in less than a minute, we face a solid wall of flame.

The fire burns so hot it scorches my face and hands. I fight the urge to cover my face and watch the trees on our side of the valley. They steam, but don't catch. At least not yet. The roar of the wind combined with the roar of the fire is deafening.

The Bloods panic. There's too much noise for them to communicate. Most follow the natural human instinct to run away from the fire. If they stopped to think it through, they'd realize the wind is too strong and the fire too hot to outrun. But it's impossible to think straight in the split-second it takes to make their life or death decision. Nine of the Bloods do the smart thing and run through the flames, toward us. Silhouetted against the wall of fire behind them, they're easy targets and we drop them. Had they all attacked us, some of them would be alive in the morning.

We watch, awestruck, as the fire leaps from treetop to treetop, whipped into a frenzy by the wind. The fire moves farther and farther away from us, leaving nothing but charred and smoking ruins behind. There's no chance for the Bloods to outrun the flames. I can't see them, but I know they're dying.

We don't sleep a wink all night. By morning, there's nothing left of the forest but charred snags. The wall behind us still stands, but much of the east wall has burned to the ground, leaving nothing but ashes and twisted, charred, melted razor wire. The wind blew the fire away from the east wall on a slight tangent, so the wall contained and dampened the flames. The forest in that direction is intact. Although I can't see far enough to tell for sure, I'll wager that wall or no wall, the forest downwind burned. Smoke rises high in the air to our south, confirms my prediction.

All three of us have cherry-red faces, scorched by the heat. I touch my face gingerly. It hurts, like a bad sunburn. "Time to leave," I say.

We wind our way forward, careful to avoid slow-burning embers and leave the confines of the "King's Game," crossing over the ruined wall. We exercise caution as we navigate through the remnants of the razor wire, but the incredible heat of the fire melted and fused the sharp edges. A mile into the forest on the other side, we stop to catch our breath.

"Do we go home?" asks Grizz.

I shake my head. "No. We have unfinished business here. Do you remember what happened to Jerald and Amigo? How Javier beat them to death? I want revenge." I remember Jerald's pathetic face as he begged me to make Javier stop beating him. Even now, I have a visceral sense of fury and helplessness. I will have my revenge.

15

We crawl through the charred remains of the forest and approach the Bloods' fortress. Even the charred remains of trees give enough cover for us to move in close. We're covered with soot from head to toe, which is unpleasant, but the ash provides us with excellent camouflage. Pillars of smoke rise miles high to the southwest, tell us that the fire is still burning. I feel guilty about destroying the forest, but if we hadn't, we'd be dead.

The wind blew the central axis of the fire to the west of the Bloods' fort. The crop fields around the walls created a firebreak that spared the Bloods' fortress from destruction. Intense heat from the passing fire burned parts of the west wall and some buildings on the outskirts of the village. I'm sure the Bloods have dealt with fire before; they contained our fire as it approached their walls.

I'm relieved. I didn't want the deaths of Blood civilians on my conscience. The Bloods' leaders are bloodthirsty, but the villagers treated us with kindness.

The village is a hive of activity. Parties of Bloods poke past the ruins of the wall that marked the border of their "King's Game" and into the ruined forest beyond, looking for survivors. They won't find any. Other workers tear down the fire-damaged wall and the few gutted buildings in the village. They'll rebuild.

Javier moves from place to place, encouraging his people. He walks to the ruins of his "game" preserve and stares at the devastation. Building a new venue for the "King's Game" will be a massive undertaking—perhaps he won't bother. The latest game should discourage him.

Grizz and I watch all day. Steve spends the morning searching through the unburned forest on the other side of the village, gathering the supplies we'll need tonight. He returns in the afternoon with vines he's collected. We braid them into sturdy ropes.

After the sun sets, we watch where the Bloods post their sentries. I'd hoped to take advantage of the places where the fire breached the wall, but they've posted sentries near the breaches. The Bloods assume my companions and I perished in the fire. A reasonable assumption: there's only a tiny sliver of the preserve left intact. The guards are watching for Crips, not us. Whatever their motivations, we'll find a way over the wall.

We move cautiously around the walls, looking for weaknesses in the Bloods' defenses. There are none. The fire left a cloud of ash and soot hanging in the air, so there's little moonlight. The dark night suits us.

After we circle the wall, I whisper, "This won't be easy. They aren't letting their guard down. The walls are lousy with sentries."

Grizz grunts, which means he's thinking. "We need a diversion," he says at last.

"We're gonna be pyromaniacs again, aren't we?" asks Steve, smiling. In his soot-darkened face, his white teeth are brilliant.

"Yep," I say. "Steve, use fire arrows to light a fire in the guard tower nearest the burned wall. The Bloods will assume they missed a few live embers. Grizz and I will climb the wall on the opposite side."

Steve nods. "I'll have a nice, toasty fire going in thirty minutes."

"After you start the fire, work around the fortress until you're back here. We'll meet you after we've dealt with Javier."

Steve nods. Grizz and I leave him and move through the forest surrounding the fortress until we reach the west wall. We don't have to wait long before we see flames leaping into the sky. The fire turns the low-hanging clouds over the fort a fevered shade of crimson. Steve did his job.

Two sentries guard the parapet in front of us. As we'd hoped, they're watching the fire. Grizz ties his rope into a lasso. He pitches it over a post jutting from the top of the wall. I climb up the rope and scramble over the top. The sentry nearest me must have seen motion out of the corner of his eye, because he turns toward me. I silence him with an arrow. The second sentry hears the first sentry fall and I'm forced to take him down. No sooner have I done this than Grizz appears at my side.

We flip the rope over to the inside of the wall and climb down. Steve's fire is billowing now, so no one notices as two shadows slip into the village.

"We need to find a lone sentry," I say. We locate one outside the door of the banquet hall where Javier feted us. Like everybody else, the sentry watches the leaping flames. I approach him from behind. When I'm near enough, I wrap my arm around him and hold my knife at his throat.

"If you make a sound, you're dead," I hiss.

He raises his empty hands, palms out. "OK," he whispers.

"Where does Javier live?"

"Javier's quarters are in that building," he says, pointing to a three-story building to the south of the banquet hall.

Grizz and I tie up the guard. We carry him into a dark alley behind the banquet hall and drop him on the ground. We leave him there, trussed hand and foot and gagged.

"Don't move until morning," Grizz warns. "We'll be right around the corner, and we'll kill you if you make any noise."

Unable to speak because of the gag, he mumbles and nods his head. He understands. The fear in his bulging eyes assures me he'll do as he's told. Unless someone comes down the alley, there'll be no problem from this sentry until daybreak.

We leave the guard and move around the banquet hall, flitting from shadow to shadow, eyes and ears tuned to catch any hint of movement. We find Javier's building and open the front door a crack. I peer in, see nothing but furniture. We push the door open, and I flinch when it squeaks, but there's no one inside. We scan the room. This must be Javier's parlor; it's filled with comfortable-looking furniture. We close the door behind us, find the stairs leading up, and ascend to the second floor.

The second floor houses several small rooms, separated by narrow hallways. A room near the middle of the floor serves as a conference room. Maps and drawings line the walls, and a huge oak table surrounded by high-backed chairs dominates the center of the room. Comfortable-looking velvet, plum-colored pillows rest on the seats of each chair. A dozen sconces line the walls, although only two are lit. Their flickering light causes the shadows in the room to jump and sway.

I've wrestled with various ways of killing Javier. I can't murder him in cold blood. Much as I despise him and what he did to Jerald and Amigo, I can't stand him up against a wall and put an arrow in him. I've thought about hauling him back to the Sanctuary with us to stand trial but abandoned the idea. There are only three of us. It'd be difficult to watch him, and he'd try to escape. And even if he didn't, the villagers have no legal system. The only law in our neck of the woods comes in the form of our archenemy, the Court. Turning Javier over to them is out of the question.

This room without windows gives me an idea. I walk across the room listening. The floor is solid; it doesn't squeak. We peer across the hall and find Javier's bedroom. A tall four-poster bed stands against the wall opposite the door and two heavy-looking chests dominate the other two walls. There's a large, comfortable-looking chair with a footstool in one corner and a table with a cup, pitcher and water basin beside the bed. There's nobody in the room. Javier is still out.

We investigate the other rooms on this floor and listen for sounds of Javier's return. We find a small dining room, an armory, what seems to be a records room, a bathroom with a gravity-powered flush toilet, and a sitting room.

"Let's wait for Javier in his bedroom," I say.

Grizz nods. "I doubt it'll take much longer to put the fire out."

While we're waiting, I tell Grizz of my plan to kill Javier.

He gives me a worried look. "Are you sure?"

"Yes, I'm sure."

Grizz shrugs. He knows trying to talk me out of it would be a waste of breath.

Sure enough, within an hour the sound of feet on the stairs announce Javier's return. "Cover the door," I whisper to Grizz. I sit on Javier's bed, so he'll see me the instant he steps into the room.

Javier opens the door and steps inside. He's deep in thought with his head down, so he doesn't see me. When he looks up, he's startled.

He receives another shock when Grizz steps behind him and rests a knife against his Adam's apple.

"You," he says, at last. His face breaks into a big smile. "Well, you won the game. I don't know how you did it..." He stops and realization dawns. "*You* set the fire."

"We did."

"No matter," he says. "There's no rule against setting a fire, you still win. We've never lost the King's Game before. You should be proud of yourselves. Leave with our blessing."

"I can't do that," I say. "Because the game isn't over."

"What do you mean? The game's over. You win"

"We've added a few rules of our own. Let's cross the hall to your conference room and I'll explain the new rules."

Javier shrugs. With Grizz's knife at his throat he's in a bad bargaining position.

We enter the room. Grizz walks Javier to the wall opposite the door.

"Here's what will happen," I say. "You and I will finish the King's Game. In a minute, Grizz will give you a knife. A knife like the one you gave us at the start of the King's Game. I have a knife just like it." I show him mine. "We'll blow out the sconces and close the door. The room will be pitch-black. Just you and me, in a dark room, armed with knives. If you make it out of the room alive, you win the game. If not, you die."

Javier looks at me as though I've gone insane. "You're crazy," he says.

"Look at it this way Javier. You'll have much better odds here than you gave us in the forest. In here it's one on one. Both armed with the same weapon."

He stares at me intently. What he sees is a girl who is much smaller than he is, and he knows himself to be a mighty warrior. "It's your funeral," he says. "I don't understand why you don't celebrate your victory and leave. Why make me kill you?" I see a flicker of doubt in his eyes. I *am* the girl that just won the King's Game.

"Do you remember our friends, the robot and the dog you killed?"

"Vaguely."

"You need to pay for what you did to them. Grizz, prepare the room."

"Once I kill you, how do I know your friend there won't run me through when I open the door?" asks Javier.

"You *don't*. But our people keep their word."

Grizz extinguishes the sconces, leaves the room, and closes the door. The room is totally dark. I wait a few moments to let my eyes adjust. They don't. There's no light. I'm locked in a dark room with a predator. A tickle of fear runs down my spine. I hope I haven't outsmarted myself. A part of me wants to turn around, throw open the door, and stop this.

*   *   *

I choke off my fear and concentrate.

I have an advantage. I've spent the last several days walking silently, thinking about the placement of every step I take. I've strained to hear every noise, knowing the Bloods could appear at any minute from any direction. I count on my tuned ears to give me the edge.

I steady my breathing and listen. I hear a footstep. It's a soft one, but unmistakable. And it's followed by another one. Javier is on the move.

Javier wins if he reaches the door. I've considered waiting by the door and letting him come to me. But that's an obvious strategy; Javier will expect it. To win, I need to surprise him.

I listen for another step. It comes from the left of Javier's starting position. There's a huge table in the center of the room, so Javier will walk around it. I know which way he's going. I take a step and listen. Javier moves again. And then again. He's moving slowly, but I now know the frequency of his steps. I time my next step to match his. I want to ambush him by the edge of the table. I listen and synchronize my step with his again. When I reach the table, I stop.

I calm my breathing and listen again. I wait and wait; There's no noise. *What's Javier doing? Is it possible he's heard me?*

Finally, he moves again. This time, he's moving right.

He changed course. He's won't be predictable!

He moves back toward his starting point. Once he reaches it, he remains silent. I listen, ears straining. Finally, he moves again, to the right. I have no choice but to retreat. If I don't stay between him and the door, he'll make one fast dash and reach the door before I can stop him. *Why did he change course? Did he hear me?* I reach the door.

As I move, I regain my confidence. I'm certain I'm making no noise. I glide to the right, listen for Javier. The sound of breaking glass shatters the silence. Javier broke a sconce. The sound startled me. Did I make a noise? Did I gasp?

I'm uncertain, but I can't rule out the possibility that I made a noise. *Best to assume Javier knows where I am.*

I'm right! Javier rushes forward. No longer worried about noise, he runs straight at me. I take a couple gliding steps to my left. Javier's on my right side, a yard away. He cuts with his knife, hoping to hit me. I back up, trying to put distance between us so he doesn't catch me with a lucky cut.

Javier realizes I've moved and abandons his knife thrusts.

"I found you, little girl," he says in a conversational tone.

His voice is not where I expected it to be. He's farther to my right than I expected. *How did he get there without me hearing him?* Panic rises. *Have I underestimated him?* I force myself to choke off the panic. If I'm not careful, panic will make me breathe heavy, and as close as he is, Javier will hear.

"I'm coming to get you," he says. "I know where you are."

How can he know? He can't. He's bluffing, trying to force me to make a mistake. A careless step or panicked breath will give me away. I calm myself again.

Everything is silent. *Is he waiting for me to come to him? Is he planning to make a dash for the door?* I've lost the initiative. I'm reacting to him. I must regain control. *What's he thinking?*

I calm myself and try to put myself inside Javier's head. He's a battle-tested warrior and the leader of a bunch of cutthroats. He's in a contest with a young girl. He won't run for the door. That would be cowardly. No, Javier won't run away. He wants to kill me.

He moves again. This time, he's coming right toward me. He's guessing, and his guess is correct. I take two steps to my left. Javier doesn't change course, he's headed where I *was,* not where I am. He's close. Very close.

"I smell you little girl. You can give up now. Don't make me kill you."

16

I'm consumed by fear. Then I realize I can smell him, too. But I could smell him ever since Grizz closed the door. His smell permeates the room. It doesn't tell me where he is.

I listen for another step. He's less than two feet away. Moving fast, and no longer worried about noise, I step in behind him. With one quick move of my arm, I bring my blade around his head, flush with his Adam's apple. Because I couldn't see him, I bring the knife closer to his neck than I intended. A trickle of warm blood runs over my knuckles. Javier gasps in surprise and pain.

He's mine now. He's helpless. But I can't bring myself to cut his throat. I visualize Javier destroying Jerald and Amigo. I focus on my rage, and still I can't make myself do it.

"Don't sport with me, girl. Kill me and be done with it."

There's no hint of fear or pleading in his voice. He's a brave man.

"Grizz," I say, trying to keep my voice level, "open the door, please."

Light floods into the room. Accustomed to absolute darkness, Javier and I flinch and squint.

Grizz looks surprised to find both of us alive.

"I can't kill him," I say. "Cover him so he won't move."

Grizz does as I ask, aiming his bow at Javier's chest. If Javier moves, he'll have an arrow through his heart.

I lower my knife. He considers his options. I'm not sure what I'll do. I decide: "I'll let you live, Javier."

If he's surprised, he doesn't show it. He looks puzzled. "Why not kill me?" he asks.

"I can't. We don't kill if we can avoid it."

"Then why did you lock me in a dark room and stalk me?"

"I *want* to kill you. I want revenge for the deaths of my friends. But I can't do it."

"What will you do with me?"

"I'll let you go," I say. "But once I let you go; I want your word that you'll return our backpacks and allow my friends and me to leave your land."

"My word won't mean much," says Javier. "I can't lead my people. A mere girl has defeated me."

"No one needs to know what happened in here tonight. And as far as me being a 'mere girl', I've defeated stronger men than you." This statement is close to being true. "How do you think a 'mere girl' with only two friends defeated one hundred of your finest warriors? I watched your people die, Javier. Dozens of them. Don't repeat your mistakes. Don't continue to underestimate me. You lost, but you lost to a worthy foe, not a 'mere girl'".

Javier takes a long moment to consider. "That's your only condition? I return your property and let you go?"

"There's one more condition. Do you still have the body of our robot? The one we call 'Jerald'?"

"We can dig him up. We threw him in the trash pit."

"Fine. You do that. And you clean him up. We'll come back for him. I want your word that you will give him back to us when the time comes."

"Yes. Your little tin man is of no use to me. Why don't you take him with you?"

"He's too heavy to carry."

"Yes," says Javier, pulling his beard. "I understand. As I recall, our people had a hard time carrying him to the dump. Don't worry. When you return, we will have your little friend polished and glowing like the sun. Except where I broke him."

"We'll leave now."

"We can throw a feast to celebrate your victory. That is the way of my people. After any victory we fete the warriors, and they stand on a table and brag about their bravery. You *are* the victors."

"Thank you for the offer. But we need to return to our homeland."

"And you don't trust me, eh?" Javier says with an ironic grin.

"That, too."

We descend Javier's stairs to the street below. The night is less dark. There's a hint of dawn in the eastern sky. Nobody is abroad at this hour, except the sentries. They reach for their bows when they see us but relax once they see Javier. I breathe in relief once I realize Javier will keep his word. One gesture from him and Grizz and I will be in a battle for our lives.

We leave the fort through the front gates. Javier turns to us before we go. "Bloods honor their oaths, too."

I turn to Javier and nod. The Bloods will never be our friends, but we can trust them.

We find Steve and head north.

"Why do you want Jerald's body?" Grizz asks. "Do you want to bury him?"

"No. Jerald told us steel surrounds his central circuits. That's what makes him so heavy. His brain *may be inside* his body. If so, he's still alive. Javier killed his sensory apparatus, his ability to see and speak. That should be reparable. With luck, his personality and memory are still intact."

Grizz grins. "I hope so. I like the little rascal."

"You have someone who fixes robots?" asks Steve.

"We have a friend named Bree. She can fix almost anything. We also have robots at the armory. They may not know how to fix

Jerald because he's not like any robot they've seen but they might be able to help. To them, maybe a circuit is a circuit. And if worse comes to worst and we can't fix Jerald, we can always take him back to Fair Haven."

"What humans did to Jerald won't improve their opinion of humans," says Grizz.

I smile. "But if they can bring Gerald back to life, it'll be worth it."

We reach the north side of the Bloods' plateau and find another series of steep cliffs falling to the desert below. We descend the cliff faces with care. Without having to hoist Jerald and Amigo, our descent is much faster than our climb up. Once we reach the bottom, we're in a desert much like the deserts of our home. Water is scarce, but we find enough to meet our needs.

Several days after we leave the Bloods, we see another city on the horizon. We have only a limited knowledge of the geography here, but I'm willing to bet we've found the home of the Sons of 1776, or as Javier would call them, the Crips.

*　　*　　*

Grizz stares intently at the city in the distance. "Do you think that's the home city of the Sons?"

"That's my guess. Steve, what do you think?"

"I can't tell. I've never seen the city of the Sons. Everybody on the road knows that you don't come anywhere near these parts. The people here are plain evil."

Part of me wants to get a better look at the home of our foe, but another wants to give this place a wide berth. "I want to get closer," I say after weighing our options.

"We should be careful," says Grizz. "They'll have their Apache scouts on the lookout for visitors."

I've tangled with the Apaches before, and they're formidable. They're masters of stealth and cunning. They cut your throat before you even know they're near. "Nobody has more respect for the Apaches than I do. But we, too, have learned a thing or two about being stealthy."

We creep toward the city of the Sons using the tangled desert plants as cover. Once, we hear a soft rustle in the vegetation ahead. Seconds later, an Apache appears, padding through the desert using a path on a tangent to our own. We go to ground and watch as he passes us. He stops once and, nose up, sniffs the air. *Can he smell us*? If he does, he gives no sign. He continues to walk. We wait fifteen minutes before moving. I'm happy we found the Apache instead of him finding us. I give Grizz and Steve a smiling thumbs-up, and we continue.

The city of the Sons turns out to be different from others we've encountered on this side of the brane. They've constructed the fort using adobe, a mixture of sand, clay, and manure. Massive timbers give structural support for the walls. The walls enclose a large area. The city of the Sons is at least half again as large as the Bloods' home city. We dealt the Sons a massive defeat in the Battle of Fort Kennedy, and, because we killed so many Sons, there are many empty beds inside those walls. I find no joy in that thought, just a weary sense of an unpleasant job completed.

Like most cities of this world, fields surround the fort's walls. We watch as miserable-looking slaves go about their chores, planting, weeding, or harvesting. Slave drivers stalk the fields with thick bullwhips. When they think a worker not moving fast enough, they give him a lash of the whip. The unlucky slaves cry out in pain and shamble on, trying to move faster. With horror, I realize scars cover the backs of every man, woman, and child in the fields.

An old woman near our hiding place falls to the ground, overcome by the harsh desert heat. A slave master crosses the field and stands over her. I expect him to give the old woman a drink or at least splash water in her face to revive her. Instead, he pulls his whip back and strikes the woman with a mighty *crack*. The old woman whimpers and tries to rise, but she fails. The master strikes her again and again. Following each lash, the old woman cries, until she's unable to make a sound. And still the master continues to whip her.

"She's dead!" Grizz whispers, his voice tight with anger.

I rest my hand on Grizz's arm. We can't help.

I've seen enough. We back away.

Alert to the possible presence of Apaches, we move stealthily until we're ten miles north of the city of the Sons.

"Once we free our own people, we'll do something about the Sons," says Grizz.

"There's much evil in this world," says Steve. "Ridding the world of wickedness will be difficult."

I walk in silence, mulling over Steve's comment. *Can I spend the rest of my life killing evil men?* I can't answer that question now, but I'm tired of war. With luck, we'll free our own. We'll see what comes next.

A series of mighty mountains rise to our west and run northward. Those are *our* mountains. We have three days to walk. After over a year on the road we're thrilled with the prospect of seeing Fort Stone. We're almost home!

A day's walk from the safety of Fort Stone, we're brought up short by a sound like intermittent thunder coming from the north. Grizz, Steve, and I exchange nervous glances. Rain is rare on our side of the mountains.

"What the…" Grizz starts, but the sight of an enormous humanoid body appearing over the horizon cuts him off.

17

We know what it is. It's Garganto. We first met Garganto over a year ago. He's well over sixty feet tall, and, as far as we can tell, indestructible. We still don't know who built him, but they programmed him to crush to death every person he encounters. By a stroke of incredibly good luck, Kenny convinced Garganto that she was his father. Strange, but true. Since then, Garganto has worked for us. I assume his presence here is intended to discourage the Sons of 1776 from sending raiding parties to harass our activities around the workshop, the chem lab, and the armory. We can't really use Garganto on the other side of the mountains because wherever the blacksuits go, they use a human shield of slaves to protect themselves. Garganto would be incapable of crushing one without crushing the other.

The ground shudders with every step Garganto takes.

"What on earth is that?" asks Steve, terror in his voice. Steve has never met Garganto.

"I'll explain in a minute, but first, we better run."

We run toward the mountains to our west. They're only a couple miles away, but I doubt we'll reach them before Garganto catches us. Garganto can't climb, and although he has arms, they don't work. If we can reach the mountains before he catches us, we'll be safe. On the other hand, Garganto moves much faster than we do.

"Do you think he'll remember us?" asks Grizz as he runs.

"I don't know," I reply. "I'm pretty certain Kenny's programmed him to squash anyone coming from the south. So, tiny little humans traveling north are all enemies to him."

My hypothesis is confirmed when Garganto begins to speak. "My name is Garganto, killer of killers. Look on my power ye mighty and despair!" he rumbles in a gravelly, stentorian voice.

Gauging the shrinking distance between Garganto and us, I realize won't reach the mountains in time. Garganto moves as fast as a freight train on a straight track though open country. Grizz and I might have a chance, but Steve, with his short legs, can't keep up. We can't leave him behind, but if we don't, we'll all die.

I stop and face Garganto.

"What are you doing?" hollers Grizz.

"We'll never make it," I reply.

Grizz answers by picking up Steve and throwing him unceremoniously over his shoulder. The dead weight slows Grizz down, but even so, we might have a chance. I leave my friends and run on a different course, to the northwest. I wave my arms around and holler insults at Garganto. I'm hoping Garganto will follow me. Grizz is faster than I am, but with dead weight on his shoulder, I'll be faster.

My ploy doesn't work. Garganto ignores me and continues to chase Grizz and Steve. I reach the safety of the mountain's talus slope and scramble up and over the boulders lying at the foot of the mountain.

I turn in time to see Garganto close the distance between himself and Grizz. They'll never make it! Garganto is too fast. Garganto's giant right foot comes down on top of Grizz and Steve.

"Noooo!" I scream. *How can this be? We've travelled for months, gotten within a few hours of home, and we lose it all to a robot who's ostensibly on our side?* The unfairness of it all breaks me. Tears stream down my cheeks. I've just lost the love of my life. I con-template climbing back down to the desert floor and letting Garganto finish me as well.

18

I watch as Garganto stomps around in circles. Befogged as my brain is, I wonder why Garganto is behaving so strangely. And then, over my sobs, I hear Grizz's voice. "We're alive, ET!"

"Grizz!"

"We're in a narrow arroyo," calls Grizz. "Garganto can't crush us because his foot's too big. But he's making the sides of the arroyo crumble. He's burying us alive!"

"I'm coming!" I cry.

Grizz's response comes back: "Don't do anything crazy, ET! Steve and I are expendable. You're not!"

If I could save Grizz's life by letting Garganto kill me, I'd do it. But Garganto would finish me before Grizz and Steve could dig themselves out. I scramble along the flank of the mountain, trying to get near enough to talk to Garganto.

"Garganto!" I holler at the top of my voice. "We're friends!"

"Only enemies come from the south!" rumbles Garganto in reply. "You come from the south. You are enemies."

"It's me, Garganto, ET! Don't you remember me?"

Garganto pauses. "ET?"

"Yes, I'm ET. You remember me! I'm your father's friend."

Garganto looks confused. His IQ is not high, and the concept of a 'friend of his father's' coming from the south leaves left him perplexed. "If you're my father's friend, then you'll know the password he taught me," Garganto rumbles.

I struggle to remember. I only heard Kenny use the word once. *What was it? Something unusual!* I rack my brain, and at last, it comes to me. "The password is Ozymandias!"

Garganto stops moving. I'm in such a hurry I fall, scraping a shin and the palm of my hand, but I ignore my injuries, spring to my feet, and sprint to the arroyo where I last saw Grizz and Steve. I reach the top and stare into the arroyo. I can't see either Grizz or Steve!

I scramble into the arroyo and dig through the sand with my bare hands. I don't know where Grizz and Steve are, so I can only hope that I'm digging in the right spot. I scrape away more and more sand, and finally touch human flesh. In a brief second, Grizz's head emerges. He's coughing and spitting, gasping for breath. Another moment of frantic digging and his shoulders and arms are clear.

I move a few feet and begin digging again. Grizz was carrying Steve, so Steve must be somewhere near. I dig more and at last; I find Steve. His face is blue from oxygen deprivation. I continue digging until his chest is clear. He won't be able to breathe with his chest buried. Once I uncover his chest, I administer mouth to mouth resuscitation. His mouth is full of sand. I remove the sand with shaking fingers. I pinch his nose and blow into his mouth again and again. I'm in despair when he coughs. Moments later he breathes on his own. I collapse in exhaustion. Grizz has freed himself and he goes to work helping Steve.

Garganto looks at us in confusion. "How did ET, friend of my father, come to be traveling from the south? Father says only nasty people come from the south."

"It's a long story, Garganto. We've been traveling."

"Will you speak with my father soon?"

"Yes, Garganto, we'll speak with your father soon."

"Will you tell him," Garganto continues in his doomsday voice, "that I am lonely?"

"Why are you lonely?"

"I'm lonely because I have no one to squash."

"There are no Apaches?"

Garganto snorts, which produces a sound like a dozen canons being fired at once. "Yes, I see Apaches. But they are sneaky little devils. I see one, and just when I'm about to stomp him, the little rascal disappears. I'm losing faith in myself. How can I be a fearsome killer if I can't squash little Apaches? I'm depressed."

"No need to lose faith, Garganto. The Apaches are very elusive. And I promise I will talk to your father. Perhaps he'll find a more interesting job for you."

"Thank you, ET," says Garganto. "I'm sure my father will not have forgotten me."

Knowing Kenny, she probably *has* forgotten him. When Kenny gets involved in a project, she forgets everything else. I've seen her go days without eating or sleeping when she's challenged. I'll let her know her "son" is unhappy.

We say goodbye to Garganto and resume our journey north.

After we've traveled a few miles I pause and peer back over my shoulder. Garganto stomps around once more, his eyes facing south.

*   *   *

We pass through the old, ruined town and approach the hill that towers over the workshop. The sentries watch us. One of them recognizes me.

"It's the Daughter of Gaia!" she yells. The others take up the call. Within minutes we're surrounded, each person trying to touch me. The attention embarrasses me. I touch every hand I can reach.

"They've missed you," says Grizz, smiling from ear to ear. He's being mobbed, too. Moments later a young African American girl runs towards us.

"Bree!" I cry.

We move toward each other through the sea of villagers. I embrace her and feel tears on my face. The bonds between my friends and I are strong ones. We were kids together in Tucson. I hate to let her go. She looks at Grizz and he scoops her up in his arms, both of them grinning.

"How you doin' munchkin?" he asks.

"I'm *not* a munchkin, you gorilla!" she objects. This is an old time-honored exchange. Grizz and Bree have good-naturedly discussed Bree's small stature ever since I can remember.

Bree beams at both of us. "We were afraid we'd lost you."

"It hasn't been easy, but here we are! I've been lucky and Grizz is too ornery to die."

"Come. Come inside," says Bree at last. "You two are thin as scarecrows."

In the excitement of homecoming, I've forgotten Steve. "Bree, meet our good friend Steve. He's one of us now. Without him, Grizz and I would have been dead long ago."

Bree hugs Steve. "Pleased to meet you, Steve. Thanks for looking after these two. They're lunks, but we love 'em."

Bree leads us into the fort that guards the workshop. I realize the fort is *much* bigger than it was when I left. "You've expanded!"

"We've become quite a commercial center," Bree says. "Once we've fed you, I'll give you the grand tour."

She ushers us into the mess hall. Within moments, a young boy brings us plates heaped with steaming food. I'm surprised meat is on the menu. "We have meat?"

"It's goat meat," explains Bree, sounding apologetic. "Raising goats is efficient. There's not much vegetation here, east of the mountains, but goats are master scavengers. It's nice to add some extra protein to our diet."

The goat has a gamey taste, but my taste buds have become much more flexible than they were back in Tucson. When you've eaten bugs, goat tastes good.

"So, tell us what we've missed!" I ask.

"The fight against the blacksuits is going well—I'll let Falstaff give you the details. The biggest problem we have here east of the mountains comes from the Apaches. They ambush our supply trains. You know how we've been trying to build solar farms so we can move technology to the villages on the other side of the saddle? Well, we need to send one hundred armed guards with every convoy. Even then, Apache ambushes cost us people and material. Falstaff grumbles over the huge number of his warriors we need over here, but he understands the problem.

The mention of Apaches gives me the willies. I've escaped from them twice, both times by the skin of my teeth. Being bested by a "little girl" has humiliated them. They hate me with a passion and have vowed to track me down and kill me. The worst part is that they're excellent warriors. They frighten me.

"Garganto told me the Apaches are frustrating him. They're too sly for him to catch."

"Well, I can tell you he's not stopping them."

After we've finished our meal, Bree takes us for a tour of the fort. The walls are bristling with armed guards and villagers scurry around, busy with their tasks.

Bree leads us out the back door of the mess hall, and I cry out in delight. Before us is a giant field of solar panels.

"We can't build the solar farm outside the walls, because it's vulnerable to Apache raids. So, we've built a nice one here."

I gaze around in wonder.

Bree introduces me to a tall villager with startling green eyes, a receding hairline, and a tidy, trimmed beard. He's a handsome man and his looks remind me of one of Kenny's many boyfriends.

"This is Richard," says Bree. "He's in charge of the solar farm. He oversees our workers, and he's our expert on setting up panels and connecting them to generators.

"Happy to meet you, Richard," I say.

"The pleasure is mine, Daughter of Gaia. May I say how honored I am to work for you?"

"You're not working for me, Richard. You're working for all of us."

There's deep adoration in his eyes and, as far as *he's* concerned, he's working for *me* regardless what I say.

Bree shows us through large warehouses which we're using to store equipment moved here from the armory. There are many weapons.

"These are motion sensitive guns," Bree explains, gesturing at a hall filled with wicked looking guns.

I recognize them instantly. These are the guns used by the ancients to guard the approaches to the Armory. The minute one of these guns detects a heat signature and something in motion it fires at the movement. Since these guns aren't shooting at us, they're powered down. I've lost members of the Daughter's Guard to these lethal weapons.

There are flying drones here, too. Thermal and motion sensors activate their weapons, too. I've lost guards to these, as well.

"Can a drone strike New Washington from here?" I ask.

"They have the range, but they're a blunt instrument. The drones kill slaves just as easily as they kill blacksuits. They can't distinguish between them. If a thing generates heat and moves, it's dead. We have them on the prowl for Apaches trying to infiltrate our lines, but with limited success. The Apaches travel in ones and twos until they're ready to attack. And they don't mass for an attack until they're right on top of us. We can't use the drones at that point because we'd hit *our* people. Also, the Apaches have an endless number of trails when they move north. The drones are good, but they're policing over five thousand square miles. They nail a few Apaches, but not enough to end the threat.

"One thing we *can* use the drones for is surveillance. We reprogram them, and instead of blowing things up, they use the cameras in their bellies to keep tabs on Salieri's goons. Unfortunately, they take a day to recharge. We can't keep enough of them in the air, because we also need to charge the airplanes and our communications equipment. Plain and simple: we need a bigger solar farm."

"I'm sure you're expanding the farm as fast as you can."

"We just finished building a big solar farm at the mines, and we've built smaller farms in every village. Small, but big enough to power communications gear."

"How's that working?"

"Great! We have instant communication with the villages now. So, every single villager knows the Daughter of Gaia has returned. Now that we have the comm system up and running and we've planted the grain crops, we're putting every ounce of energy into expanding the farms at the mines and here."

We continue our tour of the warehouse. There're tons of communications equipment, crates of ammunition, computers, electronics gear, and much else I can't name.

In the corner near the exit is a gigantic tank. "Wow!" I say in excitement. "You got a tank running!"

"We did," Bree confirms, "but getting it to the other side of the mountains where we *need* it—that's another matter."

The tank is enormous. It's at least fifteen feet tall and twice as long. The gun barrel looks to be fifteen feet long all by itself.

"I've looked at ways to disassemble the tank into smaller pieces to make it easier to move, but the people who built it didn't contemplate taking it apart. Even broken into pieces it weighs tons."

"Why is so much gear stored here?" I ask.

"We move equipment from the armory to the workshop fast," Bree says. "But it takes forever to move gear over the saddle. That's our bottleneck. So, we use these warehouses to stock our backlog. We're working on ways to get stuff over the saddle faster, but I'll let Chase tell you that story."

"Come over here," says Bree, gesturing with her left arm.

I gasp again.

Grizz, who's standing next to me, whistles in amazement.

"Airplanes!"

"Yep," says Bree. There are three small airplanes standing in the sunlight, metal wings shining.

"Do they work?"

"They work. You want to fly one?"

My innate fear of heights causes red warning signals to go off inside my head, but I know what these planes can do for us. They'll be a great weapon in our fight against the Court. "Heck, yes I want to fly," I say.

"I *have* to fly one of those," says Grizz, excitement in his voice.

Steve looks lost. "Those are airplanes," I explain. "They fly. Like birds, only much faster."

Steve glows with excitement. "Can you teach me to fly as well?"

"Not yet," says Bree. "The people who built the planes designed the seats and controls for large people. Villagers aren't tall enough to work the controls. But I'm working on installing a booster seat and changing the controls. That should make it possible for you to fly. I'll have it perfected in a couple weeks."

"How many planes do we have?" I ask.

"There were twenty of them at the armory, but so far, the only ones who can fly them are Chase, Kenny, and I. Besides, the size of the solar farm here limits us to one full charge every twelve hours. It takes thirty-six hours to charge three of them. The good news is we can fly them between the lab, the armory, and the fort here on a single charge. We can fly one to the mines and back on one charge. We don't have enough solar panels at the mines to re-charge them. So, we can't fly beyond the mines."

"I'm surprised *you're* big enough to fly one," says Grizz with a smile.

"Stuff it," replies Bree.

A whirring sound coming from above halts their exchange. I look up and watch an airplane come straight down. It kicks up dust as it settles to the ground.

"The plane lands like a helicopter?" I ask, surprised.

"Yes," says Bree, "two flying machines for the price of one."

The bubble over the cockpit rises and a tall blonde girl emerges. She scrambles from the cockpit. I run towards her. We meet and wrap our arms around one another.

"Kenny!" I cry.

"It's about time you got back to work," Kenny says. Kenny always sounds tough, but I can hear here sniffling just like me.

Kenny turns and gives Grizz a big hug.

"Careful," I say. "That's my boyfriend you've got there."

Kenny smiles. "You *did* see him first. By an hour."

Grizz's family moved into our neighborhood when we were both toddlers. We were friends at first sight, and one of the first things I did after we met was take him around the corner to introduce him to my friend Kenny.

We spend the rest of the day catching up. I tell my friends of the adventures Grizz, Steve, and I have had. Grizz and I snuggle as I tell them how we brought Grizz back from the dead. Grizz describes our adventures with the robots at Fair Haven and Steve gives them a blow-by-blow account of the King's Game.

Kenny describes the farming improvements they've made in our absence. We could only carry a limited amount of seed with us from Los Alamos, so we never intended to eat the grain from the first planting. Rather, we wanted the first crop to produce enough seed so we could plant massive amounts of grain at the mines and in at least twenty of our villages. We met that aim.

"So," says Kenny, "we're right on target. We planted seeds here, at the mines, and in most villages. A little over two months from now we'll have our second harvest. And this time we'll reap enough grain to feed tens of thousands. Our new plows are working well, and my fertilizer is producing crops so big the villagers think I'm using magic."

The key to our victory against the Court lies in the production of more food. Our people are subsistence farmers. If they don't work in the fields, they don't eat. We need to turn our farmers into soldiers. With a bigger militia and our new weapons, we'll break the stranglehold of the Court. At least, that's the plan.

"We met your son on our way back," I say.

"How's my boy doing?" asks Kenny.

"Other than almost burying Grizz and Steve alive, he seems healthy."

"Oh, my God! You came home from the south?"

"Yep.

"I'm sorry! We've been trying to figure out a way for Garganto to distinguish good guys from bad guys, so he won't stomp the wrong people. At one point, we tried tying a red armband on our people, and that worked for a while. But the Apaches figured out the scheme, and *they* started wearing red armbands. They realized they didn't have to worry about Garganto, so they didn't have to swing wide to get around him. They carved up our convoys left and right. After that fiasco, I just sent Garganto way, far south, where our people don't go."

"By the way," I say, "Garganto says he's getting frustrated trying to kill Apaches. They're hard for him to catch. He's suffering a little emotional crisis. I promised I'd tell you."

"I'll talk to my boy," says Kenny. "What he doesn't understand is that just having him where he is makes the Apaches detour around him and that slows them down. I'll try to explain that to him, but he isn't all that bright, he might not understand the subtlety."

That evening, I sleep in a comfortable bed for the first time in a very long time. I've had troubling dreams about the slave whipped to death by the master at the city of the Sons. Why *this* death haunts my dreams I don't know. Heaven knows I've seen worse atrocities committed by the blacksuits. But this dream repeats itself night after night, and it's unusually vivid.

When I awake, the sun streams through my window. I sit down for breakfast and dig into my food. I hear a familiar voice behind me. A mountain comes through the door.

Once more I fly into the arms of one of my lifelong friends. "Chase," I sob. "I've missed you."

"I've missed you too, ET. I was working on the other side of the saddle when I heard you returned, or I'd have been here sooner. We thought we'd lost you. The villagers were losing hope. People are celebrating in all fifty villages now that you're back."

Since I've been on my own for the last several months, I've forgotten the Daughter of Gaia hysteria. I've been just plain old ET.

It's been easier. I've had nothing to worry over except my friends. But now, I'm back and hundreds of thousands of people think I'm a sainted savior. I sigh. I don't want to be the Daughter of Gaia. There was no job interview. But I'm the Daughter of Gaia to these people. That's my reality.

After breakfast we make plans. I want to learn to fly, but first, I need to visit our villages. I need to discuss the military situation with Falstaff, and Falstaff and I need to visit Mother Helen. Helen is our spiritual leader. She sees visions that are uncannily accurate.

Grizz will stay here and take flying lessons. He'll also help Chase with his construction projects. Being apart from Grizz is the hardest thing I suffer. But we need Grizz here. We'll only be apart two weeks. Still the separation saddens me.

Just before our departure I pull Grizz aside, wrap my arms around him, and, standing on my tiptoes, crush his lips with mine. Our kisses are deep and passionate, and they awake something primal in me. I ache inside, and although the ache hurts, it's sweet and warm at the same time.

"I wish we could be together like this forever," Grizz sighs.

"Someday," I say. "Someday."

As thrilling as the kisses are, they make our separation even harder. As I walk away, I gaze back over my shoulder. Grizz is unbearably handsome, as always. There's sadness in his sky-blue eyes. I force myself to look away.

Chase and I will go over the saddle together. He's eager to show me the work he's done in my absence. When we reach the saddle, people work everywhere. Thousands of villagers are crating material up the steep slope, material that's bound for the mines and the villages. This much I expected. What's *new* is the series of pulleys Chase and his workmen are building.

"We've completed pulleys and carts on the steepest parts of the mountain," he says. "Soon, we'll be able to triple or quadruple the volume of material we can haul."

I marvel at the sophistication of the system of pulleys-within-pulleys that will soon become freight elevators. "I'm impressed, truly impressed. You've accomplished this in just a few months."

I get over the saddle much faster than I'd assumed. Chase's elevators take most of the work out of the journey. By day's end I'm approaching the fortress at the mines.

Once again, I'm greeted with unbridled joy. Before I left for Los Alamos, I'd grown almost used to the attention and the crowds, but today I'm taken aback. I start my "Daughter of Gaia routine," smiling and waving, touching as many outstretched hands as I can. It takes two hours to work my way through the crowds. I'm met by a joyful-looking Falstaff. We embrace.

"Let me look at you," says Falstaff with a huge smile. "Yes, you are our Daughter of Gaia, back in one piece. We've missed you. Our people have grown sad in your absence."

"I'm back for good, now."

"Splendid! You're so thin! We must fatten you up, so you can fight blacksuits!"

We head for the mess hall, but a pair of blonde behemoths intercept us. My twin brothers, Han and Luke.

"Hi sis!" says Han as he lifts me off the ground and almost crushes me in a bear hug. He releases me and Luke does his best to break my ribs, too.

"I've missed you two," I say. "And look at how tall you've grown!" They're easily six feet two. "What have you been feeding them, Falstaff?"

"Good old regulation army grub," Falstaff replies. "These two eat enough rations for a whole brigade."

"I'm so proud of you two," I say. I beam at them fondly until I realize something is wrong with their faces. I take a moment to figure out what's wrong. "What happened to your eyebrows?"

Han and Luke exchange sheepish glances.

"You know Kenny's bombs?" asks Luke.

"You know. The ones you put in the ground," continues Han.

"That blow people up?"

"Yes," I say. "Kenny's mines. We used them at the Battle of Fort Kennedy. We blew up quite a few Sons with them."

"Well," says Han. "We took one apart."

"Cause we wanted to make fireworks," adds Luke. "We borrowed cool chemicals from Kenny to make the colors."

"The fireworks were fantastic," says Han.

"A little too good," says Luke.

"Burned off our eyebrows," concludes Han.

They look at their feet. They know they're about to get a tongue lashing.

I try to hold back. I really do. "You two!" I explode at last. "What were you thinking! You could have killed yourselves!"

"The fireworks were awesome," says Han.

"Yeah, blue and yellow and red."

"How could you let them do this?" I aim my wrath at Falstaff who is nervously pulling on his beard.

"They had K.P. for a month, afterward," he says.

"Yeah," says Han. "We peeled a million potatoes."

A trumpet call rings out in the distance.

"Time for dinner!" shouts Han.

"Winner gets double dessert!" says Luke.

"Hey," hollers Han. "No fair. You got a head start. You're *not* getting my dessert! See ya later, Sis."

The two of them disappear into the mess hall.

Falstaff leads me to the mess hall, but at a more temperate pace. I meet yet another familiar face as we're walking to our seats.

"Margaret!" I cry. Margaret is the Captain of the Daughter's Guard, an elite force of one hundred warriors that's tasked with keeping me safe and sound. I couldn't take them on the road with me, because we wanted to get the grain back home as fast as possible, and the short legs of the Daughter's Guard would have slowed us.

Margaret nods her head and smiles. "If you took the Daughter's Guard with you when you travel you wouldn't get in so much mischief."

"From now on," I promise, "you go wherever I go."

Margaret looks relieved, and doubtful. "We will do our duty."

Over dinner, Falstaff brings me up to date on our military campaign. "We've hounded the blacksuits. But now we're having a rough time finding targets. The blacksuits have given up on rebuilding their outer ring of forts. With our ability to concentrate our power wherever we choose, they couldn't keep us from charging in at night and destroying what they'd built during the day. They now control their fields and slaves from hundreds and hundreds of small strongpoints. When they see us coming, they abandon the strongpoint and retreat. Since we don't have enough fighters to hold every strongpoint, we destroy the strongpoint, and leave. But, since the strongpoints are cheap and easy to rebuild, the blacksuits are back in business in a matter of days. And we're not strong enough to take on their inner-ring forts yet."

"Have you been destroying the luxury crops?" I ask. The Court has long grown crops that support their lives of luxury. Fruits, silkworms, cotton, grapes for wine, and dozens of other things the elites use for themselves but deny their slaves.

"The Court has stopped growing luxury crops. The only thing they grow now are food crops. And we can't destroy the food crops, because they'd cut the slaves' rations long before they'd give up *their* meals. The slaves are malnourished now."

I consider what Falstaff just said. "So, we have a standoff?"

"Yes," says Falstaff, pulling on his red beard—a gesture that means he's worried. "The problem is the Court will soon begin harvesting their food crops. And once they can feed themselves, they won't need the villages anymore."

"Will they harvest their first crops before our new grain is ready?"

"They'll harvest quicker-growing, short-season crops before our grain is ready," Falstaff says.

This is awful news. The blacksuits can't destroy our villages if they need the food we produce. But once they harvest their own...

"There's nothing we can do," I say. "We'll build bigger solar farms over here, and once we do; we'll bring our new weapons to bear. We're in a race against time, and we'd better win."

That night, I dream again of the old woman whipped to death near the Son's city. There's a reason this dream is reoccurring, I'm sure of it. But I can't unlock the puzzle.

The following morning, Falstaff gives me a tour of the mines. The fort, our barracks, and the fields we farm are vast, and Falstaff has built our defenses well. If the blacksuits want to take the mines from us, they'll pay. "Defense in depth is the key," Falstaff explains, "defense in depth and mutually supporting strongpoints."

Our farmers are thin and emaciated, and this worries me. The villagers are, by their own choice, on half rations. They sacrifice so more workers can carry things across the saddle. As we walk among our people, I become the Daughter of Gaia once again, smiling, waving, touching hands. It's the least I can do for men and women who sacrifice everything.

Once the tour is over, Falstaff and I leave to visit Mother Helen in the Sanctuary. We're accompanied by the Daughter's Guard. I feel much better knowing we have scouts on our flanks so nobody will surprise and overwhelm us. I've been bushwhacked enough times in this world, and I'm not keen on having that experience again.

On the last day of our journey, Sanctuary Hill rises high above the surrounding desert. I'm excited to see Helen and my fellow sisters. A long time ago, I took the oath and joined the sisterhood. The act formalized my position as the Daughter of Gaia. The vow of chastity I took prevents me from marrying Grizz, and this is a bigger burden than all the other demands combined.

Helen looks just as she did when I last saw her. She's still beautiful with her deep blue eyes and her lustrous mane of white hair. Her best trait is the peace and serenity on her face. Helen is an angel incarnate.

Helen, Falstaff, and I discuss our current situation. We spin ideas for hours but find no solution to our predicament. Our one, thin thread of hope is that it will be many months before the Court can feed itself. We're safe until then.

I make a special point of visiting Sister Juliet. She has always been Helen's heir-apparent, acknowledged by all to lead the sisterhood after Helen's passing, but when we last met, she barely spoke with me, she was so upset. She thought I had usurped her position as the heir to Helen. I tried to reassure her I don't want to be anything more than a simple sister. She didn't believe me. And her placement in charge of manufacturing the vile smelling wolfbane that keeps our people safe from the nightly predations of the dreadwolves did nothing to improve her mood.

I find her hard at work overseeing the workers creating wolfbane. The foul smell from the workshop nearly gags me.

"Hello, Juliet," I say with a smile.

Rage contorts her features, but a neutral expression replaces it so fast that I question whether I saw the rage at all. "Hello, ET," she replies.

"I just want to reiterate what I told you the last time we met, Juliet. I swear to you; I have no intention of taking Helen's place."

Juliet looks at me, suspicion in her eyes. But she forces a wan smile. "Thanks, ET. I appreciate that."

With no further word, she turns her back on me and goes back to work. She doesn't believe me.

I return to Helen's chambers and report my experience.

"There's nothing you can do to stem Juliet's anger, child. I've spoken with her several times. I cannot guarantee that she will be my successor. My visions cast her in that role, but visions change. I see visions of you leading a victory parade through the streets of New Washington, but that doesn't mean the outcome is inevitable. When people do unexpected things, especially evil things, visions change. Juliet doesn't find my reassurances comforting. Still, she is a good woman, and she works hard."

A messenger knocks on the door of Helen's chambers.

"Please come in," says Helen.

"I have a radio communication," says the messenger. "A Son of 1776 showed up at Fort Stone under a flag of truce and gave a message to our sentries. Bree sent it to us." He hands the message to me. It is in the scratchy handwriting of our communications operator, an escaped slave, still learning to write.

I read it aloud:

To the Daughter of Gaia:

By now, you have grown tired of Apache attacks on your supply trains. To prevent further unnecessary death, I have a peace offering for you. Meet me in two weeks' time at a point one day's walk south of the Workshop. I will bring two bodyguards with me. You may do the same. You must attend. If you do not, our next actions will be extremely unpleasant for your people.

The Leader

19

"What's this evil man up to?" asks Helen.

I'm silent for a long time trying to make sense of the letter. "I'm not sure." The 'Leader' is the commander of the Sons of 1776. We gave his people a tremendous beating at the Battle of Fort Kennedy. I don't think he has the resources to make another assault, and, even if he did, he's not dumb enough to try. The Apaches are a thorn in our side, no doubt about that. We have three entire brigades tied down on the east side of the saddle, just to provide security for our forts and supply trains. I'd much prefer those people building solar farms to Fort Taylor. We know that the court will soon produce its own food. When it does, it won't need our villagers anymore. Every single day matters.

Helen looks at me with concern. "Will you meet with him?"

The beginnings of a plan are forming in my head. "Yes, I will."

"But the man is not trustworthy. How do you know he'll keep his word and bring only two bodyguards?"

"I'm certain he *won't* keep his word. That's why I want to meet him."

Helen gives me a strange look. We ask Falstaff and Margaret to join us, and I sketch the outline of my plan.

When I finish, I see grave doubt on my friends' faces.

"You're sure your plan will work?" asks Helen.

"I'm betting my life on it," I reply. *Literally.*

Margaret shakes her head. "Here we go again. Our sworn mission is to keep the Daughter of Gaia alive. How can we succeed when the Daughter insists on taking such awful risks?"

"This time," I explain, "you'll be traveling with me."

Margaret beams.

I raise Kenny and Bree on the comm and tell them what I want them to do.

"Someone let crazy ET loose again," says Kenny.

"Yep. I'm on the rampage. But this plan will work. It has to."

*   *   *

I waste no time getting back across the saddle because I want to oversee every detail of my plan's implementation. I visit the Workshop, the Chem Lab, and the Armory with Margaret and my guard in tow. For a change, I don't mind the slower walking pace of my short-legged guards. I have more time to rerun every detail of my plan in my mind. It's good that I do, because I find a few holes.

On the eve of my meeting with The Leader, we gather one last time to go over every detail of the plan. Steve, Margaret, and twenty of her most trusted fighters left this morning. Steve has been working with these elite warriors for two weeks. He's drilled them on the fundamentals of moving silently through the desert. The stealthy completion of Steve and Margaret's part of the plan is essential to its success. If they don't do their job, the odds are strong that I'll be dead by this time tomorrow.

Worse than my death, Grizz and Kenny will probably be dead along with me. I'm taking them as my two allotted bodyguards. None of us sleep very well. I keep turning things over in my mind. I doubt myself. *Have I taken every possibility into account? Am I missing something?*

Kenny recalls Garganto from his patrolling and sends him north to keep him out of mischief. We don't want him squashing us, and, since the first part of the mission will take place under a white flag, we don't want him stomping on the Leader, either.

I remind myself that nothing ever goes according to plan. But I have faith in my companions and in our ability to adapt and improvise. Sleep overtakes me in the small hours of the morning—just in time for my constant nightmare in which the Son whips the old slave to death.

Bree wakes us an hour before dawn. We eat breakfast and check our equipment. My AK is cleaned, oiled, loaded, and ready. I love my bow, but nothing beats the stopping power of an automatic rifle on continuous fire. I shove a dozen extra clips in my backpack, knowing that if I need to use more than a few of those clips, my plan will have gone terribly wrong. I sling two water bags over my shoulder, clip my comm to my belt. I put new batteries in the comm last night, but I throw a couple spares in my pack, just in case. The comm is my lifeline to Bree at Fort Stone, and to Chase at Fort Carlson, near the Armory.

Grizz carries a white flag on a long pole: a flag of truce. In theory, anyone under a white flag should be safe from enemy fire. I don't expect The Leader to honor the truce, but we'll keep up our end. Grizz, Kenny, and I head out. "Good luck," cries Bree from behind us. I turn and give her a thumbs up. "See you soon," I call back.

We follow the old road south. The road itself is useless for travel. Long ago, it deteriorated into small, broken concrete slabs jutting out at every imaginable angle. We walk beside the road. This, the eastern side of the mountains, is in a "rain shadow," so the monsoons blowing in from the west dump their moisture in the cool air of the upper reaches of the west side of the lofty mountains. Rain seldom falls on this side. Few plants thrive here, so there are few places to hide.

Grizz, Kenny, and I run every day we can. Because we're fit, we're able to maintain a jogging pace alternating with fast walking for hours. The Leader's message said he'd meet us a dayswalk south of the workshop, but for us that means half a day's travel. This is important. I need enough daylight to ensure my plan develops as intended. Things go wrong much faster when you can't see what's happening.

As we get closer to the meeting place we move with more caution. Kenny, Grizz, and I fan out, check for signs of an ambush. I don't think The Leader intends to kill us before the meeting, because he'll want to gloat first. The last time I saw him, he was running away from me to save his hide, and that must rankle. He'll want to look me in the eye when he delivers my death sentence.

By early afternoon we're within sight of our meeting place. The Leader has erected a huge white tent beside the old road. The breeze rustles its roof and walls. A white flag of truce flies over the tent. The flag ripples and snaps in the strong, dry wind coming off the mountains. We stop a hundred yards short of the tent. Grizz insists on approaching the tent first. He'll check out the interior for possible dirty tricks. There won't be any. The Leader knows we won't walk into an obvious trap.

As Grizz approaches the tent, the front flap opens, and I recognize the long, lanky form of the Leader. He slaps Grizz on the back as though they're old friends. Grizz enters the tent and I hold my breath. A moment later, Grizz reemerges and gestures us forward. There are no lethal surprises waiting for us inside the tent.

Kenny and I advance. When we reach the tent The Leader smiles at me and raises his hand to slap me on the back.

"Don't touch me," I say.

"Cranky, are we?" he says, his voice jovial. The smile on his face doesn't reach his wintry eyes. "By the end of this meeting, we could be best buddies."

I keep my expression neutral, but my eyes are as bleak as his. "I'm listening."

The interior of the tent is sumptuous. A colorful woven rug covers the ground. There is a large oaken table surrounded by comfortable-looking chairs. A sidebar holds a bottle of VSOP brandy surrounded by crystal snifters on a silver serving tray. Graceful geometric designs cover the tent's inner walls.

I don't see any of this, at first. I receive a terrible shock the moment I enter the tent, a shock that stuns me. Standing in front of me is none other than Oskar Salieri, the Chief Justice of the Court, our bitterest enemy. The man he is evil personified.

20

I can't keep the surprise from my face.

"You didn't expect to see me," he says.

"I did not. How did you avoid the dreadwolves?" I'm genuinely curious. Dreadwolves have historically locked the blacksuits inside New Washington. No one travels in the forests around New Washington after dark without being eaten by packs of dreadwolves, and the forest is so large it's impossible to travel from one side to the other before nightfall.

"You have a traitor in your midst." His smug smile annoys me.

"Is that so?" I try to keep my gaze flat, but the truth is I'm flabbergasted. Our people *hate* the Court. After centuries of slavery and degradation, of being beaten and killed, of having their children stolen from them, of eating a starvation diet while the elite live in luxury, our people detest the Court. I can't imagine any of them betraying us.

"Your traitor passes us small quantities of wolfbane, has been for a while now. We've had plenty of opportunity to spy on you. And, as you can see, we've made new friends." Salieri nods at The Leader.

The Leader is beaming.

I see Kenny's knuckles go white and she raises her AK. I put my hand on the barrel of her gun. *Not now, Kenny. We're under a flag of truce.*

Next to Salieri is a blacksuit officer, the breast of his shirt resplendent with ribbons and medals. He looks at me with the cool, professional detachment of a disciplined soldier. Alongside the Leader is an Apache. Rage contorts his face into a malevolent mask of hate. His hand is on the hilt of his knife. The Leader restrains him. "Not now, Brown Wolf, not now. All in good time."

I force myself to relax. "What do you want to talk about?"

The Leader speaks first. "I assume you're tired of my Apaches and their ambushes?"

"We're managing," I reply.

"We still have thousands of soldiers we can put in the field."

"Put them in the field. We'll take pleasure in wiping out another of your armies."

Salieri speaks next: "But the last time the Sons put an army in the field, you weren't fighting a war on two fronts. Now that we can make wolfbane, we'll attack you on the west side of the mountains while the Sons attack you on the east side. You can't fight us both. We'll make mincemeat of you."

I work hard to keep a chill of fear from my face. There are too many unknowns here. Does Salieri *really* produce enough wolfbane to keep a large army on the march? And how many Sons are still alive? We decimated a force of twenty thousand at the Battle of Fort Kennedy. Still war on two fronts would be hard to win. Then I realize that if these men *knew* they could defeat us; we wouldn't be talking. If they were certain of victory we'd be fighting, not talking.

"We grow stronger every day," I say. "I don't fear either of you. I don't fear both of you." This is a lie, but I doubt they can tell.

"Then you are foolish," says the Leader.

I shrug. There's no reason for displays of bravado. Nonchalance will be a better bargaining posture. Brown Wolf, the Apache, continues to glower at me. Ignoring a murderous Apache is hard, but I must. Any sign of fear will give my adversaries encouragement.

"We're giving you the opportunity to save your people," Salieri says, his voice even. "We will defeat you if we must, but today we're offering you the opportunity to prevent thousands upon thousands of needless deaths, on our side and yours."

Salieri is a far more polished than the Leader. He knows me well enough to realize I'll respond better to a reasoned argument than to a threat.

"What are the terms of your 'peace plan'? You're not offering unconditional peace, I assume."

"Simple terms, really," says Salieri. "We grant your villagers freedom. We trade to acquire the goods we need from you. You will give us back our mines. And you will disband your militia. Our blacksuits will protect you from all threats."

The Leader adds his condition: "All *we* need is access to the Workshop and Chemistry Lab that our fathers built, which you stole from us."

"These terms are unacceptable. If we disband our militia, we're defenseless. And I didn't hear you offer to free the slaves *inside* the ring." I turn my attention to the Leader. "And if we gave you the Workshop and the Chem Lab, you'd use the weapons to expand your slaving empire. You're ruining enough lives now. I won't give you the technology to ruin more. Unless you have better conditions to offer, this meeting is finished."

"Then there will be war," says Salieri.

I nod and turn to leave.

"Oh," says the Leader, "you may run into a few Apaches on your way home."

I've been counting on this. I knew the Leader wouldn't let me go without sending his Apaches after me.

Salieri is surprised. "What?" he asks, his face red with anger. He turns on the Leader. "We invited these people under a flag of truce." Salieri is a demon, but he's a man of his word.

The Leader glares at Salieri. "I couldn't restrain the Apaches once they learned 'The One Who Got Away' would be here. And losing the 'Daughter of Gaia' will reduce the villagers to putty."

Brown Wolf, the Apache, leers at me.

"You gave your word!" cries Salieri.

Salieri and the Leader lock eyes. Salieri is angry. The Leader is contemptuous. They need one another now. But if they defeat us, these two jackals will tear at one another's throats in a heartbeat. The Leader is kidding himself if he thinks his collection of misfits can stand up to the blacksuits. The blacksuits are trained, disciplined, and lethal, unlike the Leader's collection of misfits and thugs.

"We'll take our leave," I say.

"You'll regret this," howls the Leader.

I ignore him. Grizz pulls back the tent flap and holds it for Kenny and me. He keeps his eyes glued on Brown Wolf, ready for action if the Apache threatens. I can hear the heated conversation between Salieri and the Leader as we step into the sunlight.

My eyes need a moment to adjust to the bright light, but once I recover, I see the terrifying sight of an Apache army. They're arranged around us in a semicircle and there are more than a thousand of them, more than I expected. They're determined to kill 'The One Who Got Away.'

We must keep them off balance, so we do the one thing they don't expect. Our home and safety lie to the north. So, they don't expect us to run to the southwest, but that's what we do. Surprised by our gambit, they need a moment to adjust. And when they do, arrows rain down around us. The moment of surprise we bought saves us. Had they loosed their arrows before we started to run, we would have been easy targets. As it is, they must launch their arrows on an arc and that makes them far less accurate. A lucky shot hits Kenny in the shoulder.

"Damn that hurts!" she cries. She rips the arrow out without breaking stride. "I'm mad, now!"

Once we establish our lead, our long legs give us speed that the Apaches can't match.

For an Apache, following fleeter prey is simple. Apaches can maintain a trotting pace all day. They are famous for running deer to the ground. Although the deer is much faster, it lacks stamina. The Apaches know if they follow a deer long enough, the deer will tire. When the deer is so tired it can't move, the Apache walks up and slits its throat.

Soon, Grizz, Kenny, and I are beyond the range of Apache arrows. I look over my shoulder and see them coming after us at their consistent pace. I take my comm from my belt without slowing and thumb the transmit button. "Margaret, launch your flare." The flare rises in the air in front of us. That's good. No wasted steps.

Sweating from exertion, we see Margaret's position. She's found an elevated location on the desert floor and fortified it by dragging stones to create a rough wall. The position is three miles from the Leader's tent, just as we planned. We put on a final burst of speed, clamber over the makeshift rock wall, and drop behind the rocks. I high-five Margaret, Steve, and as many of the Daughter's Guard as I can reach.

"Job well done!"

"When a job involves the Daughter of Gaia's safety, we don't fail," says Margaret.

"I feared the Apaches might encircle the tent, and you'd have to shoot your way through to reach us," says Steve.

"I'm glad they didn't. That would have made things *too* exciting."

I peer over the wall at the approaching Apaches. Surprised as they must be at our inexplicable tactic of running *away* from safety, they're still confident and eager to extract their revenge. They wear their customary dun-colored clothing, matching the color of the surrounding desert. The large number of Apaches with red or blonde hair shows that the D'Ne themselves are declining in numbers. The Apaches train promising-looking non-Apaches. And while the trainees are formidable, they're not as lethal as the native D'Ne.

They don't hide from us. They gather and discuss our strange behavior. From previous encounters, they know the range of our

AKs and are careful to stay at a safe distance. They settle on a strategy. I watch as they extend their lines to surround us. My fear of being surrounded by Apaches is visceral. Worries about my plan hammer away inside my head. *Have I thought of every contingency? Have I missed something important?* I force myself to focus.

They still haven't discovered Steve, Margaret, and Margaret's warriors, so, once they have us surrounded, their leader lets out a blood-curdling cry which every warrior echoes. They charge straight at us, willing to take casualties to end the fight right now. Their terrifying howls are enough to demoralize most people, but not our little group. And we have a surprise for them.

"Deploy the guns!" I shout.

Our people pull the nylon coverings from our thermal-imaging guns and remove the black plastic lens caps from their heat and motion sensors. These are the same guns deployed against us when we first discovered the Armory, and they cost us dearly. We turn the muzzles on our enemies. We have four guns, one pointed in each cardinal direction, and they begin their awful work. The guns search for a heat signature and fire a stream of high-explosive rounds at it. Grizz, Kenny, and I add our AKs and the others use their bows. Within two minutes, dozens of Apaches fall. If the Apaches press their attack now, they *will* overrun us. Our guns are lethal, but they're not enough to take out a thousand Apaches before they storm over our improvised walls.

21

I breathe a huge sigh of relief when the Apaches retreat. *I was right!*

Frontal assault against a well-armed foe is not the Apache way. They retreat until they're beyond the range of our guns. Within minutes, they're invisible. A thousand of them are within a few hundred yards, but I can't see a single one.

From long experience, Apaches know there's no need to suffer overwhelming casualties. Their strategy now is to wait for nightfall. From the Apache perspective, why take huge losses when you can overwhelm a foe in the dark? After nightfall, as quickly and quietly as they move, they'll crawl to within a few yards of us before we're aware of their presence.

However, they don't realize that thermal-imaging guns can see a heat signature as well at night as it can during the day. But I won't let things go that far. I remove my comm from my belt and thumb the transmit button one more time. "Send the birds," I say.

Bree's voice comes back: "The birds are in the air."

At top speed, our drones will take twenty-five minutes to reach us. But to be on the safe side, we open our backpacks after twenty minutes and pull out silver shrouds. The silver shrouds were part of the bounteous material the ancients stored at the workshop. Their immediate purpose was to seal in body heat, so people could slip into them and camp out in frigid weather without freezing to death.

We're using them for a similar purpose. Covered by our heat-deadening shrouds, we're invisible to the drones. We pay a price: under the hot desert sun, we're soon broiling. Sweat runs down my body, first in trickles and then in rivers. I look at my watch. The drones are late. *Has something gone wrong? Did we send the drones to the wrong coordinates?* The heat inside my shroud continues to climb. Sweat runs in my eyes, blinding me.

A whirring sound overhead announces the drones' presence. I relax. We put a dozen drones in the air. We've been using the solar farm to charge every drone possible for this mission. Over the next fifteen minutes they pour a withering fire on the Apaches. The Apaches are familiar with our drones—they've been dodging them for months now. But where the drones couldn't do much harm when they were trying to cover five thousand square miles, they now have their targets massed in a tiny area.

The work they do is terrifying. Apaches are on their feet and trying to get away, but the drones fire five hundred high-caliber, hollow point rounds a minute. Once a target falls, the drones search for another. The Apaches have no chance.

A body doesn't lose its warmth at death, so the drones continue to fire until the corpses have cooled.

I thumb the comm. "Recall the birds. Mission accomplished."

After a slight delay, Bree responds. "Congratulations! The birds are homeward bound."

22

We watch the drones recede. I wait a moment to be sure they're gone before stripping off my insulating shroud. My clothing is soaked. I pull a canteen from my backpack. I've probably sweated off five pounds. The water is warm, but that doesn't matter. It's delicious, the sweetest thing I've ever tasted. I quaff the entire canteen. No matter, I have another.

Once I've satisfied my thirst, I look around at my friends. They're drenched in sweat, too.

"We look like a bunch of drowned rats," says Grizz.

"Speak for yourself, big guy," Kenny demurs. "A sopping-wet goddess is still a goddess."

She's wrong. Beautiful as she is, Kenny still looks like a drowned rat. "If a goddess is present and nobody cares, is she still a goddess?"

"Like does a tree falling in a forest make a sound if no one hears it?" Kenny snorts.

"Yeah. Kind of like that."

"A goddess is a goddess, even if she's surrounded by cretins" Kenny looks insulted but consoles herself by drinking the better part of another canteen. She looks at Grizz and me and sniffs.

I tend to Kenny's injury. I lack even the most basic medical supplies, but I wash the wound and tear a strip off the bottom of my tunic to cover the wound. Kenny squawks during the whole procedure. She lost some blood, but the wound is shallow and clotting.

"Geez, ET, I'm glad you like me. I'd hate to think how much you'd hurt me if you *didn't* like me."

"Don't be a baby."

Kenny looks at me and shakes her head. "Your bedside manner sucks, Erin," she mutters.

A few wounded Apaches moan. We stand with weapons at the ready. Two Apaches see us and try to notch their bows. Margaret's warriors silence them. I'm nauseous as we walk through the field littered with dead Apaches. A high caliber, hollow point bullet does terrible things to a human body. The wounded won't last long. We have no first aid equipment with us. *Would I save a wounded Apache if I could? Yes, I would.* If I lose my sense of compassion, I become a different, lesser person. A wounded man is a wounded man, whichever side he fights for. The wounded Apaches are far beyond the help I can provide, even if I had medical supplies.

The Leader and Salieri approach the battlefield from the north. Salieri looks grim. The Leader looks stricken. Brown Wolf looks thunderstruck. With a banshee wail, he draws his knife and charges at me. But Grizz is too quick. His AK barks once and Brown Wolf falls.

The Leader's face turns red, and the veins on his face stand out. "You'll pay for this," he screams.

"I doubt it," I reply. "You're beaten. We destroyed your army, and now we've destroyed your Apaches. You'll have your hands full fighting off the Bloods. Get over it."

"I'll get you!" he shrieks. "This isn't over." He turns and storms away.

"We'll leave the burials to you," I call after him.

"Impressive," says Salieri. He's a cool customer. He might be on a stroll through an apple orchard for all the emotion he shows.

"Your drones won't work if you use them against us. Or, I should say, they'll kill more of your people than they will of mine."

"Meet us on the field of battle, your army against ours," I say. "We'll leave the drones out of it. Just your fighters against ours."

"Why would I do that? We'll be harvesting our own food soon. And once we do, we won't need you and your motley serfs. Now that we have wolfbane, the game has changed. We can attack you anywhere. You can't guard all fifty villages. We'll wipe them out one by one."

I can't argue. Now that he has wolfbane, he's right. Unless we develop new tactics and develop them soon. "You won't have us in a two-front war," I observe.

"Oh, we will." He looks around to ensure the Leader is out of earshot. "The Leader is vicious and vindictive. He won't stop coming after you until he's down to his last man. You may be right: you may have beaten him. But it won't matter to him. He'll try to extract his revenge. I'm counting on it." Salieri smiles.

"We'll see." I turn to my friends. "Let's go home."

"Do you mind if my friend and I travel with you?" he asks. "As I recall, you're a splendid conversationalist."

"Yes, I mind. Unless you want to tell me about your troop dispositions and military plans."

Salieri smiles and shakes his head.

We jog north, putting miles between ourselves and our enemies. Salieri watches us go with his patented condescending, slanted grin. He knows how to get under my skin.

The walk home is quiet. We're lost in thought. It's difficult to kill a thousand people, even in self-defense. Margaret and her warriors, with their deep-seated hatred for the enemy are a little more blood-thirsty than we are, but that's understandable. The Daughter's Guard is almost giddy. Part of that is the successful mission, but part is also the relief you feel when you've survived a dangerous mission.

"Was it hard to slip through the Apache lines?" I ask Steve.

"Falstaff spends a lot of time teaching his militia trainees to move silently through the woods. So, the Daughter's Guard was good before I started my training. They learned *my* lessons fast. We saw the Apaches a few times, but they never saw us. They weren't on the lookout. We were. We had a few dicey moments, but that's expected. The hardest part was dragging rocks to build a strong point. It's difficult to carry a heavy rock and move silently when you know Apaches are nearby."

I pat Steve on the back. "I knew you could do it. I'm so glad you and Edie joined us. We owe our lives to you."

Steve smiles and we walk on in companionable silence.

The sentries at the workshop cry out the minute they see us, and we're soon surrounded by enthusiastic villagers. We smile and join in the celebration. Eliminating the Apache threat is an enormous victory. I high-five dozens of outstretched hands.

Bree runs towards us. "You got 'em?" she asks after she catches her breath.

"We got 'em," I reply. "No more ambushes!"

When we're fed, clean, and rested we discuss the future.

"The Leader will try to keep the pressure on our convoys with whatever remains of his militia," I say.

"My boy, Garganto, will have an easier time catching *them*. Apaches may be too sneaky for him, but not that bunch of tat-tooed nincompoops." adds Kenny.

"You may even catch them in the field and engage them in a straight up battle."

Now for the bad news. I go straight to the radio room and inform all stations that the blacksuits now have wolfbane. Helen calls me back a few minutes later, using a secured line.

"The blacksuits have wolfbane?" says Helen. "That's a disaster."

"Yes," I agree. "They can strike us anywhere at any time."

"Can you and Falstaff come to the Sanctuary so we can develop a strategy for dealing with the new circumstances?"

"I'll be on my way in the morning. I'll pick up Falstaff on my way."

As soon as I'm finished talking to Helen, a call from Falstaff comes in. He understands the ramifications of the blacksuits gaining wolfbane. We make our travel plans.

I find Grizz after dinner. He sits on his bunk in the dormitory, cleaning his AK. I sit beside him, and we talk.

"The war will end in a few months," I say. "Win or lose."

"And what happens then?" asks Grizz.

"We settle down and concentrate on loving one another, as much as we can, given my vows to the Sisters."

"All I want is to love you. Your vows are your vows. You know I respect them. I'll take you any way I can get you. But do you really think we can retire, once we've defeated the blacksuits?"

I've given this question considerable thought. "Yes, I can. I'm tired of war, sick of death. The ET I was before I came here is still inside me somewhere. I can find her again. Can *you* stop?"

"Are you kidding me? I can stop. After a nice, long rest, who knows? Like Steve says, there's a lot of evil in the world. Have you considered what happens if we lose?"

I groan. "I try not to think about it." I put my arms around Grizz, and, as always, we end our conversation with kisses that leave us both short of breath and burning with desire. It takes all the willpower we can muster to pull away.

I go to sleep with mixed emotions. Having deadly Apache warriors wanting me dead has weighed on me for a long time. Knowing we've eliminated the Apaches is a huge relief. And they'll no longer be preying on our convoys, which will help us move the materials we urgently need to the other side of the mountains. But my joy is tempered. The blacksuits have wolfbane. They can strike anywhere.

I have my usual nightmare about the overseer whipping the old lady to death and I wake with a start. I know there's a reason for this dream and I struggle again to understand it. The memory isn't only of a brutal whipping. Horrible as the beating was, there's another reason the dream reoccurs. What *else* was I thinking? I'm sure it must have been important.

The meaning comes to me in a flash.

23

Thousands of slaves worked in the field that day. But we saw only a few overseers. Why so few? *The Sons are shorthanded*! I now understand the significance of that fact. We wiped out twenty thousand Sons in the Battle of Fort Kennedy. But we didn't kill any slaves. The slaves have been planting and harvesting all along, even though there are thousands fewer mouths to feed. The Sons must have a huge surplus of food!

I leap out of bed, shrug into my tunic and run to the radio room. The light in the eastern sky tells me it's near dawn. I rush into the radio room, and a startled radio operator stares at me, mouth agape. I didn't take time to comb my hair, so I look disheveled.

"Raise Fort Taylor," I say breathlessly.

The operator does as he's told and hands me the mike.

"Fort Taylor," says a sleepy-sounding operator on the other end.

"I need to speak with Falstaff," I say.

"Begging your pardon ma'am, but Falstaff is sleeping."

"Wake him."

"Yes, ma'am."

Five minutes later, Falstaff is on the line. "Daughter of Gaia, congratulations on your victory over the Apaches." Falstaff is one of those people who shrugs off the cobwebs the instant he opens his eyes. He's fully awake.

"Thank you, Falstaff, but that's not why I called." I'd never get Falstaff out of bed unless I had very important news. He knows this.

"The Sons are sitting on a huge surplus of food." I explain my reasoning. "We've bled the Sons dry. We can take their city, and, when we do, we'll have all the food we need!"

"Excellent news, Daughter of Gaia! With that food in our granary, we'll make warriors of thousands of farmers! We won't need to wait on the super grain harvest!"

"How fast can you march five brigades over the saddle?" I ask.

"I can have our veterans on your side of the saddle in two weeks, equipped and ready to march."

"Perfect!" I say. "The militia marches quietly in the dark?"

"Our veterans make no sound."

"That's good," I say. "The Leader will have his remaining militia trying to harass our supply trains. I want to sneak your warriors over the saddle without them noticing. Let's catch the Leader by surprise."

"We'll march under cover of darkness, and no one will hear us. This means we'll postpone our visit to Mother Helen."

"This means *I* won't visit Mother Helen. You should still go. We need a plan if the blacksuits show up in force at the mines."

"I understand," says Falstaff. "I hate to miss the battle with the Sons. It's been a long time since I've been in a true battle. Where the blacksuits are weak, they run when they see us coming. Where the blacksuits are strong, they are too strong for us to engage them."

"I know," I say. "For what it's worth, the campaign against the Sons will be a short one."

I wait until breakfast to break the news to my friends. When we're assembled, I ask them where Eva is. Eva was a slave of the Sons until we set her free over a year ago. In the time since, she's become an essential assistant to both Bree and Kenny. I find I've asked my question too early when Eva walks across the mess hall to join us.

I talk of the Son's food surplus. "We destroyed most of the Son's army, and we eliminated the Apaches, too. I hate to underestimate an opponent, but I'm certain we can take their city."

"Won't it be costly to make a frontal attack on the Son's walls?" asks Margaret, conservative, as always.

"Not necessarily. We can't use our wonder weapons on the west side of the mountains, yet. But the Sons are on *this* side. Bree, can we reach the Sons' city with our airplanes and tanks?"

Bree scratches her head. "Yes. The tank will run thirty hours on a single charge. It's capable of speeds up to sixty miles an hour. There'll be plenty of juice to get her into the fight. I'm not sure about getting her back. The planes can only fly for six hours on a single charge, but fast as they are, six hours gives us plenty of time to reach the Sons' city, drop a whole rack of bombs and return home."

"The Sons won't hold out long," I say. "But even if the tank runs out of charge and we have to leave it there, we have others, don't we?"

"We have six of them," Bree confirms.

"Good." I change the subject. "Let's get Chase involved with this campaign."

Bree smiles. "He'll be more than ready to take a break. He's been working nonstop on fortifications ever since he got back from Los Alamos."

I key the transmit button on my comm. "Chase Kennedy, are you out there?"

Chase's voice comes back over the static. "I am. Am I speaking with our fearless leader?"

"Nope, it's just ET," I say.

"And to what do I attribute this honor?" asks Chase.

"We need you for a mission." Since I know we have a traitor in our midst, and since this comm is on an open frequency, I decide not to discuss the specifics of our mission.

"I'm at the armory," says Chase. "I can wrap things up here and be there in four hours, easy."

I'm surprised that Chase can get here that fast but remember that we have air transport now. A journey that used to take days now takes hours. "I'll see you then."

I turn to Eva. "Eva, would you consider a very dangerous mission?"

Eva leans in. "If it involves fighting the Sons, count me in," she says with passion.

The Son's enslaved Eva's people. Her face and back still bear the scars from the many vicious beatings she's received. They Sons killed many of her relatives and friends. She'll do anything to fight them.

"I want to get a message to the Sons' slaves. Our militia will arrive there three weeks from today. The minute the slaves see our militia on the horizon, tell them to run for our lines. I want to evacuate as many civilians as possible, so they don't get caught in the crossfire once our assault begins."

"I'll spread the word," says Eva. "I'll disguise myself as an old crone. Sons think all slaves look alike, but they pay attention to the younger women. Unwanted attention. Shall I leave today?"

"Leave at your convenience."

Eva nods.

"So," I say. "Who's going to teach me to fly?"

24

Most of our planes are single seaters. We have one two-seated training model here at the workshop. Kenny instructs me to take the front seat, as she climbs into the rear seat.

Once we're strapped in, Kenny tells me to put on my helmet. As soon as I do, I hear her voice in my ear.

"There's a two-way radio inside the helmets, so we can communicate over outside noise."

"That's comforting."

"Listen, ET, this thing is easy to fly. I mean, if Chase can fly it, how hard can it be?"

Chase's voice comes over the intercom. "Thanks, Kenny."

So, they'll monitor our flight from the ground. "How many people are listening?" I ask.

Chase replies: "Everybody at the Workshop."

"Great. When I screw up, the entire world knows."

Kenny's voice comes back online. "Don't let it worry you. Are you still afraid of heights?"

"Yep."

"You gotta get over that."

"Yep."

"I'm gonna give you the controls. If you do something stupid, I'll override you. So, you can relax. You can't crash this thing, it's impossible."

I breathe a sigh of relief. "OK," I say, "I'm ready."

"There's a small round red thingy on the top, left side of the control panel."

"A small red thingy? I'm glad you're using the technical terms."

Through my earphones, I hear Kenny breathe in exasperation. "I'm trying not to use words that might confuse you, ET. Now push the small red thingy."

I do as I'm told, and the plane vibrates. "The 'small red thingy' is the power button," I say.

"You're quick, ET. Now engage the vertical takeoff drive."

"How do I engage the vertical takeoff drive?"

"There's a long stick thingy on your left side. That's the vertical takeoff drive. See why I don't use the technical terms?"

"Yep. Score one for Kenny." I pull on the stick. Nothing happens. "Nothing's happening."

"Very perceptive. That's because you've only engaged the vertical drive. Now, you gotta tell it how fast to go."

"I do *not* want to go fast."

"There's a little round gizmo beneath the small red thingy."

"I see it."

"That controls the speed of your liftoff. If you turn it just a little, you go up slow. If you crank it far to the right, you'll go up like somebody shot you out of a cannon."

"Slow sounds good." I nudge the dial. The plane rises almost imperceptibly.

"Great job, ET. At this rate we'll finish this flight by winter. Go faster."

What the heck. I crank the dial hard to the right. The speed of our takeoff forces me down into my seat. We must be pulling two or three G's. The ground disappears. The top of Workshop Hill recedes to a pinhead below.

"Geez, ET, you could've warned me. I almost had a conniption."

"You said you wanted to go faster."

"Slow down, Speedy. You'll be up in the jet stream in five seconds. If you don't slow down, you're gonna wind up in New Mexico."

The jet stream is powerful. We discovered it the hard way on my first balloon flight. I crank the dial to the left. We stop rising and hover in place.

"Watch your altimeter," says Kenny. "It's the readout on top of the displays in the center of the control panel. Anything above twenty thousand feet is a no-no."

My sole defense against my fear of heights is to avoid looking down. It worked well when I was rock climbing and for some of my more hair-raising adventures in this world. But if you want to fly a plane you gotta look down. I screw up my courage and make myself take a quick peek. The instant I do, my knees go weak. "We're a long way up," I croak.

"You doin' OK?"

"Yep." I take several deep breaths. They say that the best way to confront a phobia is to challenge it. I peer down again and fight to keep my breathing normal. I still feel weak, but I'm determined to overcome this fear.

"You're breathing hard, ET. Are you sure you're ok?"

"I'm OK."

"You wanna go somewhere or do you just wanna hang here?" asks Kenny.

"Let's go somewhere."

Kenny has me disengage the vertical drive which automatically engages the horizontal drive. She teaches me to use the pedal to control the airspeed and how to use the stick to turn, go up, and go down.

Once I've mastered the controls, I enjoy myself. The panoramic view of the desert and mountains below is breath-taking. As I gain confidence, I dive and climb, bank in great sweeping turns.

"Fun, huh?" says Kenny.

"This is easy."

I do a complete 360-degree loop. "Woo hoo!" I cry.

Kenny gasps. "I should tell you about etiquette in a two-seater," she says. "You should tell the instructor you're gonna do stuff like that *before* you do it. So, she doesn't pee her pants."

"Sorry, Kenny!"

"I'll bet you are," she mutters. "You can tell how fast you're going by looking at the airspeed readout. It's right below the altimeter."

"We're going fifty miles an hour. Is that fast?"

"No, that's slow. Goose it."

I mash the pedal to the floor. I'm thrown back against my seat by G forces. The ground speed climbs to five hundred miles an hour. We're high up, the desert below speeds away.

"Just don't do that when you're landing," says Kenny.

"No kidding?"

"Cripes, ET. No need to be sarcastic. Are you ready for a thrill?"

"Yesssss. I guess so."

"We're coming up on the saddle. At its highest point, the saddle is around eight thousand feet high. You want to be at 9500 feet before you cross it."

"Why so high?"

"Because thermals come up off the mountains. The air's choppy."

I bring the plane to 9500 feet. I get the jitters as we approach the saddle. The minute we reach it the plane shakes. "The plane's falling apart!" I cry.

"It's not falling apart."

Kenny's correct. As soon as we leave the saddle behind the ride becomes smooth again. Fort Taylor lies to the right. I put the plane into a steep dive and pull out of it at two hundred feet. We buzz across the fort and the surrounding fields. I even waggle the wings. The people below cheer and wave. They don't know the Daughter of Gaia is the one buzzing them, but a reminder that we have wonder weapons has to improve their morale.

"Nice one, hot dog," says Kenny. "It's time to go home. Do you see the readout at the bottom of the control panel?"

"Yep."

"That's the percentage of battery you have left. My readout says twenty-eight percent—one hour, give or take. We've never run it to zero before, but I'm sure nasty things will happen if we do. The Workshop's forty-five minutes from here, so let's head for home."

"Aye Aye, captain." I make a sweeping one hundred eighty degree turn and climb back up to 9500 feet to prepare for crossing the saddle again.

When we're back near the workshop, Kenny takes the controls. "I'll teach you how to drop bombs and land tomorrow," she says.

I'm exhilarated after my first flight. A large party greets me when I climb out of the cockpit. Everybody cheers. "That was awesome!" I celebrate by grabbing Grizz and giving him a deep, passionate kiss.

"You should fly more often," he says when I let him go.

After breakfast on the following day Kenny tells me it's time to learn how to land and use the bombsite.

I remember yesterday's lesson and get the trainer in the air without Kenny's help. She corrects the few little mistakes I make, explains what I did wrong. She's more patient than I expected.

"You're doing well, ET. I'm impressed. But now I want you to learn how to drop bombs."

"OK."

"There's a little round black gizmo that's smack dab in the middle of the control panel."

"Got it," I say.

"That's the cover for the bombsight. Remove it."

I do as I'm told. I'm rewarded by a display that gives me a magnified view of the ground below. In the center is a red dot.

"Do you see the red dot?" asks Kenny.

"I see it."

"On the top of the flight stick is a red thingy. When you push the red thingy, you release a bomb, and that bomb will land on the red dot. It's cool. The bomb adjusts for wind speed, the plane's ground speed, angle of approach, everything."

Kenny shows me how to maneuver the bombsight around so I can lock on a target before I even reach it. The plane's autopilot flies the plane to the location in the sight and drops the bomb when we're over the target.

Kenny has laid out several targets near the workshop, big red X's on the ground fill the bombsight.

"When you're on a bombing run, you wanna come in at a thousand feet. You should reduce your speed to around a hundred miles per hour. So cut your speed, get to a thousand, line up a target, and blow it up," says Kenny.

On my first try I miss the target by a good quarter mile. I discover that I'm not dropping real bombs. Kenny has loaded the bomb bay with big bags of gypsum. They leave a nice, big, white splatter where they hit.

"You're supposed to drop the bomb on the target. You're not supposed to blow the bejeezus out of a poor innocent cactus."

By the end of a three-hour flight, I'm able to hit my targets nine times out of ten. Even when I miss, I don't miss by much.

When we're done, Kenny teaches me to land.

"You use the bombsight," Kenny explains. "You don't want to press the red button on the stick, or you'll blow up the airport. Get near the airport, engage the vertical drive and press the blue thingy near the center of the control panel. The plane lands itself. Now mind you, the sight's *not* very smart. If you tell it to land in the middle of a lake, it'll land in the middle of a lake."

"I'll keep that in mind. Don't blow up the airport and don't land in a lake."

"You're a quick learner, ET."

I give Grizz another enthusiastic kiss when I land.

*   *   *

During the days that follow, Grizz and I become competent pilots. After the first few training missions, Kenny switches us over to single seaters. I'm a nervous wreck waiting for my first solo flight.

I'm relieved when the flight goes off without a hitch. The single-seater controls match the trainer, but it's much faster.

Bree has adjusted the seats and pedals in the tank so members of the Daughter's Guard can drive it. While Grizz and I train to become pilots, selected members of the Daughter's Guard learn to operate the tank. The tank figures in our plans to capture the Sons' city. Bree nags at us until we agree to let her command the tank. "You guys have all the adventures," she complains. "I trained the staff at the Workshop. They're good! They'll keep things running while I'm gone. I promise!" I cave. Militia members will drive and fire the tank's guns. Bree's job as the tank commander is to ride in the turret and tell the tank's crew where to go and what to shoot.

Falstaff's five brigades reach our side of the mountain in two weeks, as promised. They come in the dead of night and are so quiet they startle our sentries. My brothers, Han and Luke, are part of the militia, a fact that fills me with foreboding. I want to hold them back, keep them safe. But I can't. Every member of our militia is someone's brother or sister, son or daughter. How can I justify keeping my family safe?

The next morning, we have a major strategy session with Gretchen, who is Falstaff's second in command. She brings her five brigade commanders. Han and Luke are present for the meeting. Han now commands the Third Brigade, and Luke commands the Seventh. My wacky brothers are colonels now, and they're all business. We embrace. I want my little brothers back. But the fact is, they're warriors now.

I tell the assembled officers of my preliminary plans for attacking the fort, and they make several constructive suggestions. These men and women are veterans now, I remind myself. They've been through the crucible of battle, and they know what they're doing.

The Sons play right into our hands. As Salieri predicted, the Leader is using his few remaining assets to harass our supply columns. Only these guys aren't Apaches, so they take heavy casualties for the little damage they do.

On D-Day, we gather at sunset and review our plans. Kenny recalled Garganto for obvious reasons. Since the Sons' raiding parties are nearby, and since we don't want them to find out what we're up to, we'll once again march after dark. We equip our company commanders with flashlights, and they know to keep them shielded and aimed downward.

"You march tonight," I say. Everyone nods. "It'll be a five-day march. We get to the Sons' city, but we stay out of sight. Radio us to let us know you're there, and we'll send the tank. The tank will travel at fifty to sixty miles an hour, so it'll reach you in a couple hours. The tank will leave in daylight, so any Sons' raiding party around here will see it go. I assume a few of the Sons will follow it to find out what we're doing, but they can't get to their city before the tank does. By the time their raiding parties return, the city will be ours.

I turn my attention back to Gretchen. "Show yourselves at dawn. Make a noisy demonstration under the walls. If Eva has done her job, the slaves will wait for you. Once you show up, they'll run. Do whatever you can to help them escape. When the slaves are out of the line of fire, radio back here and we'll send the bombers. After the bombing runs, we attack. When we're inside the fort, I want the Third Brigade to make a beeline for the Sons' storehouses. We don't want them to torch their food reserves."

I watch with swelling pride as our militia marches out of camp. These men and women are professionals now. They carry themselves with pride and élan. There's not a whisper of sound to alert the Sons. They're a match for the blacksuits, now. I'm sure of it. And they're more than a match for the Sons. It feels odd to watch them go without marching with them. But I'll be flying a plane to the Son's city.

The next couple days drag. I have a case of the jitters. Our plan is rock solid, but I keep running things through my mind, looking for holes. I need to remind myself that we weakened the Sons. Even if things don't go as expected, we outnumber them, and with our airplanes and tank, we have weapons they can't match. And, as we've learned in the past, the Sons are rogues and bullies, not a disciplined military force.

I wake before dawn on the fifth day, dress quickly, and go to the radio room. Grizz, Kenny, and Chase are already there. We'll all be flying today.

25

"We need to destroy as many of the Sons' defenses as possible before our militia begins their assault. I'll take out the turrets and bartizans on the east side of the main gate. Kenny, you take out everything on the west side. Grizz and Chase, you bomb the parapets. If we do our jobs, the Sons won't do our militia much harm."

Everyone nods.

"We'll take off at ten-minute intervals, so we won't run into each other. As soon as Gretchen tells us the slaves are out of the city, we go."

We wait in tense silence. My nerves jangle. Dropping bombs in practice is one thing; dropping them on real targets is another. The sun rises. If everything has gone according to plan, the slaves are now running towards our lines. My friends and I make nervous small talk until Gretchen's voice comes through on the secure line.

"The slaves are safe and sound," says Gretchen. "They took very few casualties as they crossed over into our lines. There are tens of thousands of them! We caught the Sons by surprise."

"Expect bombers over the city in less than a half hour," I reply.

I rush to my plane and strap myself in. I'm nervous, but that's a positive. It'll keep me sharp. I'm airborne within seconds and watch Workshop Hill shrink to nothing as I execute my vertical climb. I switch to the horizontal drive, check my compass heading, and increase my speed to five hundred miles per hour. The dun-colored desert flies by below. The weather on the eastern side of the mountains is crystal clear. With blue skies and a slight tail wind, it's a perfect day for flying.

In less than thirty minutes, I see the Sons' city on the horizon. There are six bartizans on my side of the fort. I descend to one thousand feet and drop my airspeed to a leisurely one hundred miles per hour. I align myself with my first target, the huge bartizan on the northeast corner of the fort. As I approach, I lock the bombsight on the target. The bomb makes a *thunk* sound when I release it from the bomb bay. I can't see the target once I've passed it, so I need to do a sweeping one hundred eighty degree turn to make sure my bomb hit the target. The bartizan is gone. There's nothing left but smoking rubble.

I take six passes to drop six bombs. The bartizans are in ruins. The Sons' defenders scurry around inside the fort. We must terrify them. Although they've seen drones, destruction of this magnitude raining down on them is something brand new. I pity them but remind myself that I'm doing what I must do. Nothing more, nothing less. The Sons are slavers, and we must defeat them.

Kenny's voice comes through my earphones. "Nice job, ET. You must have had a fantastic instructor."

"Six for six. Let's see you match that."

"Watch and learn," Kenny says. She matches my accuracy, and her turns are tighter than mine. She destroys her targets in half the time it took me. There are no more bartizans. Grizz and Chase follow us and within minutes, large segments of the walls are smoking ruins. We land our planes just behind the lines of our militia.

Gretchen, Margaret, Han, and Luke are there to greet us.

"Nice flying, Sis," Says Han.

"Can we join the air force?" says Luke.

"Nothing doing," says Gretchen. "I need you two right where you are."

The boys swallow their disappointment. At least I got to see my brothers as enthusiastic and excited as they used to be one last time. They turn back into men again.

We walk to the tank. Bree has the hatch open and is sitting in the commander's chair. She looks at us and waves. "Time to go to work?" she asks.

I nod.

Bree barks commands on the tank's internal comm. It rolls toward the front gate of the fort. Our militia leaves a wide path through the ranks so the tank can pass. When Bree is fifty yards from the gate, the barrel of the turret slews around and the gun elevates. The gun barks once and there's an instant explosion which leaves a huge hole in the front gate. The gate is solid oak, but oak is no match for the high explosive, eighty-eight-millimeter shells Bree pours into it. Within moments the gate lies in ruins.

Bree takes the tank through the gate, or more accurately, where the gate was. With a cheer, the Third Brigade rushes through the breech. There are a few Sons still manning their positions, but the sight of our monstrous machine followed by a well-armed band of roaring warriors demoralizes most of them. They break ranks and crawl over the walls, drop to the ground and run south, trying to get away.

I ask Gretchen to send two brigades to pursue the fleeing Sons. "Take prisoners," I say. "I want them alive. Get your other three brigades ready to defend the fort. The Sons who have been harassing our supply trains will be back soon."

Bree sits high in her turret, grinning. "You want to help chase the runners?" I ask.

She gives me a thumb up, backs the tank out of the fort, and joins the pursuit.

I return to my plane and take off. Grizz, Kenny, and Chase follow my lead. Once in the air, I have a panoramic view of the desert.

In their panic, most of the Sons threw away their weapons. They haven't even formed a rear guard. With nothing slowing us, Gretchen's brigades are hot on their trail. Bree's tank passes the mob of fleeing Sons, then turns around. With our militia hounding them from the rear and the monstrous machine in front of them, the mob of Sons surrenders. The few who still have weapons drop them and they raise their hands.

One small band of Sons keeps going. This rogue group runs to the west, away from both the tank and the pursuing militia. I spot a tall figure in the middle of this group, the Leader. I count the size of the group. There are only eight of them. I bank my plane and begin pursuit.

My friends follow me. I consider dropping a bomb on the Leader and ending things right now but decide against it. Once I pass the Leader's group, I land my plane. Grizz, Kenny, and Chase follow suit.

The cockpits of our planes aren't big enough to accommodate an AK, but we carry side arms. Without saying a word, we march side-by-side toward the Leader's group. When we are within sight of them, we stop. They have nowhere to go. The only question is whether they'll put up a fight. I fire a bullet in the air to remind them that, although they have us outnumbered, we have superior weapons.

One by one, the members of the Leader's group throw away their crossbows and raise their hands. Only the Leader holds out. We walk towards him, weapons aimed at his chest.

The Leader is trying to rally his men. "Don't abandon me now!" he cries, his voice piteous. "They'll kill me! Fight them! Save me!"

When we're within ten yards, I holler at the Leader: "Drop your bow. If you don't, I *will* shoot you." I fire a bullet into the ground at his feet to emphasize my point.

He throws his crossbow to the ground. The man breaks. He falls to his knees and blubbers. "Please don't kill me. I'll work for you; I swear I will."

"We won't kill you. On your feet," I say. I'm disappointed that the Leader didn't use his bow—I could kill him with a clear conscience if he put up a fight. "Turn around and march."

Kenny says, "I'll take 'em in. I'll walk back later and get my plane."

"I'll help her," says Chase.

"Thanks," I say.

Kenny hollers at her prisoners: "Get going! Pick up the pace. I don't have all day. Leader dude try something funny. Run away. Stick out your tongue at me. Please. I'd love to have an excuse to put a bullet in you!"

"Kenny be nice," I say.

"Geez, ET, this guy lied to us under the flag of truce. Remember? He had a thousand Apaches ready to cut us into tiny little pieces! Not to mention the small fact that he tried to starve you to death at Fort Kennedy. And, in case you forgot, he's a notorious slaver."

"You don't have to like him, Kenny. Just bring him back in one piece."

She marches her group toward home, muttering as she goes. Tears stream down the Leader's face. He sobs as he shuffles forward. I'm still a compassionate person. I haven't killed off that part of myself yet. But I feel no remorse for the Leader. I turn around and head for my plane, Grizz by my side.

"You've done it again, ET," says Grizz. "Another mammoth victory."

"Not me. Us. Every one of us."

Once the group of prisoners disappears, Grizz and I do a little strategic nuzzling.

26

I land my plane just outside the shattered gate. The minute I step from my plane, I'm overwhelmed by thousands of former slaves. "Daughter of Gaia!" they chant. *Great. Now I have another group of people who have unrealistically high expectations of me.* The former slaves have their arms raised in victory.

"Make way!" says Eva as she forces her way through the crowd. "Don't crush the Daughter of Gaia." She leads me through the boisterous crowd and into the city. Grizz follows in my wake. We pass through a warren of hovels, pathetic mud huts which must be homes for the slaves. The air smells of raw sewage. Gaunt children with distended bellies watch us with dead eyes as we pass. Flies cover the face of one little girl, who's too weak to brush them away. A blind old man sits next to a mound of stinking garbage, turns his head and follows the sound of our passing.

"The sick ones can sit outside now," says Eva. "If the Sons find weak ones, they kill them. They say we mustn't feed the unproductive. These have not felt the sun's warmth on their faces in ages."

Tears well in my eyes, but I won't to let them fall. Now is not the time.

We emerge from the twisting, filthy streets to find a large palace, white and luminous in the sun. We climb a dozen concrete steps and huge, heavy oaken doors open for us. "Please," I tell the guards. "Let Chase and Kenny enter when they arrive."

Once inside, it takes a moment for my eyes to adjust to the darker interior. Eva leads me down a long hall with shining tile floors. The air smells of freshly applied wax. I peer into the rooms as we pass and conclude this must be the center of government. Most rooms contain gleaming desks, file cabinets bulging with papers, and official-looking maps on the walls. *I wish it was New Washington we just liberated. If it was, my calling would be complete. No more Daughter of Gaia. Just Erin Taylor, daughter of Eric and Marie.*

I follow Eva into a large conference room. Surrounding a large, shining wooden table are Bree, Steve, Gretchen, and a large group of elderly, withered slaves. The wizened elders rise and embrace me.

"This," says Eva, "is the Council of Elders."

The elders greet me with enthusiasm. "Thank you, Daughter of Gaia," they say, "you have freed our people from cruel masters."

Their faces are glowing, worshipful. "I'm only one small part of an army that freed you."

"Oh no," cries an old woman, "you are the Daughter of Gaia. You are The *One*."

OK. I won't win this argument. "Let's sit and talk."

Once seated, an old man at the end of the table says, "we await your commands." When he speaks, he shows a mouth missing several teeth.

"I make suggestions. I don't give commands. What is the 'Council of Elders'"?

"My name is Newt," says the old man at the end of the table. "Our people elected us to help them in the few ways we can. We provide food for the hungry, medical care for the sick, comfort for the dying. We don't have many resources, but we try to wisely use what little we have."

"The Sons allowed you to do this?"

"No. The masters kill anyone who succors another. We serve on the council a month or two. Then the masters catch us, and we die."

"Please let us introduce ourselves," I suggest. A long round of introductions follows. I try to remember everybody's name. Introductions finished, I continue, "Let me ask a few questions and make a couple suggestions. Will your people accept this council as legitimate leadership? Will they take instructions from you?"

"Yes," says Newt. The other elders nod in agreement.

"Does anyone object to having Eva serve as your chairman? I ask this because I know her well. She has been invaluable to us in our struggles. She possesses remarkable skills and I know she will lead you well."

Eva gasps. "Please, Daughter of Gaia, I am too young!"

"You *are* young, Eva. But you're wise, you know us, and you know our ways. I see a great cooperative future between your people and ours, and your leadership would hasten that end."

Newt speaks in favor of Eva. The other council members nod their heads.

"I want to ask a favor," I continue. "We are in a race against time in our war against our own slave-masters. We are *desperately* in need of food. I believe you have more than you need. We thrashed the Sons in the Battle of Fort Kennedy and killed thousands of them. So, you've had fewer mouths to feed."

"This is true," Newt confirms. "We have enough food in our storehouse to feed ourselves for over a year, even if we stopped harvesting crops tomorrow. If our food surplus helps you free your own people, you are welcome to it. And, since we have much more food than we need, we will assign many of our farmers to carry the food north for you."

That went well. "Is this agreeable?" I ask the elders for a show of hands. They agree to provide us food and transport.

At this point in our meeting, Kenny and Chase join us, back from retrieving their planes. I introduce them.

"What do you call your city?" I ask.

"I think we should rename it," says Eva. "Let's call it 'Liberty'". This measure passes without objection.

We hammer out several agreements. I realize, after a while, that the council will agree with whatever I suggest. It'll take them time to learn how to make their own decisions. We agree that Chase will stay behind to help them rebuild their walls. The world is dangerous, and people need strong walls. We agree that Han and his Third Brigade will stay behind to provide security. In addition, Third Brigade will train Liberty's militia. When Chase finishes the walls and Eva's people can defend themselves, our warriors will return home.

"But what if the Bloods attack?" asks Newt. "The masters protected us from them. Will a single brigade save us from them? They are a powerful enemy."

"I have plans for the Bloods," I say. "If we have no further issues to discuss, I suggest we adjourn. We have much to do."

The council shuffles out the door, but my friends and our military commanders stay.

"The Sons who have been raiding our supply trains will soon return from the north," I say.

"If you will allow us," says Gretchen, "my commanders and I can work out a strategy for dealing with them. You must have many other matters needing attention."

I'm pleased to see Gretchen make plans for herself without help from the Daughter of Gaia. This augurs well for the future. And she's right. I have much to do. "I have a request," I say. "Can you spare a hundred fighters? I have a very important special mission in mind."

Margaret digs in her heels. "If you think, Daughter of Gaia, that we will let you go on another adventure without the Daughter's Guard you can think again."

"I'm not going on an adventure. I'll go home as soon as we've dealt with the last of the Sons. But I have a mission for Steve, if he'll accept it."

"Anything," says Steve.

"Do you remember our friend, the little robot named Jerald?"

"Yes. I doubt anyone can forget Jerald."

Chase, Kenny, and Bree look at me with curiosity.

"Jerald is our friend," I explain.

"You have a robot friend?" asks Kenny.

"We do." I turn back to Steve. "I'd like you to retrieve him for us. Javier promised to keep him safe, and I think Javier will keep his word. I don't know if Bree can put him back together again, but it's worth a try."

Bree smiles. "Fix a robot? Piece of cake."

I turn back to Steve. "In addition, please give Javier a message. Tell him we have eliminated the Crips, (his name for the Sons). The Sons' city belongs to us now. Tell him we expect him to leave us alone. He knows what we can do. Tell him that, if he bothers us, we will destroy him, just as we have eliminated the Crips."

"Do you think he'll leave us alone?" asks Eva.

"Yep," I say. "He owes me his life. And wicked as he is, he'll be smart enough to avoid biting off more than he can chew. He has ten thousand miles of desert to terrorize. He won't take a chance on irritating the people who wiped his ancient enemy off the face of the earth. And he'll have one other incentive. Ask Javier if he'd like to play the King's Game with the Leader. I'm sure he'll enjoy hunting the leader of the Crips."

"You want us to take the Leader with us?"

"Yep. Don't let him out of your sight. I'm sure he'll try to escape, especially when he figures out where you're taking him." *He's an evil man. I can't kill him myself, but I can't let him live, either. He's caused too much misery.* Sending him to Javier seems like the best way to get a sense of justice.

"I'll get to work," says Steve.

"I'll select a hundred warriors for your escort," says Gretchen. I watch them leave.

As soon as I'm alone, I call Helen and Falstaff on a secure line.

"The food shipment is on its way," I say without preamble.

"Start liberating the slaves in the outer circle and send them to Fort Taylor. We'll have enough food to feed at least twenty thousand until we harvest the new grain crop."

"How long will it take to train the raw recruits," asks Helen.

Falstaff answers: "Two months to train regular militia, six weeks to train garrison troops."

"Let's set a goal. Can we have thirty brigades ready to fight when the grain crop ripens?" asks Helen.

"Send the new recruits to me. Thirty brigades it will be," says Falstaff jubilantly.

27

To say that the empowered citizens of Liberty celebrate that evening would be a major understatement. They dance in the streets until dawn. My friends and I watch from a balcony on the second floor of the Sons' government center. We've had a busy week, and we don't have the energy to join the party. The freed slaves throw flowers at us, and chant "Daughter of Gaia! Daughter of Gaia!" I smile and wave my right hand.

I apologize to my friends. "We're a team," I say, "a team of equals. You realize I'm not getting a big head from this Daughter of Gaia stuff, right?"

Kenny smiles and gestures at the crowd in the plaza. "You're stuck with the Daughter of Gaia stuff, like it or not."

"Better you than me," says Chase, and the others agree.

I spend the next three days inspecting the city. Despite the age of its members, the council of elders moves energetically on several fronts. They've taken over the Sons' medical clinic and are now treating their own people. The lines outside the clinic are long, but nobody complains. The council has distributed food rations to everyone. Like our own slave masters, the Sons were keeping the people weak and docile by feeding them starvation rations. From now on, everyone will eat well. They've walled off a section of the city to house the Sons we've captured, and they're helping our militia with security.

Eva has organized tours of the Sons' buildings and barracks. Very few former slaves have been inside the Sons' buildings. They're awestruck by the opulence. "Someday," I tell them, "you will live in houses as fine as these." The ex-slaves look at us with wonder and disbelief.

"Now that we've made the promise, we need to deliver," I say.

"We will, Daughter of Gaia," says Eva. "We will."

Eva has organized the mass transport of food from Liberty to the workshop. We can't start carrying food north until we've dealt with the last of the Sons, but Eva has the logistics worked out. She's gathered every burlap bag in the city. Thousands and thousands of her people will work in the supply train.

I'm lending a hand in the clinic when Margaret arrives out of breath.

"The Sons are back," she says. "Gretchen says the Daughter of Gaia should watch this battle from the city walls."

"I don't think so," I say. I run out the door with Margaret trailing me.

"You are stubborn, Daughter of Gaia," she cries.

"I am."

I take ten minutes to reach Gretchen.

"We do not need the Daughter of Gaia for this fight," says Gretchen.

"I know you don't," I counter. "But I want to be here." I scan our lines from left to right. Our fighters are formed up and ready. They exude an air of confidence. They trust in their training and discipline; they understand this is a fight they won't lose. "What's the situation?" I ask Gretchen.

"We're facing roughly three thousand Sons. We have them outnumbered. First Brigade will hold the center of our line. The other four brigades will take them in the flanks. We don't want any of them slipping away. Grizz, Kenny, and Chase are scrambling their planes as we speak. Bree is bringing up her tank."

"Won't the fighting be at close quarters? It'll be risky to use those weapons with the two sides locked together in combat."

"I don't need them for combat," Gretchen replies. "I want the planes to spot Sons trying to escape. And by stationing the tank behind them, we discourage them from running away."

"You have planned well, Gretchen. But let me speak to the Sons. I'd prefer to resolve this problem without bloodshed."

Gretchen looks doubtful.

"I want every one of our people ready to fight blacksuits. I *know* we can defeat the Sons. But if we fight, some of our people will die."

"Very well," says Gretchen.

I move toward the Sons' lines. It's obvious Margaret won't let me anywhere near the range of the Sons' weapons. "We will tackle you if you persist, Daughter of Gaia," she warns.

I smile and relent. "I can negotiate from here." We're a hundred yards from the Sons.

"There's no reason for you to die!" I shout at the top of my voice. "Drop your weapons!"

"Better to die as a man than live as a slave," says a taller man who appears to command the Sons' fighters. He makes an obscene gesture at me.

"If you lay down your arms, you'll be free to go," I say.

"I don't believe you," he replies. "Charge!" he orders, and the mass of Sons runs towards us. The Sons make a fearsome sight in their leathers and tattoos, brandishing their weapons and howling like banshees. If I didn't know them for the rabble they are, I might be intimidated.

Margaret and her followers push me back. They won't let me fight. I'm big enough and strong enough to force my way through, but Gretchen is right, they don't need me today.

First Brigade catches the momentum of the Sons' charge. The Sons fight our militia hand-to-hand. Per Gretchen's plan, the First Brigade gives ground. The Sons let out a lusty roar. Because First

Brigade retreats, the Sons think they're getting the best of us. They redouble their efforts. Experienced military men might worry that, although First Brigade is moving backward, its withdrawal is orderly. They're not running away; they're drawing the Sons into Gretchen's trap. I watch as our brigades on the left and right begin their encirclement of the Sons. Within minutes, our militia surrounds the Sons.

I'm thrilled to see the disciplined way our warriors use their shields. Fighting shoulder to shoulder they give the Sons almost no target. The Sons fight hard at first, but they soon realize they're both surrounded and outnumbered. With our warriors attacking their undefended flanks and rear, the slaughter is fearsome. The Sons don't stand a chance. They drop their weapons and raise their hands.

First Brigade, which bore the brunt of the Sons' attack, works as the security detail to herd the surviving Sons into the prison we've set up inside the city. The Sons go into captivity without a problem. As they pass me, many of them spit in my direction.

"They are spitting at the Daughter of Gaia," says Margaret, outraged. "We cannot allow them to get away with such disrespect!"

"We won," I say. "There's no honor in attacking unarmed men."

Gretchen's comm buzzes. Kenny, who's been circling the battlefield, reports that no Sons escaped the ring our militia formed around them. I feel a huge sense of relief. The Sons have tormented us for more than a year. I look at my pinky, which still stands out at an odd angle. The Sons broke it deliberately. The Sons' Apache allies almost killed me twice. Their siege at Fort Kennedy nearly starved us. But that's behind us now. Now we turn our full attention to our more lethal enemy, the Court.

There's only one task left to do before I go home. I locate Eva, who has been standing atop one of the few places where the city's walls are still standing, watching the battle.

"Our militia fought well," she says.

Eva refers to the militia as "ours." That's a positive sign. The citizens of Liberty will become a strong ally—a part of the new, democratic order we'll set up if we defeat the Court.

Eva and I embrace. "Falstaff has trained them well," I say. "What should we do with our prisoners? There are several thousand of them."

Eva looks at me, thinking. "Knowing you," she says, "I assume you don't want to put them to death."

"You're correct. We'll build our world on compassion. We'll kill as a last resort."

"Some Sons have treated our people with decency. A few have shown kindness. Many have never used the whip."

"Do you think they'll work for us?"

Eva looks thoughtful. "They might, if you separate them from one another."

"That's a good idea. We'll send some to Falstaff for military training, others to work as farmers and miners. And Bree needs workers on this side of the mountains. There's enough work to keep thousands busy."

Eva nods. "Let us assemble our people in the city's central plaza tomorrow. We can bring each Son to the platform and let the people pass judgment. What do you plan for the cruel ones?"

"Banish them. Set them free, give them a sword, and tell them we'll kill them if we ever see them again."

"Aren't you afraid they'll band together and attack us again?"

"That's not likely. We've trounced them every time we faced them. I don't think they'll be eager for more. And cruel men without a strong leader are more likely to fight among themselves than they are to do us harm."

The following morning, I address the prisoners. I climb to a third story balcony so they can see me. Looking out over the prisoners, I sense the tension in the air. They know little of us, and many think we'll either kill them or enslave them. The crowd falls silent and they strain to hear every word I say.

I shout to be heard. "If you want to leave, we will let you. We will not hold you as prisoners. If you have mistreated slaves, you will have no choice: we will banish you. Many of you have treated the slaves with decency. We will give you the opportunity to join us, helping us to free *my* people from slavery. We need farmers, laborers, and fighters. We have no slaves, only free men and women. The alternative to joining us is banishment. We will give those who leave a sword as you pass through the city gates. Leave this city and head south. If we see you again, we *will* kill you. We are merciful people, but our mercy has bounds."

The prisoners are silent as I speak. Once I've finished a buzz of conversation fills the square. I give them a moment to consider their options and then continue. "Those of you who choose banishment may leave. If you wish to live, you will never come near our cities again."

Our militia lines the route between the prison camp and the city gates. We have more militia formed up outside to make sure the ones who chose banishment head south. Almost two-thirds of the Sons leave. We vet the ones who stay in the city's central plaza. We force only a few to leave.

I stay a few days in Liberty to be sure everything goes according to plan. When I leave, as I walk to my plane, I sense the energy as the freed slaves rebuild their city. Chase is overseeing the reconstruction of the walls. He's excited to build with adobe, a material new to him. There are no trees anywhere near Liberty and we don't have the resources to drag logs from the forests to the north.

A long convoy carrying the Sons' captured food winds its way northward, protected by three of our five brigades. The trip north should be uneventful, but we'll keep our guard up.

Eva asked her people for volunteers to join Liberty's new militia. So many of them volunteered, we had to institute a lottery to select them. Gretchen will leave two brigades here, to make sure the banished Sons don't return, and because we want to guard against the possibility of Javier and his Bloods getting up to mischief. Once Gretchen's confident the city is secure, one brigade will return home while Han's Third Brigade remains behind to finish training Liberty's militia.

My flight home is smooth. With Grizz on one wing and Kenny on the other I feel secure. We fly over Bree and her tank, which left earlier. We dive and buzz her tank, and, from her commander's perch in the open turret, she throws us an exaggerated salute.

When I return, I raise Falstaff on a secure channel.

"What course of action are you and Helen taking to counter the threat the blacksuits pose now that they have wolfbane?" I ask.

"There's not much we *can* do. We've increased security around the Sanctuary. Our position there is unassailable, but we've mined the approaches, stored enough food to withstand a siege, and sent a small group of warriors to provide extra security. The villages in all fifty villages know the blacksuits may appear at any moment. As you know, we've been delivering food to the blacksuits, so we haven't seen them anywhere near the villages for a long time."

"It sounds as though you've done everything you can," I say. "On the upside, the food convoy from Liberty should arrive here in a couple days. As soon as it arrives, we'll send it across the saddle to you."

"We need it. New recruits are pouring in. We've been getting four or five hundred every day. They're slaves from the outer ring, and they're motivated to fight."

I spend the next few days poking around Fort Stone. By the end of my stay our people have become so accustomed to seeing me they don't even raise their heads when I walk past.

On the fourth day of my stay, I'm on my way to the mess hall for lunch when a young lieutenant approaches me at double time. After he catches his breath, he tells me Falstaff is on a secure line and needs to speak with me about an urgent matter.

I collect Kenny, Bree, and Grizz and we run to the radio room. I pick up the microphone, press the transmit button and hail Falstaff. He comes back: "We have a situation here at Fort Taylor. Several brigades of blacksuits just showed up on our doorstep."

28

"So, they *can* make wolfbane," I say.

"This proves it," says Falstaff. "They haven't tried to storm Fort Taylor yet, but they have catapults and they're using them to pound our fortifications."

I key the mike again. "Falstaff, I'll be with you in an hour and a half. Kenny and Grizz, will you join me?"

"You need to ask?" says Kenny.

"You two pack. I'm leaving right now. Grizz, can you grab my things?"

"I will."

Heart racing, I run to the airstrip and speak with our guards: "Is this plane charged and armed with bombs?"

The guard commander nods his head. "We loaded munitions, Daughter of Gaia."

I climb into the cockpit, do my preflight inspection and launch. Before I cross the saddle, I'm on the comm to Falstaff. "Let's take out those catapults with our bombers. I'll be overhead in ten minutes. Can you give me smoke near the catapults?"

Falstaff comes right back: "The minute we see you overhead we'll give you smoke. One at a time I assume?"

I confirm. The air is unstable today, so crossing the saddle is nerve-wracking. At one point I go into a one-hundred-foot free fall, which leaves my stomach somewhere far above me. Once I'm across the saddle, I bleed altitude, leveling at a thousand feet. I don't even need to use the radio to announce my presence. There is a plume of red smoke to my left. It's important to complete my bombing runs fast. If I take too long, my plane won't have enough charge left to return to the Solar Farm on the east side of the saddle.

I bank my plane and approach the blacksuits' lines from behind our own. I fly right through the plume of smoke and see the catapult sitting near the tree line. It hurls a stone at one of our guard towers. The blacksuits have intermingled several villagers with the blacksuits manning the catapult. If I drop a bomb, I will kill them along with the blacksuits. I do the math: I can take out the catapult and kill a few of my people, or I can let the blacksuits batter our defenses to the ground and take the mines. Not much of a choice. I lock on the catapult with my bombsight and listen as the bomb disengages from the bomb bay as I pass over the target. I bank and return; my attack reduced the catapult to splinters. There's no movement near the ruins. I curse the blacksuits for the tactic of embedding civilians with their military.

I see another plume of red smoke and end a second catapult, followed by another plume and other bomb. With my mission accomplished, I land and find Falstaff waiting for me at our airbase.

"Nice job," he says.

"I killed our people," I say with sadness.

Falstaff throws his arm around me. "You had no choice."

"I know, but it's still hard."

Falstaff changes the subject. Far from being troubled by the sudden appearance of the blacksuits on his doorstep, he's thrilled. "The blacksuits are out from behind their walls! We can engage them in the open field. It'll be easier to destroy them in the open than it would be if they're behind fortified walls!"

"What's your plan?" I ask.

"As soon as our militia is back from Liberty, I want to hit the blacksuits and hit them hard. Under cover of darkness, I want to swing our forces around through the forest and attack them from the rear. We'll annihilate them."

I share Falstaff's excitement.

"What forces are available?"

"As you know, Daughter of Gaia, we have a total force of ten fighting brigades. We have garrison troops at the forts, but those are older fighters. The blacksuits would make mincemeat of them in the open. Two brigades are providing security at Liberty, and three brigades are manning our defenses at the fort. We'll get three brigades back from the assault on Liberty tomorrow, so, bottom line, we'll throw five brigades into the fight and keep a brigade in the fort in case the blacksuits break through."

"Will that be enough? Given this situation, we can recall a brigade from Liberty."

"We shouldn't need them and waiting for them will delay our attack. The blacksuits have only four brigades opposing us. If we hit them from behind with four brigades and trap them between that force and our defenses here at the fort, we'll whip them once and for all."

"I thought the blacksuits had over four brigades. Where's the rest of their army?"

"They can't leave their inner ring forts and New Washington undefended. The rest of their army is on defense."

I'm excited. "This could be the break we need!"

The three brigades returning from Liberty arrive the next afternoon. We call our officers into a planning session.

The tension in the room is obvious as the assembled officers await their orders.

Falstaff clears his throat. "We'll assemble our brigades just after dark. We need to slip out without the blacksuits noticing, so silence is essential. The blacksuits will have listening posts all around our position. Our militia will make a very short pivot on our right flank to come up behind them. Their sentries won't have time to sound the alarm before we're behind them. The tricky part is, the left flank must travel a far greater distance than the right. They must quick march."

Falstaff stops talking and makes eye contact with each person in the room. "If we win this battle and decimate four blacksuit brigades, we'll be very near victory. We have thousands of new fighters in training. The blacksuits can't replace their losses."

"Let's win!" I cry, and the assembled officers cheer.

"Brief your warriors," says Falstaff. "We march tonight!"

Margaret approaches me after the meeting. "I don't suppose the Daughter of Gaia intends to sit this one out," she says.

"Correct."

"I understand. This will be the most important battle we've ever fought. The Daughter's Guard will be around you, ma'am. We can't guarantee we'll keep you safe, but we'll die trying." Margaret's voice is tight with emotion. Tears well in my eyes at this display of devotion. *I can't let these people down.* I've made this vow a thousand times.

Fort Taylor hums as we make last-minute preparations. Our fighters sharpen swords and load quivers with arrows. An electric excitement fills the air. I have confidence in the ability of our military: it has proved itself repeatedly. A small ripple of fear nags me when I consider the fact that we're fighting blacksuits this time and not Sons. Even with the advantage of surprise, going toe to toe with blacksuits will be a rugged fight.

We form up at midnight, but we won't move for several hours. We want to attack the blacksuits at dawn. A fight in the dark in a dense forest is a recipe for disaster. So, we begin our march at 3:00 A.M. This should bring us up behind the blacksuits' lines at daybreak. If we arrive too early, we run a greater risk of losing the element of surprise.

Grizz and Kenny stand beside me, and we're surrounded by the Daughter's Guard. Chase and Gretchen stay in Fort Taylor to manage the battle from that front. Falstaff has lined up our troops in their order of battle. My group stands in what will become the center of our lines once we spring our trap on the blacksuits. My brother Luke is with us, too. His Seventh Brigade will form the center of our lines. I study him out of the corner of my eye. He looks so tall and brave, and yet I fear for his safety. He catches my eye and smiles. *Stay safe, Luke,* I pray.

At 3:00 A.M., the order comes to move out. Marching an army through a dark forest while engaged in a complicated pivot is no easy chore. One slipup, one tiny noise, and we'll give ourselves away.

I swell with pride as our brigades execute the complex pivot in the dark.

Our timing is perfect. We arrive as the eastern sky brightens. Falstaff orders the bugle to sound. Our warriors raise a blood-curdling cry and advance toward the blacksuits' positions. As we advance, we're astonished to find no blacksuits in front of us. At this early hour we should be passing through their camp. But instead of finding their tents, we find… nothing.

29

Falstaff looks around, confused. We continue our advance. We hear a roar in front of us and find the blacksuits at last. Not only are they not surprised, they're drawn up in full battle order. They're expecting us.

"I don't know how they knew we were coming," Falstaff grumbles, "but they knew."

The blacksuits don't have any civilians embedded in their lines. They don't want civilians to get in their way. I'm struck by the confidence they're displaying. Do they still think we're still amateurs? That they'll brush us off like a fly on the sleeve? They're in for a nasty surprise.

Grizz, Kenny, and I can only use our AKs until the Daughter's Guard collides with the center of the blacksuit's lines. We rip a huge hole in the advancing enemy. We drop our AKs and take up swords. The two armies collide, and the din of battle covers every sound and drives thoughts from our heads. The forest rings with the sound of swords on swords.

Our militia holds firm. They're taking everything the blacksuits dish out, and they're giving it right back.

Despite the lack of surprise, the battle goes our way. Both sides are suffering horrible losses, but the blacksuits give ground, little by little. I feel the thrill of victory-in-the-making when I'm surprised by a roar from behind our lines. I turn just in time to see a second blacksuit force coming through the forest behind us!

*   *   *

"Where did they come from?" I holler.

Falstaff shouts, "The blacksuits left their cities undefended! They've taken a huge gamble, and we walked right into their trap! I should have left a screening force around their cities."

"No time to worry about that now. We have to fight our way out of this trap."

Falstaff orders his bugler to sound the call to form forces into fighting squares. "Rally around the Daughter of Gaia!" he cries. Caught between the two blacksuit forces our only hope is for our brigades to defend themselves like a porcupine, with bristles facing in all directions. The blacksuits have no intention of letting us make this maneuver. Our warriors try desperately to cut through the blacksuits so comrades can cover each other's backs.

In the center of our line our fighters have a limited success. Desperate fighting brings as many as a thousand of us together in a fighting square. On the flanks we're not so fortunate. Small groups of our warriors gather but they're outnumbered and the blacksuits overwhelm them. Our men and women fight well, and they inflict heavy casualties on the blacksuits, but the blacksuits are relentless. We're losing the battle on our flanks, but our center is holding.

The horrible din of battle surrounds us: the clash of metal on metal, the cries of the wounded, and the cheers as one side or the other achieves a small, momentary victory. The distinctive, metallic smell of human blood fills the air.

"We have to cut our way straight through the blacksuits in front of us until we reach Fort Taylor," cries Falstaff.

I force my way through the remnants of the Daughter's Guard. I draw my sword, deploy my shield and head straight at the center of the blacksuit line. Except for a handful of officers, most blacksuits are short, like our villagers. Grizz, Kenny, and I take advantage of our size.

The three of us fight shoulder to shoulder. I dispatch a young blacksuit with a thrust and drop another with a backhand cut. One after another the blacksuits fall, and we move forward, inch by inch. As always, the Daughter of Gaia draws a crowd. A tall blacksuit officer approaches me but Kenny intercepts him. The duel between them swings back and forth. With her broad shoulders, Kenny is strong and, except for Chase, our best swordsman. The officer puts up a ferocious fight, but he falls.

I throw a quick glance over my shoulder. In the center of our line, our rear guard is holding. Elsewhere our forces crumble. We had five brigades when we started. We have less than half that number left.

I enter the mental zone where everything in the world disappears except for the opponent in front of me. Time slows and stretches. I see each opponent with enhanced vision, and they seem to move in slow motion. No sooner have I laid out one blacksuit than another takes his place. We force our way forward, toward the fort and safety. After a while, my arm tires. *Can't get tired now*, I tell myself.

"Falstaff!" I shout over the din of battle, "should we order Chase to launch an attack from the fort to help us break through the blacksuit lines?"

"We mustn't do that," says Falstaff. "It's what the blacksuits *want* us to do. The blacksuits have only three brigades fighting our survivors here. The rest of them wiped out the brigades on our flanks, and they've gone somewhere. I'm betting they're waiting for us to bring our warriors out of the fort to save the Daughter of Gaia. They'll fall on the flanks of Chase's relief column, eliminate it, and take the undefended mines. Their strategy is brilliant. If we abandon our defenses, they'll wipe out our entire army and take the mines in one stroke."

Falstaff is right. Many blacksuits fight around us, but not their entire force. The rest hide, waiting for us to abandon our defenses. Tired or not, we must fight our way to safety.

*　　*　　*

The sun rises high in the sky. We've been fighting for hours. Around me, our warriors are tiring. We kill a blacksuit and two more take his place. Our situation is untenable. Our warriors are weary, and we're losing the fight. Defeat is inevitable. I think of everything we've accomplished and nearly cry when I think of it ending this way. But Falstaff is right. We must protect the mines. We'll die, but our cause will live.

We hear a commotion in front of us. I catch a blacksuit's sword thrust on my shield and turn toward the sound. Our people, the men and women the blacksuits' imbedded in their lines when they first arrived, are attacking the blacksuits from the rear! They've eliminated their guards, and now, these men and women armed with sticks are fighting the cream of the blacksuits' militia. The blacksuits dispatch them, but the diversion breaks the blacksuits' concentration. Because of the sacrifice of these brave men and women, we find new strength and fight our way through the distracted blacksuits and reach the safety of our fort's outer defenses. Our warriors in the guard towers and strongpoints pour heavy volleys of arrows on the blacksuits chasing us. In a moment, the blacksuits realize they've lost us, and they withdraw. Our civilians made our escape possible. They paid for our survival with their lives.

Our small, exhausted group staggers through the open gates of Fort Taylor. Our dog-tired force falls to the ground, except for Kenny. She throws her shield and kicks it. "That was a disaster!" she cries. She kicks everything inanimate she can find. "We got our butts kicked! How did this happen? The smug looks on the blacksuits' faces make me want to hurl. Owww!" This latest comes as Kenny kicks the side of the barracks. She sags to the ground, and cries.

Falstaff forces himself to stand. I join him. Gretchen and Chase appear, their faces lined with pity. We embrace, and Gretchen and Chase whisper words of comfort. I can't reply. Words fail me.

Falstaff's face is a study in misery. "The blacksuits outsmarted me. I must resign. I've failed."

"You can forget about resigning," I say. "You're the best we have. No commander wins every battle."

Besides, I failed even worse. I fell into the blacksuits' trap like a two-bit sucker. Even worse, I would have brought Chase out from the fort and given the blacksuits a total victory. Falstaff may have fallen for the first trap, but he was smart enough to avoid the second. I wasn't.

Our militia is demoralized and defeated. The cries of the wounded are pitiful to hear. Our medics work hard to set up a triage for the wounded. They separate those needing medical attention into three groups. In the first group are the hopelessly wounded and dying. Nothing we do will save them, so we try to make them comfortable. The second group comprises the ones with light wounds. These will get care later. The third group are those with serious wounds but savable. These will receive immediate medical attention.

Margaret throws her arms around me.

"How many casualties has the Daughter's Guard sustained?" I ask.

Margaret shakes her head. "We have only a dozen left, half of them wounded and unable to fight."

As I walk through our shattered army I'm overcome with grief. Even now, in defeat, they still hail the Daughter of Gaia as I pass. Dying warriors smile and reach out their hands to touch the hem of my tunic. *I promised these people I'd never fail them, but I have.* Tears form, but I don't allow myself that luxury. I limp off toward my quarters. My leg hurts. I examine it, find a wound. Blood soaks my shoe and squishes when I walk. I suffered a sword wound. *Why did I not notice that? No Matter.* A medic follows me into my quarters and cleans and bandages the wound. It's painful, but not serious. When the medic leaves, I ask her to close the door behind her, and I let the tears fall.

30

There's a knock on my door.

"Go away," I sob.

Despite my request, the door opens and Grizz enters. He's angry. "What are you doing in here, Erin?"

Grizz never calls me Erin unless I'm in deep trouble.

"I've failed my people," I say. I force the tears to stop and wipe snot from my upper lip.

"You have *not* failed," says Grizz. "It's like you told Falstaff: nobody wins them all. And even if you failed, your people need you! They're traumatized right now. They're broken. They're not a fighting force anymore, they're a whipped rabble. There's only one person who can restore their spirits, and that's *you*. So, get off your bed, get out there, and tell them we've had a setback, sure, but we haven't lost the war. Not by a long shot."

Grizz seldom scolds me, but when he does, I have it coming. "You're right," I say. Much as I want to stay in bed and cry, tired as I am, I'm still the Daughter of Gaia, and my people need me.

I force myself to stand and limp toward the door. Back on the parade ground, our fighters haven't moved. Many are in tears. Silence hangs over them. Grizz is right: this army is broken. I limp to the platform that dominates one end of the parade ground.

I muster up what little energy I have left. "The blacksuits caught us in a trap today," I shout. "They've given us a good beating. But let's not forget the many times we've thrashed *them*. They haven't won the war! In fact, the only way they *can* win the war is if we stop believing in ourselves. I believe in you, and I hope you still believe in me."

"We believe!" they roar.

I pause and scan the expressions on the faces looking at me. Resolve starts to replace despair.

"The blacksuits suffered terrible casualties today. We can replace our casualties. They can't. Look around you at the training fields. We have thousands of warriors learning the art of war. Every day, hundreds more arrive. We're unstoppable. I wish I could promise you we'll never lose another battle. I can't make that promise. But I can make you this promise: we *will* win the war! Our cause is just, and if we stand together, we are strong enough to overcome *whatever* the blacksuits throw at us. The day is coming when we will march shoulder to shoulder through the streets of New Washington!"

The tired warriors stand and cheer. God knows we're tired and disappointed. But, as I look at the grim determination on the faces of our cheering warriors, I realize we are no longer broken.

Falstaff stands beside me and addresses the militia: "Take off the rest of this day. Tend to your wounds. Rest your sword arm. Regain your strength, because tomorrow the fight continues!"

Our warriors continue to cheer. We *will* rise and fight another day.

We assemble our senior officers after dinner. Falstaff addresses us. "The blacksuits' plan was brilliant," he says. "They left their cities undefended to throw every man they had into this attack. They must have marched in small groups, and after dark. Our drones would have seen them if they marched during daylight. And they must have moved fast, or our network of spies would have sent us warning. They have wolfbane now. Their spies must have known we'd dispatched several brigades to the east side of the saddle. They took their best shot. It wasn't good enough.

"I fell into their trap. *But they did not achieve their objective.* Fort Taylor stands. The mines are still *ours*. The Daughter of Gaia lives! Our scouts have confirmed that the blacksuits are running away. They're going home."

We cheer. Despite the terrible losses we've taken, from a strategic standpoint, we've denied the blacksuits the victory they needed.

Falstaff continues. "Our losses were horrific. We've had small groups of fighters filtering in throughout the day. But by our latest count, we lost four brigades today. We can't know what losses the blacksuits suffered, because they took their fallen comrades with them. But they lost at *least* two of their own brigades. The Daughter of Gaia is right. *We* can replace our losses. The blacksuits cannot. Our day will come."

Later, as I lie in bed trying to sleep, I flash back to awful memories of the battle. In my mind's eye, I once again see the blacksuits surrounding and carving up the brigades on our flanks. I see our unarmed civilians attacking the blacksuits from behind and dying, buying our survival with their lives. Despite this, my exhaustion prevails, and I fall into a deep slumber.

The following day, we complete the grim task of burying our dead. Falstaff's estimates were correct: we dig over four thousand graves. Our overall strength has fallen from ten brigades to six. We recall one brigade from Liberty, leaving only Han's Third Brigade to train the Liberty militia. We're weak on the east side of the mountains now, but with the Sons gone, it shouldn't matter.

The training ground for new recruits has grown spectacularly in the time since I last saw it. Falstaff explains that he knew he'd be getting thousands of new recruits as soon as the new super-grain crop came in, so he prepared in advance. Now, with the extra food coming up from Liberty, we'll use the larger training ground sooner than expected. Hundreds of new recruits pour in each day, most of them liberated slaves from inside the blacksuits' ring. Helen's infiltrators inside the ring work overtime recruiting men and women for our war machine.

I spend the next two weeks helping train our new recruits. As always, our trainees are enthusiastic and eager to learn. Our officers must chase them off the training field at day's end. They'd work twenty-four hours a day, if we let them. We work from sunup to sundown strengthening their bodies, teaching them to use their weapons, and working on military maneuvers.

During a training exercise involving the obstacle course, I'm shouting words of encouragement to the trainees when a messenger beckons me to the radio room. As I follow him, I'm filled with a sense of foreboding. *Is there any chance good news awaits me? Not likely.*

Falstaff and Kenny are in the radio room when I arrive. Their faces are pale and grim.

Falstaff takes a deep breath when he sees me. "The blacksuits destroyed Topeka."

31

"What do you mean 'destroyed'?" I ask.

"They've burned the village to the ground, destroyed the crops, and murdered every villager they could find. A few villagers escaped to Omaha, and it's their story we're hearing."

I'm stunned. Grizz enters the room just as Falstaff is delivering the news. He throws an arm around my shoulders.

"I guess this means the blacksuits' first crops came in," I say at last.

"We knew this would happen," says Grizz. "We just didn't know when."

Kenny's face darkens in anger. "We gotta pay them back! We can't let them get away with murder!"

Falstaff shakes his head. "There's nothing we can do now. Without leaving Fort Taylor and Liberty undefended, we can put only two brigades in the field. We can't take New Washington with two brigades. We can't burn the blacksuits' crops because they'll starve their slaves before they'll starve themselves. There is nowhere for us to strike."

Kenny hits the wall with her fist and then examines her skinned knuckles.

"Patience," Falstaff counsels. "The blacksuits are harvesting only a few early season crops. Their full harvest is still a couple months away."

"We're in a race with time," I say. "But we *can* do some things. Kenny, we need to get those solar panels moved across the saddle so we can use our planes and tanks on this side of the mountains. Help Bree speed things up. Speak with Eva. See if she'll loan us people to help move panels."

Kenny nods.

"Can we train our new recruits faster?" I ask.

Falstaff shakes his head. "We're working as fast as we can. We mustn't skimp on training. If we send untrained fighters to face the blacksuits, the blacksuits will cut them to ribbons."

Falstaff is correct. I nod agreement. "I want to go to Topeka. It's only a one-day walk."

Margaret snorts. "It's a two-day walk for the Daughter's Guard."

"I'm sorry, Margaret. I must travel alone."

Margaret shakes her head in frustration.

"I need to do this," I explain. "Grizz, will you join me?"

Grizz nods. "If we leave now, we'll make it just after nightfall."

With my wounded shin, I can't run. So Grizz and I settle for a steady walking pace.

As we walk, I have hours to think. I try to swallow my guilt over our defeat. I can't let my guilt impair my judgment. The memory of blacksuit attacks on our flanks and the massacre of our warriors will stay with me always. But I will also remember our people fighting bravely, standing up to the blacksuits and making them pay for their victory. And I remind myself again and again that the blacksuits won only a tactical victory. Strategically, they accomplished nothing.

The forest is peaceful around us. I remember the first day we saw the forest, after we came through the brane. The trees looked stunted, and the heat unbearable. I've learned to appreciate the beauty of this landscape, and the heat is something I no longer think about.

"Do you remember the first day we came through the brane?" I ask Grizz.

"I remember how hot it was, and I remember how afraid I was. And that first night, the howling dreadwolves scared me to death."

"You never looked afraid," I say, surprised and curious. "I always took strength from you, because you looked so stoic and brave."

"That's funny," Grizz says, "because I took strength from *you*."

"I guess that makes us a good couple. We feed off each other's strength."

"We're a good couple in more ways than one," says Grizz as he puts his arms around me and gives me a lingering kiss.

Despite my sorrow and the pain of my wound, or maybe *because* of them, Grizz's passionate kiss overwhelms me. I need to push him away. Short of breath, heart racing, I say, "We'd better stop or we'll never make it to Topeka." I want to spend the rest of the day and night here with Grizz, holding him, loving him. I'm ready to grab him again and crush his lips with mine.

"Duty first," says Grizz.

I struggle with my emotions and master them at last. "Duty first," I agree. My voice shakes.

Near nightfall, I can tell we're near Topeka by the smell. Dead bodies putrefy fast in this hot climate.

*   *   *

We find the burial party, just arrived from St. Louis. Despite the tragedy, they're overjoyed to find the Daughter of Gaia among them.

Between my depression from our lost battle and my lingering passion following our last kiss, it's hard to pull off my Daughter of Gaia act. But I do my best. I smile and mingle.

The leader is a short man named Iago. "It's too dark to dig," I say, and he agrees.

There's a soft breeze blowing, and we find a place to camp, upwind of the massacre site. I find it hard to sleep and wake up many times during the night. Dawn finds me awake but far from rested.

We eat a quick breakfast and walk to the massacre site. I'd prefer not to see what the blacksuits did. If I could, I'd leave the burials to the team from St. Louis. But I can't.

I've seen awful things in this world, but nothing worse than the scene before me. Dead bodies cover the ground in every direction, as far as I can see. I follow the lead of the diggers and tie a cloth over my nose and mouth, but it doesn't help much. The stench of death is nearly unbearable. Several members of the burial party rush for the bushes and lose their breakfasts.

The blacksuits massacred everyone, and while it's difficult to look at the dead men and women, looking at the dead children is even worse. They died with expressions of terror on their faces, expressions that death has preserved. Mothers lie on top of their children, striving to protect them in those terrible last moments. But the blacksuits are efficient. There are few survivors. I choke back my tears but can't hide my grief. Grizz looks stricken, too. Many members of the burial party can't control their tears. A keening, wailing sound fills the air as they react to the surrounding horror. I want to scream and cry, but don't. The villagers will draw energy from my stoicism. We're shattered, but we have a job to do.

Just before we dig, Iago approaches me. "The Daughter of Gaia should not dig graves," he says.

"The Daughter of Gaia *must* dig graves," I reply. Iago seems ready to say something else but holds his tongue.

We dig. The sound of wooden shovels breaking through the crusty surface fills the air. Within minutes, sweat runs off my brow and into my eyes. I pause and mop sweat from my forehead with the back of my hand. Sweat drenches my tunic and runs down my back in torrents. It's hard to dig a grave with wooden shovels.

As the sun rises in the sky, my sorrow turns into anger. *How can the blacksuits do this?* I take comfort in knowing we will make them pay. I don't know when or how, but I know we'll have our day. *Will I be able to slaughter the blacksuits in retribution for this awful thing they've done? I doubt it. But I will take my revenge.*

We work until nightfall. I'm grateful when the sun sets. My arms ache and my shoulder muscles spasm. I've opened the cut on my leg and must clean it and put a fresh bandage on it. Still, hard work gives me temporary relief from my grief. I'm sure a psychiatrist would tell me I'm putting myself through penance to absolve me of my inability to protect these people. But the truth is far simpler: I won't ask anyone else to do something I'm unwilling to do. I'm learning to be a leader and pitching in is what a leader does.

I fall asleep next to Grizz, my arm across his chest.

In the morning, the Daughter's Guard arrives. Falstaff and Margaret have replaced the casualties suffered in the Battle of Fort Taylor, and I spend an hour learning the names of the new members. This is melancholy work. I remember the ones who fell.

We bury corpses all day, and into the next. We dig thousands of graves. It's hard work with our primitive tools, and my hands blister. I ignore the pain and continue digging. We lose enormous amounts of water through perspiration. A good mother hen, Margaret makes sure I stay hydrated and take my salt pills. When we're done, I thank the people from St. Louis, and promise them the blacksuits will pay for their crimes.

I linger long after the burial party from St. Louis leaves. I sit alone among the graves with Grizz by my side. We don't speak. There's nothing to say. We mourn the loss of so many innocent lives, but the horror of the blacksuits' cruelty strengthens my determination. I'm tired of being the Daughter of Gaia. But sitting in this lonely field reminds me why I need to be who I am. We *must* win this war.

The next few weeks fly by. Falstaff tells me he's seen nobody who can be everywhere at once, as I seem to be. We have dozens of projects, and I want to help with every single one. I work with our new recruits, but I want to help with the work on our solar farm, too. The work involved in setting up and wiring solar panels is far from trivial and constructing generators to turn the sun's energy into electricity is even more complicated. But the size of the solar farm grows. At our current pace, we'll bring our planes and drones over and fly missions from this side of the saddle within a matter of weeks. I spend time in the fields with our farmers, watching impatiently as our new super grain turns from green to gold. The seed pods grow.

I cross the saddle several times and find the work Chase has done amazing. It's no longer necessary for a worker to cross the saddle with his or her cargo. Elevators and pulleys simplify the work. Our workers move loads from one elevator to the next. They crank the pulleys by hand, and Chase has organized his workers in teams. As soon as one set of workers tires, another, rested team replaces them. In many places, Chase has built secondary and tertiary elevators so we can hoist up multiple loads at the same time. From a distance, the elevators and pulleys look like the framework for a monstrous castle built by a deranged giant. The ingenuity of the design and the vast manpower required to put everything together are mind-boggling.

Eva agrees to send thousands of her people to help us. With their help, caravans crisscross the desert nonstop with goods destined for Fort Taylor. Kenny and Bree dismantle a tank so we can move it across the mountains. "The people who built this tank didn't intend for anyone to disassemble it," says Kenny, "but the *real* problem will come when we try to put it back together." Still, the tank has been half disassembled, and Kenny and Bree have drawn up copious blueprints which should help them put the beast back together.

32

Several weeks after our defeat in the Battle of Fort Taylor, Mother Helen calls for a council of war. There are, she says, important matters we must discuss. She doesn't say what the "important matters" are. Maybe she's realized what an inadequate leader I am, and she wants to replace me. Bree, Kenny, and Chase join Grizz and me at Fort Taylor. Chase has just returned from the work of rebuilding Fort Liberty. "It's not finished, but it's reached a point where the locals can handle the rest," he explains.

The five surviving members of the Tucson Ramblers enjoy the walk from the fort to the sanctuary. We're scarcely ever together as a group anymore, so we welcome this opportunity to catch up and reminisce.

"Does anybody regret staying on this side of the brane?" I ask with real curiosity.

"Nah," says Grizz. "I like it here."

Kenny takes a moment before she responds. "There's nothing I could have done in Tucson that would've been half as important as what I'm doing here. Still, I miss the boys. It's hard when you don't have a dozen guys asking you to go to the prom."

Chase rolls his eyes. "All my life, I've been the one who wasn't very smart. But here, I've found something I excel at. I'm proud of the forts and the elevators. I miss Charity. Until the day I die, I'll live with the fact that I brought her here to die. Still, I'd do it again."

Bree is the last to answer. "I miss my family. But if I weren't here, I'd miss my friends. Maybe someday, after we've won the war, I'll check out the action at the brane. But I doubt it. How do you go back to peaceful Tucson and hang out with kids whose biggest concern is which shade of nail polish to use? There'd be a big disconnect there."

"How 'bout you, Taylor?" asks Kenny.

"I wish I could be a kid again. Just a regular kid. But Kenny's right. I couldn't do a thing in Tucson half as important as what I'm doing here."

So, there we have it. Reluctant warriors, but warriors.

When we arrive at the sanctuary, Helen greets us. She hugs each of us.

"Everyone looks well," she says. "And you, Daughter of Gaia. You're no longer a child. You've become a beautiful young woman."

I blush.

Helen has assembled the village elders for a major council of war. It's too late in the day to meet now, so we wash off the dirt from the road, eat a late supper, and sleep.

In the morning, Helen convenes the council after breakfast. She calls our meeting to order and gets right to business. She looks at me and says, "I want to discuss a sensitive issue. We will soon have flying vehicles capable of striking the blacksuits in their lair?"

"Yes," I say.

Helen continues, "The blacksuits imbed slaves with their military units so that, in attacking them, we must destroy our own people along with our enemies."

I nod.

"The question I pose is this: do we kill blacksuits knowing we'll also kill our own?"

The buzz of conversation fills the room.

Helen cuts through the noise, and her voice rings out loud and clear. "It's time to settle this issue. I will now poll the village elders.

The results will be binding. I ask *this* question: Will we kill blacksuits knowing that doing so will result in the deaths of our own? You may answer the question yes or no, or you may abstain."

A hush falls over the room.

"What says Detroit?" asks Helen.

I wizened old woman responds in a strong voice: "Detroit votes 'aye.'"

"What says Fargo?"

"Fargo votes 'aye.'"

Helen polls the forty-nine surviving villages. The outcome is unanimous.

"The council has spoken," says Helen, looking at me. "Daughter of Gaia, have you heard the council's decision?"

I'm uncomfortable. "Yes," I say reluctantly.

"And yet the council's decision troubles you?"

"Yes."

"I knew it would. That is why I assembled the council of elders. I know the Daughter of Gaia will hesitate to use force if it puts our own people in jeopardy. You need to understand that every one of us, and I include myself, will die for our cause. We cannot defeat the blacksuits if we are reluctant to attack them. For centuries the blacksuits have held us in servitude. They have slaughtered us on the slightest whim. They have taken our children from us. They have forced us to work in the fields with no compensation. They have fed us meager rations that left us on the brink of starvation. They have denied us health care. They have denied us an education. The hatred we feel for them is stronger than our wish to live. I repeat, every slave is willing to die to win our freedom."

The village elders look at me. "I hear the council," I say. "You are right, Helen, I am reluctant to kill our own people. But I will do so, when necessary."

The elders nod their heads in agreement. "Mother bless the Daughter of Gaia," they say, in unison.

"With this business complete, I adjourn the council," says Helen.

The elders file from the room. "That was it?" I say.

"That was enough," replies Helen. "I knew the toll that killing our own would take on you. If you were *not* reluctant to kill, you would not be the Daughter of Gaia."

"Thank you. Helen. I'll do what I must."

"And yet, you will suffer."

"I will. Less, now that the council has spoken."

"Then I've accomplished what I wanted," says Helen smiling. "Now, go win this war."

It's noon when I finish my conversation with Helen. My friends and I debate whether to spend the rest of the day at the sanctuary or return to our work. We decide on the latter. In our race against time, we don't have a second to spare. We must defeat the blacksuits before they harvest their crops.

33

Two weeks later, Kenny invites me to join her at Fort Taylor's airfield. I arrive with the Daughter's Guard, followed by Grizz, Falstaff, and Gretchen. Bree is still disassembling the tank and Chase is working on his elevators in the saddle.

"Thought you'd want to look at this," Kenny says.

"Look at what?"

"Look at our first flight in a plane charged using the solar farm on *this* side of the mountains," Kenny says with a smile. "It took us twelve hours to charge this baby, but once we get our second generator online, we'll charge our planes in half the time. And at our current pace, in a month we'll have another genny and enough solar panels to cut the time in half again."

"Let me fly," I ask, embarrassed by the pleading in my voice.

"Not gonna happen. If this thing falls out of the sky, I don't want everyone mad at me for killing the Daughter of Gaia."

I'm tempted to beg, but it'll do me no good. So, I watch Kenny climb in the cockpit, go through her preflight check, and launch her plane. She levels off at three thousand feet and heads northwest. I watch until the plane vanishes in the distance.

She returns three hours later.

"Just dropped a few bombs on New Washington," she says as she clambers from the cockpit.

We give each other high fives and embrace. The day has come. We're bringing our wonder weapons to bear on the Court. I wish I could have seen the expression on Salieri's face when the bombs fell.

Kenny looks at me. "You wanna make the next flight?"

"Well, *yeah-ah*. When can I go?"

"Dawn tomorrow?"

"Yep. I can't wait."

I awake at 3:00 A.M., far too early, but I'm excited. I wait impatiently at the airfield for dawn. Kenny and Grizz join me as we wait for first light.

"What are you gonna target?" asks Kenny.

"What did *you* hit?"

"I knocked down a few defenses."

"Then that's what I'll hit."

I walk around the plane, give it a careful once-over, just as Kenny taught me. In the cockpit, I force myself to go slow and remember my training. I don't want to forget something stupid in my excitement. Confident I've done a thorough pre-flight check; I power up the engine. I take off and climb to three thousand feet. Then I set my compass heading at three hundred ten degrees and goose the controls.

I achieve maximum velocity while I'm flying above the forest that surrounds the blacksuits' ring. But once I leave the trees behind, I resist the temptation to go as fast as possible, because I want to examine the fields below me. I drop to an altitude of five hundred feet and reduce my groundspeed to fifty miles per hour. At this speed, I can study the blacksuits' fields. They have indeed changed their crops. Where silk trees were growing, beans grow. They now use fields that used to be fruit orchards for mixed vegetable cultivation. They've converted their agricultural priority from luxury goods to food. And while it's hard to tell for sure from above, lots of fields appear almost ready for harvest.

Although my plane's electric engine makes little noise, people on the ground notice me. The slaves working in the fields drop their tools and raise their hands in joy at the sight of this silver hawk shining in the sun. News travels fast inside the ring, and word of Kenny's first bombing run has spread.

I increase my speed and altitude. An hour later the spires of Fort Grant rise on the horizon. Fort Grant is one of the blacksuits' three inner ring forts. I'm not interested in Fort Grant today. I'm headed for the capital. In minutes I'm over Fort Grant, and New Washington appears in the distance.

The fort surrounding New Washington looks even more imposing from the air. It's huge. Its walls bristle with bartizans, turrets, embrasures, and watchtowers. We'll need to drop thousands of bombs to give ourselves a chance of success when it comes time to storm this massive citadel.

I overfly the city and see the turret Kenny bombed yesterday, damaged but only half destroyed. The blacksuits have surrounded the turret with a group of slaves chained to one another and to the turret. They've done something similar with every major defensive position.

I keep reminding myself that the council has told us to drop bombs even if we kill slaves. I don't like what I must do, but I'll do it. I take another pass over the city as I screw up my courage. My first bombing run is at a height of five hundred feet. I line up the damaged turret in the bombsite and press the release button. The bomb detonates, and I'm low enough that the turbulence from the explosion buffets my plane.

I make a wide, sweeping turn and fly over the turret to inspect the damage. The turret lies in ruins. There's no sign of the slaves who surrounded the turret. I can't worry about that. On my second run, I target the blacksuits' central headquarters building inside the fort. It's a grand palace and I know it well from the time I spent imprisoned there. It's not a defensive target per se, but it's a target that will strike at the very heart of the blacksuits' power.

Once more, I release my bombs and the turbulence from the explosion rocks my plane. I bank the plane and fly over the palace a second time. The bombs have obliterated the top two floors. We'll need several more bombing runs, but we'll bring the building to the ground.

I set course for Fort Taylor in a happy mood. I banish thoughts of the slaves I've killed.

*   *   *

For the next two weeks we bomb New Washington twice a day. Grizz and I take turns flying the bombing runs. Bree puts the finishing touches on her disassembly of the tank, Chase is building more elevators, and Kenny is working on a mysterious project. The only thing she'll say is that it's "radically cool" and it'll "knock our sox off."

The blacksuits try to rebuild what we bomb, but they can't build as fast as we shatter. Still, we need to mount more raids if we're to reduce their defenses and give ourselves a chance when we storm the capital.

The day following our twenty-fifth bombing run is special. We have three causes to celebrate. First, Falstaff invites us to the commissioning of six new brigades. The spectacle is thrilling to behold. The new brigades march past the reviewing stand in arrow-straight lines and in perfect lockstep. Our militia is, as always, dressed in homespun clothing, much of it patched and threadbare. But what they lack in splendor, they make up for in discipline. I know Falstaff is a genius in training warriors, so I'm certain these men and women are ready to fight. Falstaff, Gretchen, and I make short speeches. I wish I had something to offer other than the old nostrums promising the ultimate deployment of wonder weapons and the impending demise of the Court. They've heard it many times. Still, they interrupt my brief speech with cheering several times.

After the commissioning ceremony, Richard, the villager who manages our solar farm, announces that we now have enough solar panels and generators to charge a plane in six hours. I smile and hug him, which causes him to go limp with a silly grin on his face. Four bombing runs a day! We can double the destruction we rain on New Washington.

Late in the afternoon, Kenny arrives. She removes a heavy storage locker from the bomb bay of her plane. She grins.

"You have a surprise for us?" I ask.

"I do."

She doesn't continue. "And?" I prompt.

"I need to put a few finishing touches on it. Cool your jets, ET."

With no other choice, I feign patience. "Should I invite Grizz, Falstaff, and Gretchen to the show?"

"Good idea," Kenny says as she disappears into one of our warehouses. When I try to follow her, she closes the door in my face. "Don't be nosy, ET. I'll bet you sneaked into your parents' closet to figure out what you were getting for Christmas."

In fact, I did. But only once. I know arguing with Kenny is futile.

Two hours later, Kenny invites us in. We find her sitting on a bench facing a computer monitor, complete with a keyboard and a joystick. A closer look shows that the keyboard is not an ordinary keyboard. Besides keys, it has a variety of switches.

"I've wanted to work on this for ages, but I was always too busy working on other stuff," she says. "Watch this."

Kenny presses a button on the keyboard, and we hear the unmistakable whirr of a drone taking off from the airfield next to the warehouse.

"Did you just launch a drone?" I ask.

"I did," Kenny replies.

On the computer's screen is Fort Taylor, viewed from above. The size of the fort grows smaller, and soon we can see our whole complex, the training fields, the crops, and the mines on the display.

"You're controlling the drone's flight using the remote control," I say, excited. In the past we've had to control the drones by programming them before they took off, typing in sets of coordinates. Once air bound, the only control we had was to recall the drone.

"I am," says Kenny with an impish grin. "But that's not all." She punches more buttons and enters commands from the keyboard.

The pictures the drone sends back are of the forest surrounding the blacksuits' ring. Kenny is sending the drone over the forest.

"I'm starved," says Kenny. "Let's get something to eat."

"You've figured out how to have the drone send back images in real time?" Until now, we've had to wait for a drone to return before we could review the pictures it had taken. "That's nice, Kenny. Now we can see what the blacksuits are doing the instant they do it."

I must have sounded insufficiently impressed. "Geez, ET, we can watch a battle from above and use our radios to tell our militia on the front line what the blacksuits are doing. No more surprise attacks like the one they pulled on us at Battle of Fort Taylor."

"That's *great*, Kenny!" I try to infuse my voice with the enthusiasm I'd have if the walls of New Washington fell.

"Of *course*, it's great," says Kenny, mollified. "Now, dinner?"

We make small talk over a meal of beans, broccoli, and greens. Kenny urges us to eat faster near the end of the meal.

When we're finished, Kenny jumps to her feet. "OK," she says mysteriously, "now I can show you the rest."

"There's more?" I ask.

"Much, much more."

When we return to the warehouse, the drone's camera displays an overhead picture of New Washington. The picture isn't changing, so I assume the drone is not moving.

"Prepare for amazement," says Kenny. "And here's yet another proof that Kenny is not only a goddess, but a genius, too."

What I see next boggles my mind.

34

Kenny adjusts a control on the keyboard. The camera zooms in on New Washington. We're now looking at the shattered remains of the top floors of the palace. Kenny nudges the joystick and shows the plaza between the palace and the barracks next to it. More control changes and the camera zooms in even further. We see a patrol of blacksuits marching past the palace, headed north. Kenny punches a button, and the blacksuits fall to the ground writhing, their bodies jerking the way bodies do when struck by heavy caliber, rapid-firing guns. In less than five seconds, the blacksuit column lies unmoving on the ground.

"Holy smokes!" I say. "You chose the drone's target!" Until now, the drones have used thermal images to decide when to fire. If they detect body heat, they shoot. If they don't detect body heat, they don't.

"Yep," says Kenny. "We can use the remote control to direct everything the drones do. Sorry to rush you through dinner, but drones have only enough charge to hang out for ten minutes over New Washington."

I'm trying to get my mind around being able to control everything a drone does in real time. We have another wonder weapon! "Did you send these drones from Fort Carlson?"

Kenny nods.

"Given the size of the solar farm at Fort Carlson, how many drone strikes can we mount every day?"

"Six at most, but I'd count on four or five. We still need to charge planes and comm equipment."

"Let's sleep on this new information and meet tomorrow morning to discuss our strategy," says Falstaff.

Just as we conclude the meeting, an operator from the comm center enters the room panting. "Begging your pardon, Daughter of Gaia, but we've just received word that the blacksuits have destroyed another city. They burned Seattle to the ground and massacred its citizens."

*   *   *

I flash back to the massacre at Topeka, the sight of thousands of blank eyes staring at the sky, of mothers desperately trying to protect their children in the instant before death, of the sickly-sweet smell of decomposing bodies.

I rise, but Falstaff puts his hand on my arm. "I need you *here* this time, Daughter of Gaia. We must discuss how we can best deploy our new brigades and our remote-controlled drones. I need you to help me make plans for our attack on New Washington."

I fall back in my seat, numb. My heart compels me to go to Seattle, to help dig graves, to offer whatever comfort I can to the burial party. But Falstaff is right. Seattle is on the far side of the ring, out of range for my plane. I'd have to walk at least part of the way, and things are moving so fast now, I can't afford to leave for a week. I nod.

Falstaff gives a gruff grunt of approval.

Sleep eludes me. I'm thrilled that we can put six new brigades in the field, and that we'll now be able to conduct four bombing runs a day. Kenny's remote-controlled drones will wreak havoc on the blacksuits. But I can't get the massacre of yet another village out of my head.

After a light breakfast, Falstaff calls our planning conference to order. The smudges below his eyes tell me he has had little sleep. And yet there's excitement in his voice as he speaks. "By the end of this month, we will commission another six brigades. We'll have the numbers to attack the blacksuits home cities."

We've known this day was coming, but we can't suppress our joy when we hear the news formalized by Falstaff. We shout approval and thrust fists in the air.

"Payback time!" says Kenny.

Grizz, who is not very demonstrative, surprises me: "At last!" he says. We exchange high fives.

Falstaff waits for quiet and then looks each of us in the eye before proceeding. "I think we need to redirect our bombing campaign. Until now, we've concentrated on New Washington. But when it comes time to attack the blacksuits in their own lair, we must put at least one of their three inner ring forts out of action. If we don't, our supply lines will be in constant danger."

I agree with Falstaff. We'll outnumber them by a wide margin. Our best intelligence tells us the blacksuits have only seven brigades. "What about the other two ring forts?" I ask.

"We place a screening force between each of those forts and our supply lines. If the blacksuits come out to fight, we'll give them a hearty welcome. The brigade screening the fort will give ground until we bring our superior numbers into play. But this won't happen. The blacksuits are too smart to fight us in the open. They know their chances are better when they're behind fortified walls."

I clear my throat. "So, we must destroy the battlements of one of the ring forts and continue our attacks on New Washington. That's a tall order, but we'll have a month to work on it. We can drop lots of bombs now that we can fly four sorties a day."

"I agree with the priorities you've set for bombing targets," says Falstaff. "Hit the fortifications but at the same time, hit their barracks, and their administrative centers."

"And don't forget," says Kenny, "we'll have a tank ready for combat in a week. The tank's sabot munitions will penetrate the armor of another tank. I think it'll be dandy for penetrating the concrete emplacements of the blacksuits defenses."

Falstaff agrees. "Keep drones over their cities as often as possible. Make the blacksuits sweat every time they leave a building. Don't make your runs on a regular schedule. Let the blacksuits know they're vulnerable every minute of every day."

"We won't win this war with drones," says Grizz. "But we can work at lowering the blacksuits morale. *We* control this war from this point forward."

"Daughter of Gaia," says Falstaff, "do you approve these plans?"

Falstaff knows more about military planning than I ever will, but he still shows deference to me. "Yes," I say. "I agree. Four weeks from this day, the final battle begins."

Falstaff speaks again: "We should not let our numerical superiority or our wonder weapons lull us into a sense of overconfidence. The blacksuits are superb warriors, and an animal is most vicious when it's cornered."

We leave the room on this sobering note.

The four weeks before our assault on the blacksuits' inner ring pass in a blur. We're busy planning for the upcoming campaign. We decide we'll take Fort Grant before we attack New Washington. One look at a map of the inner ring forts convinces us that Falstaff is correct: with Fort Grant in blacksuits' hands, the blacksuits can disrupt our supply trains with impunity.

The details of launching a major military campaign are complex. From which direction or directions will we launch our assaults? What is our objective on day one and for following days? What will we do if the blacksuits try to reinforce Fort Grant? How can we best deploy our tank and our bombers? What do we do if our advance falters? Which units will screen the other forts? Which brigade will lead the assault through the breach? I am thankful we have Falstaff and Gretchen. They have a natural talent for detailed planning.

Bree has changed the seats in our planes so the small villagers can fly them. I still fly a bombing run every day. I use my time over the cities to draw maps of the streets and buildings inside the walls. Once our militia breaks into the cities, we need to know where to direct our attacks. Our spies have smuggled out maps of the city, but the maps don't show the height of the buildings or which ones the blacksuits are likely to defend.

I treasure my time in the cockpit because flying helps me dispel the jitters I feel when I consider the coming campaign. We have the advantage of greater numbers and better weapons, but the blacksuits are fighting for their homes. The coming battle will be difficult. Can the blacksuits use their defensive positions to inflict enough casualties to defeat us? Despite our best plans, this outcome is entirely possible.

From the air, I get a sense of how effective our bombing has been. Many of the defensive positions of Fort Grant and New Washington have been leveled. We also fly bombing runs over Fort Williams and Fort Lewis. We don't want the blacksuits to stack their defenses in Fort Grant.

The blacksuits destroy two more of our cities. Dallas and Chicago suffer the fate of Topeka and Seattle. I agonize over these losses, but there's nothing any of us can do to prevent them. We must end this war. That's the only way to prevent the blacksuits from committing further atrocities. But victory is far from certain. I don't let myself dwell on what happens if we lose.

Kenny and Bree reassemble the tank. Bree is eager to drive the tank right into the inner ring, but Falstaff convinces her to wait. "I'd prefer the blacksuits not know of this weapon," he says. "That way they won't be able to make plans for stopping it. It's a powerful weapon, but it's not invulnerable."

Two weeks before the assault, we go on half rations. We've exhausted the food we carried north from Liberty. We won't be hungry for more than a few days, because our grain from Los Alamos is being harvested. Chance's mills are grinding the seeds into flour.

At last, the day comes. We've spent years getting ready for this moment. We assemble our forces. Our plans are complete. We've hit the blacksuits' defenses hard. We've briefed our commanders. Everybody knows what's expected of them. We assemble our forces in our order of march. At dawn, we move out.

We need a week to bring our forces into battle lines outside Fort Grant. Falstaff has added a wrinkle to our plan. He takes the brigades we'll use to screen the other forts and has them demonstrate in front of Fort Lewis. We've bombed each of the three of the ring forts, but any fool can see we hit Fort Grant the hardest. And as a result, the blacksuits have placed their largest garrison there. By threatening Fort Lewis, we hope to siphon off troops from Fort Grant to reinforce Fort Lewis.

We're using our hot-air balloon to watch the battlefield. It's flown by Falstaff's troops. From high over the battlefield, they watch as a large contingent of blacksuits abandons Fort Grant, and heads for Fort Lewis.

"The blacksuits took the bait!" they say, over the comm.

Once the blacksuits commit their troops to Fort Lewis, the screening brigades wheel into position. One brigade will screen Fort Lewis, one will screen Fort Williams, and one positions itself in front of New Washington itself. From now on, there'll be no reinforcements for Fort Grant without going through our lines.

We bring our tank and bombers into the battle. The tank batters the front gate while the bombers concentrate on a twenty-yard segment of the north wall of the fort. Our intention is to destroy that twenty-yard segment, so we can attack the fort from two directions at once; one group will go through the front gate, while the other enters through the bomber-created breach. Getting through the breach is likely to be the hardest part of the assault, as the blacksuits will concentrate their fire on our militia while it's bunched up in the twenty-yard bottleneck of the breach. But our attack from two directions will force the blacksuits to split their forces.

By nightfall of the fourth day, the tank and bombers have done their work. Our brigades position themselves for the assault. We begin at dawn tomorrow.

I'll be a part of the force that goes through the north wall. Gretchen will command this front while Falstaff will lead the attack through the front gate. I surprise myself by sleeping through the night before the attack. As I dozed off, I reminded myself that we've worked for a long time to get ourselves in position. We've planned our attack to the minutest detail. Everything we can do is done. It's time to settle the fate of our people.

We launch our attack at dawn.

35

I'll go with the first wave through the breach. Gretchen has, with much exasperation, OK'd my participation. She knows she'd have to tackle me and tie me down to stop me. Her sole condition is that I deploy half the Daughter's Guard in front of me. I chafe at this but agree. Nothing says I must *stay* behind the Guard, once the arrows fly.

While waiting for the order to advance, my serenity of last night gives way to a serious case of the jitters. The blacksuits will use every bit of their cunning and skill to stop us. By day's end, many of us will be dead.

My friends will go with me. Their faces show determination and unavoidable nervousness, but our militia is joyful, almost giddy. They want revenge for a thousand years of oppression. They're fighting for their parents, grandparents, and great grandparents, back to the founding of New Washington.

Gretchen's bugler sounds the charge. Our first wave raises a throaty cheer and runs for the breach.

Our bombers collapsed the wall, but the bombs left a pile of rubble which we must climb. We expect massive problems getting through this bottleneck. We're correct. Hundreds of blacksuits pour arrows down on us from two buildings just inside the breach. The vanguard of our first wave falls in the first few seconds. The rest of us try to pick our way through the rubble, but the blacksuit fire is withering. Our attack loses momentum, and they pin us in the rubble. Over half of our first wave lies dead or wounded. I try to bring my AK into play, but the minute I raise my head, two dozen arrows strike around me, forcing me to duck.

"I don't think I'd try that again," says Kenny. Grizz shakes his head. Margaret gives me her "that-was-pretty-dumb-now-wasn't-it?" look. She's right.

Gretchen sees our predicament and orders the second wave to attack. The second wave advances past us but the blacksuits halt it, too. Murderous fire cuts the second wave to pieces. We can't get through the rubble. Chase and Kenny carry grenade launchers, and they've been practicing with them. They launch grenades through the windows of both buildings. Kenny's first shot bounces off the wall just below the window. The grenade falls to the ground and explodes harmlessly. Her second shot is right on target. The grenades make a "thump" sound as they detonate.

"Let's go!" I cry. We're on our feet and moving. The blacksuit fire is diminishing, but it's still too concentrated. We take dozens of casualties. Our advance stalls once more.

Falstaff gave us the tank to support our attack. His part of the assault will go through wide plazas, barracks, and parade grounds, which will offer the blacksuits fewer opportunities to lay down fire, so we get the tank. Gretchen orders Erin to move the tank forward.

"ET, you still alive up there?" asks Bree from the tank's comm.

"I am."

"Where are the bad guys?"

I use my collapsible periscope to examine the buildings without lifting my head. The blacksuits have knocked holes in the sides of the buildings and they shoot arrows through the embrasures. It's no wonder grenades through the windows didn't knock them out. I key my comm. "They're concentrated on the second floor of the building to the left. Then direct fire at the third floor of the tall building next door." The tank fires and I watch through the periscope as a section of the second floor of the building collapses into dust. A second shot takes away another section. A third volley exposes the interior of the second floor of the building. Bree then concentrates her fire on the building on the right.

"Let's move out!" I shout and jump to my feet. I fire my AK at the tank-created hole in the building on the left and my friends follow suit. Bree slews the turret of her tank to the right and fires two more shells. A few desultory arrows fall around us, but they can't stop us from crossing the rubble. We're through the wall and into the fort itself.

A four-story barracks is my group's first objective. The other half of our force advances toward a supply depot across the street. I sprint forward until I'm near the front door of our building. Blacksuits inside wait to riddle the first person through the door. We follow our training. We plant three small dabs of C4 explosive on the door, near the hinges and the doorknob. We retreat a few yards and detonate the charges. The door collapses. Grizz and I pitch grenades into the room and enter together, back-to-back. He sprays the left half of the room with AK fire while I spray the right. Four blacksuits lie on the floor, but six civilians lie dead, too. I take a deep breath.

Chase, who followed us through the door, places a hand on my shoulder. "We can't help it, ET. We'll kill good guys every time we kill the bad ones. Remember the council's decision."

I nod my head. Chase is right. And if we'd stopped to figure out who was in the room before we opened fire, *we'd* be dead.

We clear the building, room by room. Most rooms are empty, but blacksuits hide in others. They hope we'll miss their room and give them an opportunity to come up behind us. But Falstaff's training thwarts them. *Clear every single room* is the directive he's drilled into every warriors' head. *Leave no enemy behind you.*

Grizz and I stand ready to clear a room on the top floor when Margaret places a hand on my arm. She points to the floor. At first, I don't see what she's pointing at, but as I look closer, I see it: a trip wire. We lie on the floor and I use the barrel of my AK to trip the wire. Six crossbow bolts embed themselves in the wall behind us.

"Thanks, Margaret," I whisper. "I'd be dead if you hadn't seen the booby trap."

"Just doing my job," says Margaret.

We take half an hour to clear the building, and we lose seven more warriors. We kill a dozen blacksuits and at least two dozen civilians.

At this rate, it will take us days or even weeks to take the fort. And the butcher's bill will be outrageously high. I take a deep breath. *It's not like I didn't know this.*

Chase and Kenny join another fire team at this point. Our groups will attack the two toughest streets because of the advantages our AKs offer.

The complicated part of our mission is now before us. The streets of the fort run parallel to one another, and forty of them run from north to south. We have a fire team assigned to each street. Our plan is to advance along each of the streets in lockstep. We'll clear each building as we go, using our comms to stay coordinated. The advantage is, there's no way the blacksuits can attack our flanks. The disadvantage is, our whole line will move only as fast as the slowest fire team. Still, that's a price worth paying. There's no reason to hurry.

We leave a small screening force of warriors on the street as we clear each building. We can't give the blacksuits an empty street to maneuver through while we're busy inside the building.

I'm on the second floor of a building when I hear a commotion in the street. I peer out the window. The blacksuits have mounted a counterattack in force. They're overwhelming our screening force. I set my AK to single fire and bring down a couple blacksuits, but the fighting deteriorates into a hand-to-hand battle. In the melee, I can't be sure I won't hit one of *our* people. "Back to the street!" I holler hoping most of our group in the building can hear me. Grizz moved the second before I yelled, so he leads the way down the stairs. At the bottom, I rest my AK on the wall by the door, draw my sword, and unsling my shield. The AK is worthless when fighting at close quarters.

Grizz and I are the first ones on the street. Our screening force has only three warriors left. The blacksuits have their backs to us, so we're able to take out several before they realize we're there. Once they do, they turn and attack. Grizz and I stand side by side with our backs to the wall, shields overlapping. We slash and cut but for every blacksuit we bring down, another takes his place. A blacksuit officer comes at me from the side. He's held his attack until I'm off balance from a thrust at the blacksuit in front of me. The officer's raises his blade is, and I won't have time to bring my sword around to parry it. I'm saved when the blacksuit cries out and falls. Margaret drops him from the side. I smile at Margaret. "I know," I say, "you're just doing your job." Margaret nods.

The battle is short. Our team from inside the building has made it back into the street. Outnumbered, the blacksuits retreat. We pursue them for a few minutes, but I call off the attack when it's clear the blacksuits have established a disciplined rear guard. Since we have no easy targets, if we pursue them any farther, our team will be out of sync with the other fire teams. If we get too far ahead of the others, we'll expose our flanks and leave them vulnerable. I'm almost certain the blacksuits *want* us to do this. I can't see, but I'll bet there are blacksuits poised on the side streets ahead chomping at the bit for an opportunity to hit an undefended flank.

At noon, as per plan, we halt our advance. As we eat a hurried lunch, each fire team reports to Gretchen over the comm. Our losses have been heavy, and Gretchen will send reinforcements to the groups that have suffered the greatest casualties. Our team needs to make good its losses. We've lost half our warriors.

The blacksuits don't defend every building. They pick their spots, defending where they can best concentrate their fire. This is an open invitation for us to barrel through the openings and advance toward the center of the fort. After discussing our options, we continue with our plan for methodically clearing the enemy as we advance in sync. We need Fort Grant one-hundred percent secure before we attack New Washington.

Gretchen reports that Falstaff's group has had a terrible time advancing. The blacksuits are allowing him to cross the broad plazas uncontested, then defending a handful of choke points, and they're inflicting horrendous casualties. Falstaff has recalled the tank to help him fight his way through the choke points. The grenade launchers help, but the blacksuits know we have them, and avoid windows like the plague. Their strategy of knocking small embrasures in the sides of buildings is working. They fire through the small holes, and the holes are too small to hit with grenade launchers. The tank, however, has no problem clobbering blacksuits behind embrasures of any size.

We continue our advance in the afternoon, stopping only when we lose the day's light. We're nowhere near our first day's objectives, but we're working our way forward. Our left flank has met Falstaff's right flank. Since we're attacking from both the north and the east, our two forces will advance on a shrinking front. If everything goes according to plan, we'll push the blacksuits into an ever-smaller box in the southeast corner of the fort.

We mount a heavy guard before nightfall. We have several large, portable spotlights from the armory, and we use them to illuminate the street in front of our positions. I'm dead tired after a day of heavy fighting, but my mind is still racing, so it takes a while for me to fall asleep. As always, I plan to rise early and take the predawn watch.

A jarring noise interrupts my sleep. I blink the sleep out of my eyes. A battalion of blacksuits is counterattacking. They outnumber us and will soon break through our lines. Margaret, who was on guard duty when the attack started, hails Gretchen on the comm, tells her we need reinforcements, and soon.

36

Grizz and I drop several blacksuits with our AKs, but their charge brings them into our lines. The fighting is again hand-to-hand. As always, the Daughter of Gaia draws a crowd. Margaret rallies the Daughter's Guard around Grizz and I, and our part of the line stands firm. I glance to my right and realize the blacksuits will break through that flank. There are hundreds of warriors packed into a small space between the buildings on either side, so movement is difficult, but the blacksuits push hard and turn our right flank. They pour through the breach and attack the rest of us from the rear.

Falstaff has trained our warriors for this situation. What's left of our right flank gives ground, curls around, and makes their stand behind my group, shows the blacksuits a "hedgehog defense." We're surrounded, and my worst fear comes true. Another blacksuit battalion was waiting, out of sight. It pours through the opening they've created on our right flank, bypasses us, and charges forward. They aim to penetrate deep and attack fire teams on parallel streets from their flanks.

Surrounded by the Daughter's Guard, I'm in no immediate danger. I thumb my comm to alert Gretchen to the danger, but as I wait to get through, the reinforcements she's sent pour in and check the blacksuits before they exploit their breakthrough. But the relief force isn't large enough. The blacksuits outnumber them and will soon overpower them.

"Gretchen," I say, "we need more reinforcements! The blacksuits have committed two full battalions to their attack. They've surrounded and cut off my group, and they'll break through the relief force in a matter of minutes."

"Got it," says Gretchen. "I'll send 4th and 5th Battalions right away. They'll be there in ten."

We fight to avoid annihilation, but the blacksuits keep coming. Grizz and I force our way through the Daughter's Guard so we can contribute to the fight. Side by side, we use our superior size and try to turn the tide. We pour everything we have into the battle, and still, our losses mount, and we're forced to give ground. We have only six warriors left.

I take a quick glance at the action behind me, just in time to see the blacksuits overpower the last of our relief force. Still, the reinforcements broke the blacksuits' momentum. The minutes they take to regroup give Gretchen time to bring her second group of reinforcements into the battle. And this time, she's sent a huge force.

I'm too involved in my fight to watch the other. Our small group of survivors fights shoulder-to-shoulder, shields interlocked, but we're back against the wall. Our position is precarious. But before the blacksuits can finish us, the second relief force breaks through and comes to our rescue.

The tide of battle turns. It's now the blacksuits who are outnumbered and surrounded. They make one mighty effort to break through our lines to safety. We resist, but those of us who've been fighting for over an hour are tiring. Many blacksuits trickle through our lines and escape. I watch as they go. I want to go after them but realize doing so would be an unwise tactical decision. We know we've made the right decision when we train our spotlight once again toward the blacksuit lines. There's at *least* one more battalion queued up and ready to advance. If they could have forced their way through, the blacksuits might have exploited the hole in our lines and wreaked havoc on many of our fire teams. Had Gretchen been a few minutes slower, the situation might have spiraled out of control.

I slide my back down the wall until I'm seated. Corpses litter the street. The blacksuit casualties are heavier than our own, and this gives me some satisfaction.

Grizz slumps beside me. "That little attack cost them plenty."

"But," I reply, "they'll do everything they can think of to turn this thing against us. They almost succeeded."

"The important word is, almost."

I nod in agreement. "Our militia fought well."

Margaret, who is sitting on my other side, joins the conversation. "The blacksuits are fighting for their homes. They're desperate. But *we're* fighting for our freedom. When the issue comes down to a strong arm and the point of a sword, we're more desperate than they are. The blacksuits are good. We're better."

Gretchen's reinforcements take over security for the rest of the night so the rest of us can catch some sleep. By dawn, they've removed the corpses.

After a cold breakfast, we renew our attack as though nothing happened during the night.

The blacksuit resistance is light this morning. We make good progress, moving farther forward in a few hours than we did the entire day yesterday. Maybe the losses we inflicted on the blacksuits last night have left them too weak to mount an aggressive defense. We break for lunch and discuss the situation over the comm.

The news is positive on every front. Falstaff is moving fast, too. "This battle isn't over," says Gretchen. "Let's not get cocky."

We resume our advance, but late in the afternoon, we run into a barricade. A quick check on the comm lets us know that they've barricaded half a dozen streets on our front and several more on Falstaff's.

I study the barricade. The enemy has piled furniture, bricks, carts, pottery, and everything else they could find into a mountain that's ten feet in height and several yards deep. It'll be no picnic climbing over that wall under fire. But we don't have a choice.

I give the order to advance. The blacksuits check our advance the minute we reach the barricade. As we try to pick our way over the barricades, several hundred blacksuit archers pour down a torrent of arrows on us. The warrior in front of me falls and then the one beside her. We continue to climb doggedly but more and more of our people go down. Within minutes over two dozen warriors are out of action. Freshly spilled blood stains the debris of the barricade. I look at Grizz and he shakes his head. "This is crazy," he says.

"Take cover!" I order. I raise Gretchen on the comm. "We're stuck. If we continue to advance, the blacksuits will wipe us out. How is Falstaff doing?"

"They're facing the same problem," Gretchen affirms. "They're tied down, too."

"We need the tank."

"We'll send the tank back as soon as Falstaff breaks through. It won't be soon. He' taking heavy casualties."

I thumb the comm again. "Let's have our bombers blow the bejezus out of the buildings the blacksuits are using to pour plunging fire on us."

"That'll be risky," replies Gretchen. "If the bombs are a few yards off-target, they'll hit *you*."

"What if we pull back thirty yards once we hear the planes coming?"

"You want to try it?"

"Let's go for it. We trained those pilots well. Every one of them has flown dozens of missions. They can land their bombs on a fly's eyelash. Let's try."

An hour later, our planes are overhead.

"Fall back," I holler. We hear bombs detonating and the concurrent sound of buildings collapsing. None of the bombs fall near our party.

We move back to the barricades. The buildings across the street have suffered serious damage. Their roofs have collapsed, and the weight of the falling roof tiles has collapsed several floors beneath. "Let's cross that barricade!" I shout.

As we advance, the blacksuits continue to take a heavy toll, but the bombing has eliminated many of their positions. We lose another dozen warriors but we're able to climb the barricade and begin clearing the buildings that harbor surviving blacksuits. Once again, we catch dozens of civilians in the crossfire.

When we've finished, I call back to report our progress to Gretchen. "We're over the barricades and we've cleared the buildings of blacksuits."

"Good work, Mother of Gaia. But don't advance any farther. We have other streets to clear, too. We'll need more bombing runs to advance on the other fronts."

"They're *daring* us to advance along the streets they're not contesting," I say.

"I know," replies Gretchen. "Falstaff and I have been comparing notes. Our best guess is that they *want* us to advance down the 'undefended' streets. The minute we do, they'll pinch off our vanguard and wipe it out."

"I guess we stay patient."

We must recharge our planes after each mission, and that takes time. Two hours later bombs explode on streets up and down the line, but the afternoon light turns to evening shadows. We call a halt.

During the next two days, we advance against light resistance. Our losses are light, but we don't kill many blacksuits either. By nightfall of the day after, we've taken over three quarters of the fort and backed the blacksuits into the southwest quarter. In another four days of heavy fighting, we drive the blacksuits into a tiny wedge. The problem we have now is that with so little front to defend, the blacksuits can cover every angle of our advance. Every move we make draws a torrent of arrows.

We take the next day off to rest our weary militia. Our senior officers meet to discuss our options. The strain of constant combat has drained everyone. The faces of my friends look drawn and haggard. Our uniforms are dirty, and many show bloodstains.

"We'll take heavy losses as we penetrate the blacksuits' last redoubt," says Falstaff. "We've backed them into a corner, and they're fighting like mad dogs. Every time we raise our heads, we draw fire."

37

I ask the obvious question. "Do we have a better choice?"

Falstaff tugs on his beard. "We might. As you know, we've had our balloon over the city observing blacksuit movements. The warriors in the balloon report a high level of activity around one building near the south wall. Blacksuits arrive and leave from dawn to dusk. We think that building is their command-and-control center."

I'm excited. "If we destroy the head of the beast, the body will die." Faces that showed nothing but weariness a moment before now show animation.

Falstaff smiles, "Ideas for taking the blacksuits' control center?"

"We can destroy the building by bombing it," suggests Gretchen.

I consider this suggestion. "It'll take time and many raids to level the building. Their brain trust will move to another building. To end this battle, we must take the building with the officers still in it."

Margaret groans. "I imagine the Daughter of Gaia fits in your plan for taking the building."

I grin. "She does. Here's what I suggest: we choose the weakest spot we can find in the blacksuits' lines. We have every bomber hit that part of the line at once. Then we send the tank through, followed by the Daughter's Guard, Grizz, Kenny, Chase, and I. We make a bee-line for the command center."

Margaret is happier knowing that I've included the Daughter's Guard in our plans. "We'll attack the command center before the blacksuits can react. They'll guard it well, so taking it will be no stroll in the park. But the tank and our AKs give us a huge advantage in firepower. If our attack works, the battle for Fort Grant will be over, and we'll have just one more nut to crack."

I look from face to face. We are in agreement.

"Can you be ready at dawn tomorrow?" asks Falstaff.

I nod. "We'll move out as soon as the bombers finish their work."

*   *   *

The skies grow pink just before dawn. Undeterred by all the fighting, birds sing. Within a matter of minutes, our bombers are over their target. Four bombing runs leave the buildings across from us in total ruin.

"Let's go," I say into my comm.

Bree brings the tank out of hiding and heads through the debris left by the bombers. The rest of us follow. We're over the field of debris and behind the blacksuits' lines in less than five minutes. We meet no opposition. The bombers have done their job.

We advance down the street which leads to the command center. Grizz, Kenny, Chase, and I ride on the back of Bree's tank, which advances at a crawl, so we don't leave the Daughter's Guard behind. The slow pace of our advance frustrates me, but we'll need the Guard to secure the building. Still, we must reach the control center before the blacksuits can organize a counterattack, or, worse yet, move their officers elsewhere.

Within fifteen minutes, we see our target. The building is tiny compared to the palace in New Washington, but it's still an impressive piece of architecture. The Command Center is four stories tall, made of reinforced concrete. Two massive oak doors sit atop a set of broad stairs. During our bombing campaign, we hit the roof, so the top story has a distinct lean to it. They've carved the words "Judicial Center" in stone just above the front doors. I'm riding behind the turret of the tank using my binoculars to find defensive positions around the building when the ground drops out from under me.

My jaw rattles when my fall comes to a sudden stop. My butt slams into the unyielding steel surface of the tank. The blacksuits built a pit trap in the street. The front end of the tank rests in a large hole in the ground. Blacksuits lined the bottom of the trap with large, sharpened stakes. This tells me the blacksuits wanted to catch people, not armor. The tank's nose rests on the bottom of the pit, but its tail is still on the street. We clamber up the canted surface of the tank's rear onto solid ground.

"Are you all right?" asks Margaret.

"My butt's sore, but other than that, I'm fine."

I check on my friends. They're unharmed. Bree pops out of the turret of the tank. "What happened?" She looks around and sees the blacksuits' trap. "Those weasels!" she says indignantly. She scrambles out of the turret and examines her tank.

"Can you get it out of there?" I ask.

"Piece of cake." She climbs back into the turret.

The tank's electric engine whines as Bree tries to reverse the tank out of the hole. But in its present, diagonal, orientation, the treads have little traction. At first, the tank won't budge, but Bree guns the engine and the treads dig in. Bree backs the tank up and out of the hole.

The hole stretches all the way across the street. There's no way around it. My heart sinks. "How do we get the tank to the other side of the hole?"

Bree sits high above the ground in her turret. She examines the buildings on either side of the street. The building on the right is four stories tall. The one on the left is a one-story carpenter's shop. Bree thinks, then nods. "Follow me."

She disappears inside the tank and pulls the turret hatch closed above her. She backs the tank up three yards, guns the engine, and aims it at the front wall of the carpenter's shop. The tank crashes through the wall of the shop, splintering the wood. The roof of the building collapses on the tank, but Bree guns the engine again and knocks down the side wall. She runs the tank through the next building. When she's past the hole in the street, she makes a sharp right turn, pulls the tank back onto the street on the far side of the trap.

The rest of us follow the trail of destruction left by the tank. We pick our way through the debris of the shattered buildings. I climb back onto the tank, and holler, "Let's go!"

We halt fifty yards from the control center. I examine the building through binoculars. There's a wide plaza around the building, so we need to take out as many defenders as possible before we cross the open space. "I see four guards by the front door and several more in the windows of the third floor."

Margaret, who's been studying the defenses through her own binoculars, agrees. The blacksuits were not expecting an attack on this building so soon, and they haven't knocked embrasures in the walls. That means we can take out the sentries on the third floor with grenades.

"OK," I say, "here's what I'm thinking. Grizz and I take out the sentries by the front door while Chase and Kenny put grenades through every window on the third floor. While we're doing this, Bree takes the tank up the front stairs and drives right through the front doors."

"Good plan," says Bree and the others nod.

We advance until we're thirty yards from the building, just out of range for the blacksuits' bows, but an easy shot for our AKs. I set my weapon to single fire and look at Grizz. "You take the two on the left?"

"Yes," he says.

Grizz takes out both of his sentries and I get one of mine. The other one ducks when he hears the bullets flying. Kenny and Chase take aim with their grenade launchers and lob grenades through each of the six windows on the third floor. Bree's tank climbs the front stairs and crashes through the sturdy oak doors. She backs the tank down the stairs and turns it around, facing away from the building. No blacksuits will enter the front door behind us.

"Go!" I shout.

We run across the plaza. We've missed a few sentries and arrows strike six of the Guard. I reach the front door and pause while the Daughter's Guard catches up. There's a large entry hall just inside the front doors. Stairs on both sides lead to a second-floor balcony. A dozen blacksuits surrounded by at least twice as many civilians have taken up positions on the balcony. They shower us with arrows the instant we rush through the doors. I hesitate a second, but hear the civilians on the balcony hollering, "Shoot, shoot, please shoot." With no other choice, we set our AKs to rapid fire and clear the balcony.

"Grizz and I will take the first floor. Kenny and Chase, please clear the second floor. Margaret, can your people take the top two floors?"

"The Guard can clear the top two floors. But I am staying with the Daughter of Gaia."

Opposite the front door is another set of doors leading into a room with the words "Fort Grant Military Court" embossed in gold on a plaque beside the left-hand door. Grizz and I repeat the procedure we've practiced a hundred times in the last week: we plant three small dabs of plastique explosive by the hinges and the door handle of both doors, back up, detonate, and charge through the open doors with AKs blasting. The room is empty. There are doors inside the courtroom, one for the judge's chambers, one for jury deliberations, and one that turns out to be a small holding cell for prisoners. Every room is empty.

We hear the chatter of AKs above us. Kenny and Chase are at work on the second floor. Faint sounds of battle from the higher floors tell us the Daughter's Guard has found blacksuits on the two top floors.

We return to the entry hall and see another set of oak doors leading off to the left. There's a golden eagle painted on the door. We storm through the doors and find a large room. The Blacksuits barricaded themselves in back. A sharp firefight ensues. Margaret takes an arrow through her shoulder, but with the superior firepower of our AKs we gain the upper hand. Still, brave blacksuits stand and launch arrows at us. Before they can take proper aim, we take them down. After a furious five-minute fight, a white flag waves above the blacksuits' barricade.

"Come out with your hands raised," I say.

Five blacksuit officers stand, hands in the air. One wears a tunic with a breast covered with metals and ribbons. "I am," this one says, "Major General Edgar Wiley, commander of Fort Grant. You are the Daughter of Gaia."

"I am," I say. "We will soon have this building cleared of your people. We have our tank positioned just outside the front door, so no one will come to your rescue. Do you surrender the city? With you in captivity, and with us in control of this building, your soldiers cannot mount a cohesive defense. We prefer to end the slaughter here and now."

Kenny and Chase arrive, followed by the Daughter's Guard. "The building is secure," they report.

Wiley and his fellow officers confer, whispering quietly. "Do I have your promise that you will not harm my soldiers?" asks Wiley.

"You have my word. We will take your people into captivity, but we won't harm them."

"Then I surrender Fort Grant. Allow me to send runners to take the message to the front lines."

"You may do so."

The other four officers look at Wiley for confirmation. Wiley nods unhappily. "Tell our forces to stand down. They are to drop their weapons and surrender to the rebels." The officers leave the room, heads down defeated in mind, body, and spirit.

38

I bring out my comm. "Falstaff, do you read me?"

A split second later, Falstaff is on the line. "I hear you Daughter of Gaia."

"Tell our militia to cease fire. General Wiley just surrendered Fort Grant."

"Thank you, Daughter of Gaia. I will send an immediate order to cease fire."

Falstaff's voice is level, but I know him well enough to read the joy beneath the stoic, military correctness.

Grizz tends to Margaret. Her wound is painful, but not life-threatening. I sit next to her. "Let's take care of that."

I find the arrowhead imbedded deep inside her shoulder. I examine her back and see the very tip of the arrow protruding through the flesh of her back, two inches above her shoulder blade.

"This will hurt," I say.

Margaret nods. "Do what you must, Daughter of Gaia."

Margaret grimaces as I extract the arrowhead. She refuses to cry out, even though the pain must be brutal. I clean the wound, apply disinfectant, and stitch the wound.

Falstaff arrives at the control center half an hour later. "The blacksuits are surrendering," he says with a grin that stretches from one ear to the other. "I've ordered our militia to treat them well. Since they know that directive comes straight from the Daughter of Gaia, they will obey."

I ask Falstaff what he intends to do with so many prisoners.

Professional that he is, Falstaff planned for handling blacksuit prisoners before our assault on Fort Grant even began. "I prefer to prepare for every eventuality," he says modestly.

"What were your plans if we *didn't* take the fort?" I ask.

"I had none! Why prepare for something that's impossible?"

*   *   *

In the ensuing days, we celebrate. It tempers our joy to bury the dead. The battle cost the lives of two thousand militia members, and the blacksuits lost nearly as many. This troubles us, of course, but what is even more heart-rending is the burial of over four thousand civilians. But the slaughter will end soon.

With the burials completed, we plan the final assault on Fort Washington. We think once the capital falls, Fort Lewis and Fort Williams will surrender. With their capital gone, further resistance would be futile.

Ten days after the fall of Fort Grant, we position our militia for the attack on Fort Washington. Our planned assault will replicate the one on Fort Grant. We'll attack from two sides. This time, we'll attack from the north and south. This maximizes the length of the fronts the blacksuits must defend.

We have a council of war the afternoon before D-Day.

Falstaff looks grim. "The Battle for Fort Washington will make the Battle of Fort Grant look like a Sunday afternoon stroll. Fort Washington is over ten times the size of Fort Grant. From every-thing our spies tell us, the blacksuits have left Fort Lewis and Fort Williams lightly garrisoned. So, we'll tackle the vast majority of the blacksuits' remaining forces in Fort Washington. And you can bet that the brigades defending Fort Washington are their elite. They've had months now to prepare their defenses. They know every trick in the book, and they'll use every single one. The number of civilian casualties in Fort Washington will dwarf the number in Fort Grant. We'll kill tens of thousands of innocent people."

Falstaff pauses, then continues. "I don't speak these words to discourage you. I speak them to prepare you. We have no choice. We *must* take Fort Washington. And we will. Our militia has proven itself a match for the blacksuits. We outnumber them, and, thanks to the Daughter of Gaia and her friends, we have wonder weapons the blacksuits cannot counter. Tomorrow we begin the final battle. Many will die. But those who survive will be free!"

Every officer stands and cheers.

Late in the afternoon, I sit with Grizz and my friends, talking softly about things that have nothing to do with war, when a messenger arrives. He lowers his head and shifts his weight from one foot to the other.

"Please, speak," I say.

"I beg your pardon, Daughter of Gaia," he says, "but Falstaff requests your company. We've had a startling new development, and he needs your counsel."

Mystified, we congregate in Falstaff's tent. The minute I walk through the flap I'm dumbfounded to find myself, once again, face-to-face with the Chief Justice of the Court, Oskar Salieri. My draw drops.

39

"Daughter of Gaia," Salieri says with a pleasant smile, "I'm happy to see you again."

I struggle to regain my composure. "What are you doing here, Oskar?"

"Straight to the point. as always. Fine, I'm here to make an offer that will end this senseless slaughter. You have won the war. I concede If you attack, your militia will take Fort Washington, and my army cannot prevent it. You have the numbers and the weapons to make our position untenable. We have lost this war, and we know it."

"So, you're here to surrender?"

"In a way, yes."

I scoff. "You either surrender or you don't. There's no middle ground."

"Ah, but there *is* a middle ground. Allow me to make my proposal."

I nod. "Go ahead. We have nothing to lose by listening."

"I propose one final battle, a battle to the death between the Daughter of Gaia and a swordsman of my choosing. If the Daughter of Gaia wins, my warriors will surrender their weapons and go without hesitation into captivity. I include myself; I will become your prisoner."

"And if I lose?"

"My warriors will leave New Washington and its surroundings forever. We will leave and you will never see us again. New Washington will become yours in perpetuity. You have nothing to lose."

"Except my life."

"Except your life."

"So, what you want is *your* freedom."

"If you take New Washington," says Salieri, "you will either kill us or put us in prison. Am I correct?"

"We will not kill you, but yes, we will imprison you. You, the members of the Court, and your other senior leaders. You must pay for your crimes against my people."

"Then you are correct," Salieri says, "what we hope to gain is our freedom. But you will take possession of New Washington either way."

"And if I refuse your proposal?"

Salieri shakes his head. "Then there will be a terrible slaughter. Tens of thousands will die."

"How do we know we can trust this weasel?" sputters Kenny.

I look into Salieri's eyes. "I trust Oskar. He's cruel, and he's a tyrant, but he *will* keep his word."

Salieri smiles.

Falstaff looks at me with alarm. "To win the war but lose the Daughter of Gaia? That is an awful bargain!"

"If we refuse the bargain," I reply, "*many* will die, most of them innocent civilians. If I'm defeated, the only thing we lose is the ability to put the blacksuits' leadership on trial for their crimes. I hate to let them walk away, but when I balance that possibility against the slaughter of thousands; I'm inclined to accept his proposal. Remember, whether I win or lose, our people will be free!"

Falstaff's reddens with anger. "Salieri, you insist on picking your champion. Allow me to choose ours."

"I cannot do that," replies Salieri. "The Court insists we fight the Daughter of Gaia."

Apart from Salieri, I'm the only one in the room willing to accept the proposal. Grizz and Kenny oppose the bargain. Falstaff and Gretchen shake their heads and mutter. But I am the Daughter of Gaia, and the decision is mine.

"Who will I fight?" I ask.

"Our champion will be our Swordmaster, Brutus Napoleon. I should warn you; he is *extremely* good."

"We will fight with swords?"

"Yes."

"I accept your challenge. I will meet your champion in front of the gates of Fort Washington tomorrow morning at sunrise."

"Very well," says Salieri.

"You are a man of your word, Oskar. But we can't risk one of your subordinates deposing you and refusing to honor our bargain. Your entire garrison must leave the fort *before* the fight begins."

This troubles Salieri. "Away from our defensive positions, your people could massacre mine. Your militia is much larger than my few remaining brigades."

"We are people of honor too, Oskar. That's my offer. Take it or leave it."

Salieri looks at Falstaff. "Do I have *your* word as well?"

"If the Daughter of Gaia makes a promise, our people are duty-bound to honor it."

"Even if the Daughter of Gaia dies?"

"Even if the Daughter of Gaia dies," says Falstaff. Tears form, but he doesn't let them fall.

Salieri nods his agreement. He turns on his heel and leaves, accompanied by his bodyguards.

Falstaff fumes. "To buy victory with your blood is dishonorable, Daughter of Gaia. Please don't put us in this awful position! This proposition is unthinkable!"

"Your people love you," adds Gretchen imploringly. "Your

death would cast a pall over our victory. We want to win. But your death is too steep a price to pay!"

Grizz has tears in his eyes. "You've sacrificed everything for this fight," he says. "Please, Erin, don't give up your life."

"Who says I'll lose? I've fought many blacksuits including big, strong ones and I haven't lost yet." I hope my words sound confident, because I don't *feel* confident.

"You fight well with your sword, Daughter of Gaia," says Falstaff. "But to defeat the blacksuits' Swordmaster? You are not *that* good."

"I know you don't want me to do this," I say. "But I've decided. I *will* fight the blacksuits' champion tomorrow. With their entire army outside the walls, they can't renege on their agreement. And, I don't intend to die." *Even though the chances are very good that I will.*

Dinner this evening is somber. I try to stimulate conversation, but nobody is interested. It doesn't matter, because I don't feel like talking either. *I know I'm not a match for the blacksuits' Swordmaster. Barring a miracle, I will die.*

40

I wake up just before dawn. I listen to the birds as they begin their morning song; they're early risers, just like me. I watch as the sun paints the bottoms of clouds, listen to the sounds of a military waking. Grizz rises and joins me. We stand side by side, holding hands, as we watch the coming dawn. When the sun peeks over the mountains, I turn to Grizz, throw my arms around him, and kiss him fiercely. When I let him go, his eyes well with tears. One escapes and rolls down his cheek.

"I love you, Grizz. Regardless what happens today, you are the love of my life, and you always will be."

Grizz nods his head. I know he wants to speak, but he won't because he's afraid he'll break down. I'm thankful for his silence. If he were to break down, I would, too. And that would not be a good preparation for fighting the blacksuits' Swordmaster.

The camp bustles around us. Falstaff has fifteen brigades formed up and ready to march. I walk beside Falstaff at the head of our militia as we march to the main gates of Fort Washington. On my other side are my friends. Grizz holds my hand tight.

When we reach the gates, we find the blacksuits' army formed in ruler-straight ranks, waiting for us. Falstaff halts our march twenty yards from the front rank of the blacksuits. That'll leave plenty of room for Brutus and me to fight

"You don't have to do this," says Kenny, tears streaming. The sight of Kenny in tears brings a lump to my throat. I struggle to keep my composure. "Yes, I do, Kenny."

I brush Grizz's lips one last time. I turn and approach Salieri. "I'm ready."

"Let me introduce you to our Swordmaster, Brutus Napoleon," says Salieri.

Napoleon steps from the front rank of the assembled blacksuits. He walks up to me and offers his hand. I shake it. I'm surprised. He's short and thin, my height. I thought I'd be fighting a six-foot four-inch gorilla with bulging muscles.

Salieri steps away and Napoleon and I draw our swords.

The high-ranking blacksuit officers I have fought have been large men. They've tried to overwhelm me with their superior strength. My success has come in allowing them to tire themselves, counterattacking when their sword arms have weakened. That strategy won't work today. Napoleon isn't big enough to overpower me.

Napoleon holds his sword in front of himself, tip pointed straight at my heart. I do the same. I wait for him to attack, but he's in no hurry. He examines me with clinical interest, sizes me up.

At last, he moves forward and touches my blade. With the speed of a striking snake, he comes at me, trying for a quick kill. I barely avoid the point of his blade. I spring back at him, hoping he's left himself off-balance. He parries my thrust with ease. Napoleon is the fastest swordsman I've seen—much faster than me.

The fight settles into a rhythm. Napoleon attacks, I parry at the final instant. I counterattack and he parries with ease. I try to anticipate his moves, because with his speed, eventually he will strike before I can defend.

The killing thrust comes sooner than I'd expected. I know the minute his sword pierces my abdomen that the blow is mortal. I'm beyond the help of any healer on this side of the brane. I fall to my knees, and then on my face. I crane my head to see Napoleon, arms raised, standing over me, glorying in his victory.

41

I can't let it end this way. I look for one last morsel of strength and find it. I grasp my sword in both hands. Napoleon doesn't see me move because he's basking in the admiration of his comrades. With one last effort, I rise to my knees and hold my sword like a dagger over my head.

Napoleon has his back to me. He sees concern on the faces of his comrades.

"Hey, Brutus," I say, my voice a hoarse croak.

He turns to face me, and with one last burst of strength, using both hands, I bury the blade of my sword in his chest. He falls, dead before he hits the ground. I collapse on top of him. I feel a coppery taste in my mouth and spit out blood. There is darkness rising behind my eyes. I'm surprised that there is no pain. I feel warm all over. My head faces the blacksuits' lines. I watch as blacksuit warriors lay their weapons on the ground. And then the darkness overtakes me.

42

GRIZZ

I've written this story exactly as Erin told it to me. She dictated it
the night before her fight with Napoleon. She knew she'd lose to
the blacksuits' Swordmaster but willingly gave her life to save
thousands of others. Her decision was no surprise to anyone who
knew her.

After the fight, we carried her into New Washington and laid
her on a cot in the barracks just inside the gates. Erin lived for a
short while. Her stamina has always amazed everyone around her.
At the end, her voice was weak, and I had to hold my ear next to
her lips to hear her final words. She said, "Grizz, I want you to live
a long and happy life. But I'll be waiting for you on the other side.
If you live to be a hundred, I promise you that when you cross
over, my love will be every bit as strong as it is today."

She closed her eyes and died. The only dry eye in the room was
Falstaff's. When she was gone at last, even his strength crumbled.
Gruff as he is, he sank to his knees, his body shaken by sobs.
Kenny let out a keening wail and Bree's tears and Chase's fell like
monsoon rain. As for me, I held Erin for hours, rocking her back

and forth, feeling as though someone has ripped my heart from my body.

In the weeks that follow, as I struggle with grief, I draw solace from the knowledge that Erin Taylor loves me and will from now through eternity. That's all I could ever want.

www.ingramcontent.com/pod-product-compliance
Lightning Source LLC
Chambersburg PA
CBHW020346180626
46812CB00001B/367